Faithless

Shaune Lafferty Webb

Book 2 of the
Safe Harbour Chronicle

FAITHLESS

Book 2 of *The Safe Harbour Chronicle*

The moral rights of Shaune Lafferty Webb to be identified as the author of this work have been asserted.

Copyright 2017 Hague Publishing

Hague Publishing
PO Box 451
Bassendean Western Australia 6934
Email: contact@haguepublishing.com
Web: www.haguepublishing.com

ISBN: 978-0-9925437-8-5

Cover Art: 'Faithless' by Jade Zivanovic http://www.steampowerstudios.com.au/

Typeset Garamond 12/14

Acknowledgement

Special thanks, as always, to my husband, Gregory, for his tireless support and insightful critiques and to Danielle de Valera, Anneque Malchien, and Pamela Cooper for their enduring encouragement through the years. My thanks also go to Nick Wiggins in recognition of his technical assistance and reader feedback and for generously offering his time and enthusiasm during a recent and lengthy book signing.

I would also like to express my sincere thanks to Andrew Harvey, principal of Hague Publishing; it's been a genuine pleasure and privilege to continue this collaboration; and to Jade Zivanovic, cover artist, whose commitment and gracious cooperation is greatly appreciated.

To all the readers of 'Cold Faith', the first installment of *The Safe Harbour Chronicle*, welcome back and thank you for your company as, together, we journey further on down the road.

Chapter 1

RAB headed through the gate into the underground city, barely aware of the near empty packs hanging limply from each shoulder. He would stay only a few days—long enough to rest and restock his supplies, maybe find a new pair of boots—before he set out once again. There was time. Lately it seemed that snow time was taking just that little bit longer to come and leaving just that little bit sooner. Intuitively, he should find that a good thing. Instinctively, he couldn't. Little about this planet inspired trust.

It was easy going through the dark and narrow upper tunnel, all just second nature to him now. Each bend, each irregularity in the floor had simply become part of him. Reaching out, Rab's hand went immediately to the lock on the heavy metal door. He turned the key, heard the lock tumble, then, depressing the handle, shouldered it open. The air inside 'the house' felt warm against his face. In the middle of the far wall, a small fire was burning in the large hearth.

Cloud!

Somehow she always knew the very day he'd come walking back down the tunnel.

The fire lent him just enough light to see. Having spent weeks top-side, his eyes weren't adjusted to the dark. If the old overstuffed chair had still been there, he might have stayed and warmed himself in front of Cloud's fire a while before facing the inevitable below, but the chair had disappeared long ago—no doubt scavenged by some resourceful tunnel-dweller during one of Rab's forays on the surface. It would have been no mean feat to manoeuvre something that size down the lower tunnel. All that was left in the room now was a battered container, looking lonely in the far corner of the room.

Rab dropped his packs and began shrugging off his heavy coat as he made his way across the room towards the container. Bits of wadded-up paper fell to the floor as he walked. He stooped to collect each one. On reaching the container, he found it almost empty. No surprise. Hardly anyone ventured outside anymore; why waste a precious fuel on the off-chance someone might take it in their head to go top-side? One by one, Rab tossed the loosely wadded balls of the fine insulating paper into the container. They'd be there waiting for him when he came back up in a couple of days. No one would take them in the meantime.

Thrusting a hand into the pocket of his coat, he rummaged around until he found the small draw-string bag, which he transferred to the pocket of his trousers, then dumped his heavy coat on the floor beside the container. No one would take that, either. The rare person who visited 'the house' knew he'd be needing it again, too, and would leave both his coat and the paper alone. He had learned very quickly that these tunnel-dwellers weren't prone to steal. It was more than he could say for his own kind: the Top-siders. In the ten snow times, ten years, he'd been living on and off among the tunnel-dwellers, Rab had never heard of or seen a single incident of theft or assault, nor had he ever had even the slightest inkling that anything improper might be going on quietly beneath the surface. That is, aside from the callous handling of returned captives, a matter which seemed entirely outside the accepted rules of underground conduct. At first, Rab had felt morally compelled to challenge the city administrators whenever some unsuspecting tunnel-dweller was duped into accepting a returned captive as *their* child; now he didn't even notice when it happened.

Retrieving his packs, Rab stamped out the fire. Before starting down the lower tunnel towards the city, he dropped the keys he'd used to open the gate and the big, heavy door into one of the packs and then slung both over his shoulder. The keys clanked against the jumble of rocks at the bottom of the pack. Knowing he wouldn't have to look at those keys again for a couple of days was always a great relief; they were too sad and galling a reminder of Sunny. Ten years dead now and still he couldn't shake her. She'd set his path—left him with those keys, an impossible challenge, and the blood he couldn't wash off his hands. If all were fair in this world she should be rotting in hell right now, not resting with her task complete and her dead flesh mummifying on cold bones, inside the carcass of that wrecked spaceship out in a dry river bed. But nothing was fair in this world. Not one damn thing. If it were, Gift would never have been taken from him. It didn't seem a lot to ask under the circumstances.

The shimmerers lit Rab's way down the lower tunnel. They always seemed happy to see him back. It was imagination, of course. The tiny little beasts that lined the walls of the tunnel didn't glow any brighter for him than they did for anyone else. But after each cold and miserable stint top-side, it was comforting to believe there'd be some sort of welcome waiting on his return. Cloud would be pleased to see him—too pleased. She was starting to become a genuine problem. Someday she might just wear him down, convince him to stay. She deserved better.

Rab passed through the end of the lower tunnel onto Main Street and continued into Market Square, glancing, as was his habit, up at the light-peppered ceiling overhead. Just like it had seemed in the tunnel, for one instant, the brightworms there appeared to flash more intently to greet him. Usually he didn't pay much attention to the vendors assembled in the Square. Today he did; he was on the lookout for that new pair of boots. It didn't look hopeful, but he gave each stall a thorough inspection as he passed. Seemed there were fewer goods each time he made his way back to the underground city. A scarcity of pots here. A sparser selection of cloth there. Less variety in the kind of foods available for barter and the baskets and metal trays that held it all just looked that little less full.

They were going down and it was a surprise that it had actually taken this long.

Every now and then a vendor or customer nodded to Rab and he briefly inclined his head in reply. No one bothered to ask about his forays top-side anymore. They were accustomed to his coming and going and, if he came back alone—as he had so far—then there was nothing to ask about, nothing they needed or wanted to know.

He stopped at Lilly's pots and pans stall out of a sense of obligation. Pots and pans were of no use to him top-side and he left the matter of stocking the space he lived in while underground entirely up to Fin.

Lilly Benson was something of a fragile woman. She managed the day to day well enough, but there wasn't a tunnel-dweller in the city who'd say she was wholly sane. Harmless? Yes. Predictable? No. Sunny had known exactly what she was doing when she'd declared that Cloud was Lilly Benson's lost girl. If there's a problem, fix it; if there's one looming, forestall it. Good old Sunny! She'd forestalled Lilly's total collapse, all right. And Cloud *had* gone on to keep a close eye on the poor woman so that most of the time no one was concerned about her little oddities. And because she was a pots and pans vendor, the tunnel-dwellers were more than happy to trade for her wares, though none were keen to engage her in a protracted conversation. She tended to wander off topic.

Lilly quickly spotted Rab picking over the bits and pieces at the far end of her stall and hurried his way.

"Half trade today, Rab," she said, pouncing as she usually did on anyone who seemed even remotely interested in her wares.

"I just walked in from the surface, Lilly, and I'll be leaving again very soon. Can't use them top-side," Rab replied, replacing the battered pan back onto the top of the precariously stacked pile.

Lilly's face went blank, light grey eyes and down-turned mouth frozen for a moment in time.

"Oh, yes, top-side." Whatever it was that had stalled inside Lilly's head stirred again. "I keep forgetting."

She certainly did.

"Did you bring back anything I can use?"

Rab thought about the worthless stones weighing down his pack. If only!

He shook his head and smiled. Not everyone put in the effort to summon up a smile for Lilly. But then the woman could exhaust even the most patient person; Rab didn't have to contend with her that often.

Lilly's grey eyes began to dance, shifting focus from a spot somewhere over Rab's left shoulder to the farthest end of the Square, then back again to Rab.

"You don't know where my daughter is, do you? I haven't seen her since this morning."

Rab had lost count of the number of days since he'd last seen Lilly's daughter. Lilly had already forgotten what he'd told her just moments ago.

"Sorry," Rab said nevertheless. "Maybe she's down in the field."

"Oh," Lilly said thoughtfully, then brightened. "Everything's half trade today, Rab. Just pick anything you want."

"Nothing today, thanks, Lilly," Rab said, then, with a shake of his head, took his leave.

The remaining stalls looked equally unpromising, so Rab left the market, empty-handed, and turned into Braham Street.

A little extra flicker. The shimmerers there saying hello. When he came on a tunnel-dweller heading in the opposite direction, Rab offered a little smile and received the same in return. He was in the residential sector where that kind of courtesy was more or less expected.

If he could have brought the tunnel-dweller's name to mind, he'd have said 'good afternoon', although perhaps to this tunnel-dweller it wasn't afternoon at all. Having just come down from top-side, Rab knew the time of day and season but those who lived in the permanent semi-light of the world below tended to set their own personal calendar for work and rest.

The fire wasn't burning inside John Braham's space. Like his grand-daughter, Sunny, old Braham had been dead and gone these last ten years. Still Rab always thought of the space as Braham's, though he owned it now—or rather he shared it with Stitch and Fin. He could have moved into Sunny's space instead but he could never bring himself to go there. He didn't have a clue what it looked like, who had taken possession of it and what, if any, of her possessions they might have found there.

Well, at least Cloud hadn't wasted any fuel lighting and warming his space. It wasn't necessary; Rab was used to a more bitter cold than this and could purloin enough warmth from the space next door. His neigh-bour was a quiet, solitary man who divided his time between labouring in the 'shroom field and sleeping in front of his fire. Barely a word ever passed between them.

Something seemed a little off inside but, without the glow of the fire, Rab couldn't immediately identify what it was. His eyes hadn't fully adjusted to the diminished light underground.

He stepped across the floor and, despite its progressive thinning over the years, registered the soft carpeting underfoot. That wasn't what had changed. He gave a mental shrug, headed for the niche in the left wall and threw the two packs through the opening into his own personal space. Stitch and Fin each had a space of their own. It was sheer opulence considering where they had come from.

"Heard you were back."

Rab nearly jumped out of his skin. He was simply too weary to call up blindsight, though thank God it had finally returned. During his first months down in these caves, it had abandoned him completely. Only after frequent forays top-side had he been able to coax it back.

"Hello, Cloud."

He turned around and was dismayed to see something draped over her left arm. The last time a woman had stood in his doorway bearing gifts, it hadn't worked out too well. There had been one long unbreakable string attached. Looking up, he caught the shadow of a frown cross Cloud's pretty face. She'd been on her hands and knees in the 'shroom fields again. Her dark hair that this morning must have been tied up neatly on top of her head was hanging in tangled knots about her shoulders and there were smudges of dirt on her face.

"My mother doesn't like it when you call me that."

Rab casually lifted an eyebrow.

He knew. She knew he knew. Lilly Benson was not Cloud's mother.

"Pardon me." Rab dipped his head in mock apology. "Hello, Abby."

"Better," she said with a small smile and stepped into his space.

"May I come in?"

"You just did."

"Funny! Here," she said, extending her arm. "I made this for Stitch. Waste of time making *you* any more sweaters."

"Have to agree, considering what I really need is boots."

Rab slipped the sweater off her arm. Just the touch of it was enough to remind him why Cloud's hands were invariably swollen and raw. The weave was coarse and it felt scratchy; nothing that wasn't expected considering Cloud's dwindling supply of thread. The threader farm wasn't producing as much thread as it once did and there'd been some speculation that overcrowding among the population of the fragile weaver insects might be at the heart of the decline. The dim lighting couldn't conceal that the sweater Cloud had made was the most colourful of her creations to date. Though she'd tried to disguise it by frequently swapping the red, yellow, pink, green, and purple threads, there was no getting away from the fact that the garment was the gaudiest piece of wearing apparel Rab had ever come across.

Though ostensibly she was a reweaver, Cloud's real talent lay in horticulture. Damn good luck for the city. Cloud, or Abby as everyone else in the city called her, had been brought back from more than a decade of captivity with the Top-siders at the very time the city's mushroom crop was failing. Rab had been the first to notice the disease. Cloud soon saw it and had proposed a radical solution—the sacrifice of the diseased portion of the crop in order to salvage the rest. It had been a stroke of genius that led to a modified strain of 'shroom much smaller than any they had ever seen before but one that was highly resistant to disease. Rab often wondered what the young girl's fate might have been had her gamble not paid off. But she'd saved the crop and secured herself a privileged place among the tunnel-dwellers as a result.

Rab glanced up to find Cloud looking down at his worn and tattered boots.

"I'll look around," she said, turning her eyes back to his face.

"I can't pay you," he reminded her.

She sighed—once and loudly—then began a slow study of his space. Her gaze settled on Sunny's rusted gun, lying in its usual place in the far corner of the room. For a second Rab thought she was going to ask for it. Why not? Maybe she could have it melted down? It had long been out of bullets and although Rab had once lugged the useless thing out and back through the wasteland on the pretext of its value as a deterrent, it just hadn't been worth the effort.

Her glance slipped away without asking for it. Maybe melting it down wasn't worth the effort, either.

"Got any more of this?" she enquired, gently scuffing the pile of the old carpet in front of her with the toe of one shoe.

Rab pointed towards the niche that served, off and on, as his room.

"There's a threadbare one back there."

Cloud pushed past him and peered through the narrow opening.

"Done," she said and, turning around, began to wander here and there about the outer room, inspecting every nook and cranny along the way.

"Just that carpet. And only *after* you get me those boots."

"Of course." She stopped beside the cold hearth. "Your table is all busted-up," she said.

Rad glanced towards the table—or rather towards the spot where the table should be. So that's what was different. The table was missing. He shrugged when he spied the splintered wood haphazardly stacked by the hearth.

"Fin must have busted it up for fire wood."

"That's the way it goes," Cloud replied over her shoulder. "Don't suppose you found us a new supply while you were otherwise wasting your time up there?"

Rab shook his head. Once he'd been able to pay his dues underground by occasionally locating a cache of untapped fuel or stumbling on an exploitable stand of clean wild mushrooms. It seemed those days were gone.

"You going back up?" Cloud asked, turning around.

Rab nodded.

"Soon?"

Even from a distance, Rab could detect that familiar old expression in those deep brown eyes of hers. Aside from Gift, she was the only person to regard him both warmly and critically at the same time. In the long ago, perhaps there had been occasions when his mother had cause to look at him the same way and he had simply forgotten.

"Couple of days."

Numbering among Cloud's many other talents was the irritating ability to make Rab feel miserably guilty, although he was never really sure what he had done to earn her disappointment. His search for Gift had begun when she was hardly more than a kid; it had had nothing to do with her then and, as Rab saw it, had nothing to do with her now.

"When will you give up, Rab?" Cloud asked at last. "What difference do you think finding her would make now? She was born a Top-sider. Let her be a Top-sider."

Rab shook his head. "Not *that* kind of Top-sider."

Cloud stiffened. "I spent more than ten years of my life with Top-siders who were probably pretty much like them, Rab. You do what you have to do to survive."

Had he heard right? Had she really said that?

"What?" Rab flung Stitch's new sweater to the floor. "Steal young city girls because too many of your own die in childbirth?"

Cloud's right shoulder lifted slightly. "If that's what it takes," she replied evenly.

Striding forwards, he grabbed a hold of her arms a little more roughly than he'd intended.

"You can say that because you were rescued, Cloud. What if you hadn't been rescued and brought back here?" he said, loosening his hold a little. "What if you'd been forced to spend your life as a breeder and nothing more?"

"Well, I wasn't," Cloud countered defiantly. "Gift was. . .is. And that's all there is to it."

"Fair trade? Is that what you're telling me?"

"Why not? We steal their fuel and their food, don't we?"

"What are you talking about?" Rab demanded irritably.

"Every time we find a new source of fuel or food top-side, we don't ask for it or trade for it. We just take it. That's theft, isn't it?"

Rab had never really looked on his scavenging quite that way before. "Yes, but—"

"But nothing! Top-side is their space. *Down here* is ours."

Cloud shouldn't have had to remind him of that. Fin, Stitch, Gift and him, they had been born Top-siders. Maybe the life of a village Top-sider was just that tiny bit easier than the life of a nomadic Top-sider. Maybe it wasn't. There was such a minor difference in the degree of deprivation, hardship and despair, what did it really matter? Rab, born Top-sider, was now living city-dweller. Cloud, born city-dweller, had lived a good part of her young life Top-sider. The two of them—they were kind of mirror images. Cloud came at life from one side, he from the other.

Rab let go of her arms.

"Not easy to have your sympathies split down the middle, is it, Cloud?"

"No. I'm sorry," she said and quickly swiped the side of her face with a shoulder, smudging dirt. "And you're right, of course. It's not quite the same. Stealing children and stealing food and fuel. It's just that. . .oh, Rab," she stamped her foot in a gesture that almost made Rab laugh, "you make me so mad. Sooner or later you have to stop searching. She's gone now. I know you promised her. But how long do you think a promise like that has to last?"

For a long silent while Rab just stood there looking down at her. He didn't feel like laughing anymore.

"You came back," he said at length.

"Yeah, I did, didn't I? And at the back of your mind you still have that niggling little suspicion that I'm hiding something, don't you?"

"I—" Rab began.

"There's only one thing I'm hiding," she snapped, cutting him off, "and you and I both know what *that* is. But I'm sure you'll agree it's a secret best kept. Some are, you know."

Cloud's little fit of temper struck a raw nerve.

"Or maybe you'd like me to come clean on absolutely everything and tell Lilly the truth," she said. "Because I swear that's the only thing I've ever kept from anyone. I don't know one damn thing about those Top-siders who took your precious Gift. I don't know where they came from or where they were going. If I did, I'd tell you. It would stop this useless traipsing around, wouldn't it? Save you from ending up dead out there some day. But they weren't *my* Top-siders just like they weren't *yours*."

At that less then subtle reminder of their common past, she gave him a shove and struck off towards the entrance to his space. As she passed by Stitch's discarded sweater, she stooped and gathered it up. At the opening she stopped, swung around and flung the sweater right into Rab's upraised hand.

She never missed.

"I'll keep an eye out for those boots," she said, leaving Rab, sweater dangling from one hand, looking at an empty doorway.

Chapter 2

RAB was too spent after Cloud left to consider much else but sleep. After all, that's what he'd come back to the tunnels to do—rest and restock his supplies before heading top-side again. But when Rab ventured back into his own small space, he discovered that all his bedding was gone. When old John Braham had lived here, there'd been an abundance of soft cushions scattered all about the floor. Now there were only a few. Rab dragged a couple inside the inner niche and fashioned himself a bed that was, in comparison to what he was used to, absolute luxury. Tossing his ruined boots aside, he collapsed, clothes and all, into the inviting softness. When Stitch had been small, Rab used to have the boy walk gently up and down his back to loosen the knots in his aching muscles. But Stitch had grown so big, the boy would break his spine now. In fact, Stitch was bigger than him nowadays and all Rab could put it down to was the magic of living underground in the warmth with the prospect of a solid meal every day, although the absence of day light had heightened the boy's natural fairness and, if possible, sapped more of the colour from his already light blue eyes. Even Fin had filled out a little although there remained a certain hollowness and angularity about his face that spoke of those formative years spent on the surface.

Vaguely, Rab wondered where Stitch was now. Trailing after Fin most likely. And God only knew where Fin was. Both brothers seemed to have adapted to tunnel life better than Rab had anticipated, better than he ever would. Born surface, Rab dearly hoped that, when the time came, he'd be lucky enough to die surface. If he kept tramping top-side after Gift much longer, that day might not be too far off.

Gift!

Was he truly so obsessed with finding her as Cloud believed? Likely so. And the odds were that, after all these years, Gift had probably forgotten him.

With the nagging pain in his lower back threatening to keep him awake, Rab struggled onto his side and faced the inner wall, where the light that filtered in from Braham Street failed to reach. Semi-light. Semi-dark. Didn't matter. Rab could usually sleep in either, but his argument with Cloud threatened to snatch away from him the one thing he'd been craving these last few days. Cloud was right about a lot of things. She'd been right about how to avert a complete annihilation of the 'shroom crop. She'd been right when she claimed that by reweaving old thread, they could produce more clothing. And, all right, she was right that he'd become hopelessly obsessed. She was way off the mark when it came to the promise he'd made though. The real promise he'd made to Gift had been fulfilled long ago. If you have to make a choice about who to save, she'd said, then choose Stitch. And although maybe it hadn't been a conscious decision to save Stitch, by stumbling on Sunny and having her bring them to the relative safety of her city, he had done exactly that. He really hadn't had any other option, not with the boy's leg so badly broken. Stitch still walked with a bit of a limp, but not much really. There were things he could not do, like descend into the valley with the rest of the youngsters to collect oil for the city from the dwindling seep, or harvest too long in the 'shroom field, but without Sunny Stitch would have died up there on the surface. It was a fate that was probably still lying in wait for *him*. What were the odds he wouldn't slip and fall up there sooner or later?

No, the promises he was so obstinately holding onto were the ones he'd made to Sunny and to himself after the young woman had died. Died! Not an entirely accurate description of how Sunny had met her maker. Though she was quickly heading in that direction anyway. All he had done was hurry the process along—just as she'd asked him to do. And so, to the accompaniment of a sharp and terrible sound that still haunted him, the last of the bullets for Sunny's gun was spent, leaving him with only the dead for company in the wreckage of the crashed spaceship and the pledge he'd made to protect not only its location, but the truth behind the legend he'd left his own dying village to pursue. Unbearable promise number one. And, yes, by consciously agreeing to guard Sunny's secret he'd brought that one tumbling down on himself.

Unbearable promise number two had come of its own accord—the second he found Gift gone from the place where they had left her, safe Sunny had vowed and lied, waiting for their return. To this day, he was never sure just how complicit Sunny had been in the young girl's abduction. There were days when he was convinced that Sunny really had bartered Gift for a sweater, a set of gloves and a second-hand pair of boots. There were days when he couldn't conceive that even Sunny could have, at her core, been so cold-heartedly cruel. To his dying day the woman seemed destined to remain an enigma. Maybe Gift, when he found her, would have the answer. Maybe when he found Gift, having the answer wouldn't matter anymore.

At the sound of laughter, Rab turned and caught a glimpse of someone moving around in the space outside his small niche. The brothers were back. One of them was laughing. Fin? Unlikely. Probably Stitch. Rab rolled back to face the unlit wall, sleep finally seeping, warm and calm, through the channels of his weary mind. He'd kept his promise to Gift. He was keeping his promise to Sunny. Maybe two out of three was enough.

***

Rab could hear the brothers talking quietly when he woke up. Rising stiffly, he stumbled to the narrow opening of his niche.

Stitch stopped talking and looked over at him. Fin glanced his way, nodded briefly, but kept on eating.

What was that he had in his hand? Dinner or breakfast?

Rab couldn't decide. Just how long had he slept?

"Breakfast," Stitch said.

Was the kid a mind-reader?

"Do you want some?"

Rab shook his head. He'd grown accustomed to one good meal a day and it wasn't time yet.

"Find any wood this time?" Fin asked before stuffing his mouth again.

"Not this time," Rab replied, obliged to hold onto the edge of the doorway for support.

The rock felt warm to the touch. Rab glanced towards the hearth and found a fire glowing. It was only a small fire and the pile of busted-up wood from the table looked hardly diminished at all.

"Any 'shrooms?" Stitch reached towards the old bowl that was balanced on his knees.

"No."

Neither brother had asked about Gift. They hadn't for a long time.

When Rab stepped away from the doorway, Stitch shied the last of the cushions in his direction.

"Then I'm guessing you didn't bring me anything, either."

"Guess again," Rab said, folding himself awkwardly into the low seat. "They're still in my pack."

Stitch bounded up from the floor and, without invitation, made straight for Rab's niche. When he stepped back through the doorway he was carrying one of the packs as though it contained precious cargo. He didn't bother to avail himself of a cushion, just dropped to the floor and cautiously upended the contents of the pack onto the thinning pile of the carpet. The ring of keys came tumbling out with the rest.

This rock-gathering had become something of a ritual and literally a pain in Rab's neck. He'd thought Stitch would grow out of the fascination, which had actually begun not long after they had left their village, when Stitch was just a little kid. But no. Each time Rab left the city, he went charged with another promise to bring back more rocks. And each time he came back, Stitch was just as anxious to discover what Rab had brought him. There was little hope now of having the lad's enthusiasm wane. Though the carrying had quickly grown old, Rab didn't mind the foraging. It gave him an excuse to look for one particular type of stone.

Although he hadn't managed to find it yet, some day he would and that elusive little chunk of blue rock, like the one he kept inside the small draw-string bag in his coat pocket, might just lead him to Gift. For now though, for Stitch's sake, he'd continue to carry back those useless lumps of stone and count himself lucky that the lad had found a healthy diversion, although a bit of an unlikely one considering he lived, day in day out, surrounded by rock. Rab had given up arguing the point once Stitch informed him that the rocks top-side were different. They were. But lately the rocks he came upon during his forays were all starting to look the same and Rab was having a hard time finding anything even mildly unusual to add to Stitch's collection.

"Abby brought you a sweater," Rab said. "Did you find it?"

"Who me?" Stitch asked, glancing up from his sorting. "I thought that was yours."

Fin snorted.

He understood how things stood between Rab and young Abby.

"Yours," Rab said, reaching out, a little stiffly, to retrieve the discarded article. The stretch nearly dumped him out of his seat. Holding the garment up from the shoulders, he gave Stitch a quick study.

Could the boy really have grown so much in a couple of weeks? "Looks a good fit."

"Always is," Fin said, getting up lithely from the floor.

Rab felt a pang of jealousy. Had he ever been that young and agile? His fruitless treks top-side had made an old man of him before his time. Fin wasn't really all that much younger than him; it just seemed that way.

"How long are you staying?" Fin asked.

He'd disappeared into the smallest of the alcoves, where Rab heard water running.

The same old question every time. First from Cloud. Then from Fin. Stitch never asked.

"Couple of days."

Same old answer.

"Then you won't be interested in helping out on the carts," Fin said, stepping out from the alcove.

When he wasn't off somewhere doing God knew what in the farthest reaches of the tunnels, Fin worked down in the mushroom field maintaining the tracks and carts. He was pretty good with his hands and Stitch was beginning to show the same promise. Well, at least the boys had proved their worth to the tunnel-dwellers even if Rab hadn't. Ironic really considering, when all was said and done, Rab was the most valuable asset they had. They just didn't know it and never would as long as Rab kept his promise to Sunny.

Rab glanced down at his worn and battered hands. All right, maybe he could coax those bent fingers into helping Fin out some. Maybe Fin would cut him a little bit of slack if he did.

"This afternoon," he said, looking up. "How's that?"

Fin seemed genuinely surprised, faltering before he replied.

"Good." He turned to Stitch, "Will you stop messing around with those rocks?" then stepped athletically over his abandoned seat. "Swear to God you'd rather play with them than eat."

When Stitch looked up, Rab lobbed him Abby's new sweater.

"She'll be mad at you if you don't wear it," he said.

Actually she'd be mad at *him*, insisting he'd forgotten to give it to Stitch.

"Hurry up," Fin snapped from the doorway. "Just bring it with you," he called over his shoulder.

His old sweater was half over his head as Stitch hurried back to Rab and the bowl he'd left abandoned on the floor by Rab's feet.

"Sure you don't want it?" he mumbled, nodding at the bowl.

When Rab shook his head, Stitch snatched the last of the food and, with his new sweater tucked under an arm, bolted for the doorway.

"See you this afternoon," he said.

At least that's what Rab thought he'd said. It was a bit hard to tell since he was jamming crumbling bits of food into his mouth as he spoke.

The boy disappeared in a flurry of feet, crumbs, and a shout to Fin to 'wait up'.

There hadn't been a word of complaint about the outrageous colour of the sweater. Stitch, like anyone else would have been, was pleased to have it.

Rab picked up the bowl Stitch had left on the floor, sniffed at the remnants lying in the bottom, just a few scraps, but enough to tell him it was Sunny's own recipe for 'shroom loaf. Beat him how or when Fin had figured out how she'd made it.

For a moment Rab debated how he was going to get back onto his feet with the bowl still in his hand. In the end, he placed it on top of Stitch's seat, rolled onto his knees and pushed up from the ground with his hands. When he bent to retrieve the bowl, he almost toppled over. How the hell could he keep this up? Take on another trek? A couple of days from now, he knew the question would be gone from his mind. It always was.

What first?

Sort his stinking clothes? Wash them? Find something lying around the place to barter with down in Market Square for a new supply of food? The latter didn't look at all hopeful, the former just an agonising chore. As he went to dump Stitch's bowl in the little alcove, he settled on a wander down to the library. A morning wasted among old books wasn't going to gear him up; it would clear his mind though, and right at that moment a clear mind was exactly what Rab felt he needed most.

He'd change into new clothes first. It was a bit of a surprise that neither Stitch nor Fin had said anything. Or maybe his clothes always stunk that bad. On his way back to his niche, Rab collected his pack and the keys Stitch had left on the floor.

***

No sooner had he stepped onto Braham Street than Rab had a change of mind. After so much solitude, what he really craved was the communion of people, specifically someone who wouldn't shout at him or challenge him or dart off within a few minutes of seeing him. The library was widely regarded by most tunnel-dwellers as redundant; there would be no company for him in that cold place where even the shimmerers failed to thrive. The someone who came to mind was Ruby. Of all the tunnel-dwellers, Ruby had been the one to accept him unreservedly. Perhaps it was a matter of conditioning and a higher tolerance born out of years caring for returned captives. So Ruby it had to be. When he came to the intersection of Braham and Main streets, Rab kept going straight into the opposite tunnel. There were a number of minor functionary passageways that branched off from that main tunnel: one led to the hospital; another to the library; others Rad had never bothered to investigate, but the council chamber itself opened directly onto the main tunnel. Rab had never been invited behind its large and very heavily panelled door. When he came to the chamber, he wasn't too surprised to discover a thick somewhat threadbare carpet now hanging from the frame where the big old door had once been suspended. He'd often wondered how long it would take before that substantial bit of tinder was consigned to fire.

Reaching the end of the minor passageway he had taken, he found the door there still intact. Considering what lay behind, it would likely be the last to go. Opening the door, he spotted Ruby right where he had expected her to be, perched on the same rickety old chair behind the same rickety old desk, looking for all the world as though she hadn't budged from the spot in front of the hospital's brightly blazing hearth since he'd left. At first, he thought Ruby was alone until he spied a bundle of something lying on top of one of the beds near the door and realised it was a small person. Not one of Ruby's usual break, sprain or cough victims but something else.

He jerked his head, indicating the bed, as he continued on towards Ruby behind her big old rickety desk.

"The Pigeon Brothers brought her in last week," Ruby said by way of greeting.

The Pigeon Brothers! Three words that, whenever mentioned, were sure to set Rab's blood boiling. From the disparate look of them, Rab doubted the pair were actually brothers and of course their name wasn't really Pigeon. That was just a title old John Braham had dropped on them long before Rab had ever encountered the repulsive duo. Something to do with homing pigeons, Ruby had once explained, although she couldn't tell Rab exactly what a homing pigeon was and Rab had never been interested enough to find out. On the day he'd found Gift missing, Rab, in his naiveté, had believed it would be a simple matter to enlist those two bounty hunters in the search for her. He needed someone who knew all about the nomadic Top-siders. Where they went. What routes they took to get there. How long they stayed. For that kind of expertise there were none better than those bounty hunters.

Rab hadn't counted on the price the Pigeon Brothers would demand though. He had little to offer them and they could easily find more affluent victims to bleed. No deal had ever been struck although Rab suspected that, deal or no deal, the pair kept an eye out for Gift just the same, reasoning that when push came to shove, he'd find the bounty somehow. Well, he couldn't. But let the brothers think what they wanted. All he had to know was *where* to find her; the rest he could do for himself.

Rab bypassed Ruby and walked directly to the small recess where she stored patched and repatched linen, some of the more robust medicines, and a small cabinet full of dust-covered reading glasses. He glanced overhead, towards the barely visible hole in the roof there. The battered, rusting old chain was hanging down; hard to see way up there in the gloom unless you knew what you were looking for. The chain hanging down like that meant the bounty hunters hadn't departed the city yet. They'd draw it top-side again once they left and drop it through the small jagged hole in the roof of the recess when they returned, an alert for Ruby that they required access to the city again. Once Ruby had neglected to monitor the comings and goings of the chain until it was almost too late to rescue a couple of bounty hunters who had been left up on the plateau. Confused by cold and hunger, they hadn't thought to attempt to bust the lock on the city gates and at least gain access to the upper tunnel where pounding on the inner door might have eventually raised someone. Ruby monitored the chain every day now.

"You could have asked me if they are still here instead of making yourself at home in my hospital," she said.

Satisfied, Rab wandered back to Ruby and propped himself on the edge of the desk, about to enquire about Gift, when Ruby shook her frizzy head, anticipating his question.

"They didn't see her," she lifted a shoulder, "well, anyone around her age anyway and I can't get a thing out of that one." She gestured towards the crumpled-up bunch of bone, skin and sheeting in the bed. "I think she's a *true-breed*," Ruby part whispered, part mouthed.

It never ceased to amaze him how even Ruby, with the years she had spent patching up these returned captives and sending them on their way towards mostly productive lives in the city, never understood that, to a Top-sider, *being* a Top-sider was not a matter of shame.

Rab glanced slyly back towards the bed. The girl was curled up, fetal-like, knees to chest. Beneath a loosely hacked mop of matted brown hair, her face was all cheek bones and big round eyes that stared but didn't seem to see him. Yes, she had the look of Top-sider about her for sure. Ruby was probably right.

"She doesn't look too good," Rab observed quietly.

"Isn't," Ruby admitted, just as guardedly. "She won't make it. That's why I agreed to take her."

With the passing of Sunny and old John Braham, it had fallen to Ruby to step forward and fill the void. No one else in the city was prepared to have any lengthy dealings with the Pigeon Brothers and since Ruby was invariably charged with the initial care of the returned captives down in the hospital, it was the logical decision.

"You paid the bounty for a girl you knew from the start was Top-sider?"

One of Ruby's eyes began to twitch. "Now I wouldn't go saying that I knew from the start she was Top-sider."

No, Rab wouldn't go saying that. Ruby could get into a whole lot of trouble for that kind of mistake.

"I had to have a good look at her first. Decide if she was too young."
Sure she did.

Briefly, Rab glanced back at the bed. In the last ten years, not a single girl had gone missing from the city, not since old Braham had erected that old heavy door at the base of the upper tunnel. The bundle of bone and rag in the bed looked hardly any bigger than Gift had been the last time he'd seen her. But top-side kids were commonly undersized and there was no telling how old this one might be.

"No one came to consider her?" he asked, turning back to Ruby.

Ruby shrugged. "Prue did. Wouldn't have her."

Rab struggled to put a face to the name. Then it came to him. Prue. Pots and pans Prue, Lilly Benson's strongest competition.

Sunny, with her inimitable talent for contorting the truth, would have had Prue bundling the girl out the door in no time, happy in the misbegotten belief the girl was hers. . .for a while anyway. . .until the kid up and died on her.

"She probably isn't one of us," Ruby was saying, "but even a poor miserable thing like that deserves to die in comfort, instead of up there. . ." she waved a hand in the general direction of the ceiling, ". . . out in the cold with those surface-roaming *animals*."

Surface-roaming animals who might just have loved her, Rab thought. God, he was growing soft. Or perhaps Cloud's latest tirade was getting to him. Village Top-siders loved their children. Why couldn't nomadic Top-siders? Maybe they even loved the stolen ones. He didn't share that notion with Ruby. She had a good heart and all in all, did a better job than Sunny. An honest one. Well, mostly.

"How long?" Rab asked although he wasn't sure he really wanted to know.

"Tomorrow. Day after. Hard to say."

He didn't need to ask anything more; Ruby would sit right there in that chair until the very last breath left the little girl's body. It was Ruby's way. And at the end, she'd probably be holding the little girl's hand. She really did have a good heart.

"If you want," Rab said after another quick glance towards the bed, "I can stay here in the hospital tonight. Give you the chance for some rest."

Why not? The hospital had the best, very likely the only real, beds in the city. And after Sunny, well he could watch the young girl die without even blinking an eye. Just like Ruby. Didn't mean they didn't care.

"No need unless. . ." Ruby faltered, ". . . unless you want to."

"All the same to me," Rab said with a shrug. "Just thought I could be useful."

At least he could show that he could be for a change.

"Got to wonder, haven't you," Rab said thoughtfully after a moment, "how big a part Sunny might have played in some of the later disappearances from this place?"

"She never did such a thing," Ruby snapped. A florid crimson wave that began at her neck surged upward until it reached her cheeks and the exposed tips of her ears. "Sunny was well respected here and if you're half as smart as you think you are, you won't go around say—"

Ruby's tirade ceased midword with her mouth left hanging open.

Rab was about to ask what was wrong, but was interrupted by a great clatter and bang as the door to the hospital hit the inside wall. Ruby jumped to her feet; Rab slipped off the desk; and someone was leaning, hanging off the door, half-in, half-out of the room.

Rab knew the name of the man hanging there, but again just couldn't put the name to the face for the moment. The big man was breathing hard and his face was flushed. From a distance it looked as though he was trembling and, if Rab hadn't known better, covered from knee to shoulder in grey 'shroom dust.

"Max!" Ruby called as she shot around the side of her desk. "What in heaven's name is wrong? Are you hurt?"

That was it. Max Something-or-other. Worked with Fin down on the tracks sometimes.

Rab made to help Ruby get the injured Max into one of the beds, but stopped when the man began violently shaking his head.

"Not me! Not me!" Max had finally caught enough breath to speak. "There's been a terrible accident. Down in the mushroom field," he wheezed. "One of the carts has tipped over. There's people trapped."

Rab shot a glance over at Ruby, who was pushing the frizzy fuzz that passed as hair back from her face.

Down in the mushroom field!

"Who's hurt? How many?" Ruby cried as she belted back past the bed containing the motionless girl to retrieve her medicine bag.

"Don't know. I was hauling, right up front, when I felt this awful kind of wrench, then heard an almighty crash and someone started yelling that the middle cart had overturned and I should start running and get you fast."

Rab wasn't about to wait for an invitation. He shoved Max aside and pitched himself down the passageway, speeding towards Grocer's Alley and the offshoot tunnel that would take him directly into the 'shroom field.

As he ran, he was vaguely aware of two sets of feet pounding the hard ground behind him. Max and Ruby were right on his tail. Rab didn't spare a thought for the delicate shimmerers every time he bounced off a wall because he'd taken a turn too sharply.

By the time he reached Market Square, Rab was absolutely convinced it was Fin who was lying injured in the mammoth cave down below. He shot through the Square, heedless of vendors, carts, and customers, knowing but not caring that he'd left a couple of tunnel-dwellers on the ground in his wake. Faces blurred in front of him. Shouts followed behind. He made it to Grocer's Alley, still at speed, and if it hadn't been for Max anxiously calling him back, he'd have continued on at the same breakneck pace down that lane.

"Can't go that way."

Rab swung around to find Max pulled up, bent over crookedly at the waist, gasping for breath. Behind him, Ruby's face was vibrant red. She was listing sideways, hand clutched to one hip, with the big medicine bag firmly clasped in the other.

"The tunnel's full of mushrooms," Max panted noisily. "We'll step all over them. Got to go—"

"Through 'the house'," Rab finished for him impatiently and, without waiting for confirmation, raced off ahead of his two companions towards the tunnel that meandered upward to 'the house'.

At all costs, spare the crop!

Rab was accustomed to the falls and rises and the insensitivity of the top-side world. His companions were used to the more reliable and gentler nature of the world below. While he took the twists, turns, and bumps of the tunnel easily, he could sense Max and Ruby falling behind. If it hadn't been for the shimmerers lighting their way, one or other of them would likely have taken a tumble in their frantic uphill dash towards 'the house'.

As he'd expected, the fire hadn't been lit in that upper space. Max and Ruby—they could see better than he could in the dark, so as loathe as he was to do it, Rab drew up. Though blindsight allowed him to sense the location of the ancillary tunnel, to the left side of the hearth, lacking light, he was more likely to stumble into the hearth than find the entrance. The seconds wasted waiting for Max and Ruby at least afforded him the opportunity to snatch a few deep breaths. Like Ruby, he had a stitch developing in his side. Max, having already run the distance from the 'shroom field to the hospital, had to be relying wholly on nervous energy. He was a big man and if he was obliged to speak, he usually did it in a mutter, and when walking, tended to do so at a leisurely pace. There was nothing leisurely about his pace now; as he shot by in the dark, Rab plainly felt a gust of wind on his face. Ruby came hard on his heels and Rab fell in behind. Once they started down the narrow and seldom used ancillary tunnel towards the 'shroom field, there'd be shimmerers to light the way, but it was too cool up in 'the house' proper for the lovely little beasts to thrive.

Rab listened intently for each and every one of Ruby's footfalls, following as best he could directly behind her, and made the ancillary tunnel without incident. The walls were too close, the floor too irregular and rock-jammed to allow them to do anything but walk carefully in single file. Last time he'd been down this tunnel, Gift had been with him. The tunnel had been in poor condition even then, but he didn't remember having to work quite so hard to squeeze past every jagged obstacle in his way or, for that matter, that there had been quite so many rock falls. Maybe it was he, not the tunnel, that had been in better condition. He hoped to hell there was a gang at work clearing the main tunnel because if they had to get an injured Fin up this way, he didn't see how they were going to do it.

Ahead of him, Ruby was having a rough time of it. She wasn't a young woman, good enough for her years, Rab supposed, but clearly pretty well spent.

How much farther was it? God, why couldn't he remember? Couldn't be far. Just couldn't be. And then suddenly, it wasn't. Over the top of Max's large head, in the glow of the shimmerers, Rab could make out the blunt end of the tunnel. They'd have a scramble to the bottom, he recalled. Not too bad a scramble but enough to challenge Ruby. When they reached a stretch of rubble-free ground, just shy of the exit, Rab slipped the medicine bag off Ruby's shoulder. She glanced back briefly, but never said a word. Very likely she couldn't even if she'd wanted to. In the light from the shimmerers, Rab had seen in her face what her faltering gait had already hinted at. Ruby was tapping the limits of her strength. Thank God it wasn't too far now, yet each step still seemed agonisingly slow.

Max emerged first and took the scree beneath the tunnel exit at a trot. Ruby held back, allowing Rab to tackle the loose slope at high speed. If his feet hit the ground at all, Rab wasn't aware of it. All that registered was a constant pinging sound as he sent small rocks, grit, and dust in a cascade ahead of him down the hill and Ruby's voice calling frantically to him from above.

"Be careful!"

Was she kidding?

He simply didn't have the time or the patience. Fin was down there! Halfway down the hill, Rab shot past Max. He guessed Ruby was making a more cautious descent. He didn't look back to find out. The floor of the massive basin ahead of him was deserted of workers. There were crops aplenty though and, although it pained him to do it, Rab slowed down as much as he dared and threaded a watchful path through the densely planted field heading for the track that would bring him to the service tunnel in the opposite wall of the basin. The track was his best and only clear route forwards. To sustain the city, every feasible patch of ground had to be given over to cultivation and so the 'shroom fields extended right up to the very edge of the track and almost to the entrance of the tunnel itself. Long before he reached the tunnel, Rab could hear shouts and yells and a persistent droning kind of sound much like the wind sometimes had when it sang to him top-side. No wind here, just a haunting draught of whispers breathed from the mouth of every cropper who had gathered at the far end of the track.

Rab pushed, shoved, and shouldered his way through towards the front of the crowd. Every time the medicine bag became snagged, Rab was obliged to wrench it free. He ignored the occasional protests, ducked whenever an errant elbow wheeled too close. These tunnel-dwellers hardly knew him; there'd be no reasoning with them to let him pass. He just hoped they'd make a clearer path for Ruby; otherwise, he couldn't see how she could drive a way through the impasse of emotionally-charged croppers. He had the medicine bag, but Ruby had the skill and Rab feared there was little he could do without her.

Breaking through the front rank of onlookers, Rab finally got his first real look at the accident. It hadn't been some small maintenance cart that had overturned, but one of the larger transfer carts. Since they ran the carts in tandem, three at a time, the toppling of the middle cart had tipped the trailing cart onto its side. This last cart was blocking much of the entrance to the tunnel where, some distance in, the middle cart lay upside-down. Rab couldn't make out much about the condition of the first cart but it must have toppled, too, because just as Max had claimed, there were 'shrooms spread everywhere. In some places the pile was as high as Rab's shoulder, in others, just a scattering of 'shrooms littered the floor. As Rab had hoped, there was a gang of croppers working furiously to gather the fallen load. But there were too few of them to make much of an impact and the business of gathering up the 'shrooms and getting them to safe ground was an infuriately slow process. Most of the croppers were scooping the fallen 'shrooms up in handfuls; others had stripped off their outer shirts and were using them like baskets. There simply wasn't enough room for more croppers to work, not without trampling a good part of the harvest underfoot. When one of the precariously stacked piles of salvaged 'shrooms threatened to tumble, a cropper jumped forwards from the mob of bystanders and began to try to right it. The well-intentioned gesture just made matters worse and the destabilised pile collapsed. They were getting nowhere.

Rab rushed forwards, a little too heedlessly perhaps. One of the croppers yelled at him. Rab didn't bother to reply, but kept on leaping up and over the mound upon mound of 'shrooms. He crawled onto the top of the trailing cart, the side of it really, and that allowed him to make better time and at least spare the 'shrooms that had spilled from it. Ahead he could see clearly now where the middle cart had come off the track. It lay wedged between the track and one side of the tunnel wall. The back end of it appeared to be sitting higher off the ground than the front, suggesting that the front end had crumpled completely. Had the cart tipped the other direction, it would have been an inconvenience to right, but all in all, a minor incident. The track ran hard against the side of the tunnel there; the cart couldn't have rolled right over and there'd have been minimal spillage and no one on that side of the cart to be trapped beneath it.

Rab hesitated, torn between waiting for Ruby and jumping down off the trailing cart into the heart of the trouble. He looked back and spotted her squeezing through the front of the crowd. Rab raised his arm and dangled the medicine bag, hoping to attract her attention. He had no idea what had become of Max. Ruby must have seen him, because immediately she began running towards him. No one yelled at Ruby as she wove a crooked path through the delicate wreckage. In fact, one of the croppers, on catching sight of her, immediately stopped his gathering and rushed for her. When the cropper, just another nameless soul to Rab, glanced away from Ruby and noticed the medicine bag hanging limply from Rab's hand, he began to shout.

"Clear the way! Clear the way! Ruby's here. You there," he bellowed, rough handling a cropper who was bent to his haunches and blocking Ruby's path. "Move aside."

Rab hurried to the back of the trailing cart again, dropped to his belly and waited for the cropper to get Ruby to him through the scattered 'shrooms. As soon as she reached the back end of the cart, Rab reached down, caught hold of her outstretched arms and began to pull. The cropper's big hands circled Ruby's waist and together they lifted her onto the side of the cart. Once Rab had Ruby onto her feet, he looked back and found the cropper gone.

With Ruby in tow, Rab headed to the front of the cart again. He was desperate to sight the people trapped beneath the middle cart, but there were workers in the way. Those directly below him were frantically gathering 'shrooms, adding them, handfuls at a time, into unstable piles as close to the entrance to the tunnel as possible. A small patch of ground had been cleared to one side of the overturned cart, where a couple of croppers were lying flat on their bellies. The other croppers, those collecting up the 'shrooms, were obliged to jump repeatedly over their outstretched legs to make any headway with the 'shrooms that had spilled between the two carts. Beneath the intermittent shouts from the croppers gathering the 'shrooms and the constant drone bleeding from the onlookers behind him, Rab thought he could hear someone, one of those croppers who was lying on the ground, softly talking, but kind of on and off, as though they were waiting for a reply in between.

Good! That was good!

It meant that Fin and whoever else was trapped beneath that cart were probably responding. Rab's hopes began to rise. Everything was going to be all right. Sure, they'd lost part of the crop and, by the look of it, at least one of the big carts, maybe all three of them. It wasn't the first time these tunnel-dwellers had faced that kind of hardship. It wouldn't be the last. Max had panicked—of course, why wouldn't he? Rab would have panicked, too.

But then Rab recognised one of the croppers lying on the ground towards the back end of the cart—almost at the same moment he spotted a patch of colour extending out from under the crumpled front end. The cropper was a dust-covered Fin—and the patch of colour, the gaudiest Rab had ever seen.

It wasn't Fin beneath that cart; it was Stitch!

Still the 'shroom-gathering croppers continued to shout the occasional order. When the rescuer lying beside Fin rose from the ground and leaned against the cart, there was an ominous-sounding screech. Just one. Behind Rab, the onlookers continued to shuffle their feet and spread the meagre but dire news. Inside his chest, Rab's heart continued to beat. But Rab was only vaguely aware of any of it until Ruby started shaking him by the shoulder.

"Get down there. Find out what's happening." She gave him a shove to get him moving. "Better I stay up here out of the way until I'm needed."

Yes. Why had he hesitated? He had to get down to Stitch.

The patch of cleared ground was barely wide enough for Fin and the other cropper, but if he jumped well, Rab might manage to land clear of the spilled 'shrooms and Fin's head. So he swung the medicine bag back into Ruby's hand and leapt, landing hard against the shoulder of the standing cropper and just shy of Fin's head.

Startled, Fin shot up from the ground, arms raised, clearly prepared to go for someone's throat. When he saw it was Rab, Fin grasped his shoulder instead and dragged him down to the ground.

"I can't get to them," he said, breath hurried, ragged. "Abby's directly under the cart. See?" He pointed. "She's been talking to me but Stitch hasn't said a word."

"Abby's trapped, too?"

"Rab? That you?"

Cloud's voice—strong and steady.

Rab lowered his head to the ground and tried to peer underneath the overturned cart, but saw nothing.

"It's me, Cloud. How can we get you both out? Can you tell us?"

"Move the mushrooms," she snapped out of the darkness, "and I can get myself out. That's what I've been trying to tell them but no one's listening."

"They're doing it, Cloud," Rab explained, glancing up and back at Fin who was trying to wipe the dirt, sweat, and mushroom dust from his eyes with the tail of his shirt.

"What about Stitch?" Rab called.

It took Cloud a moment to answer but at last her voice sounded from beneath the cart. "He can wait too."

Rab stood up and, peering around the side of the cart, located Stitch's gaudily clothed arm lying motionless among the mushrooms. No one could get close enough to reach it.

Dropping back down to his knees, he called again to Cloud. "He's pinned."

If he couldn't see her, then maybe she couldn't see Stitch.

"I know," she replied. "When the cart began to fall, I dove under it, but Stitch tried to stop it. I called to him to let it go, but there wasn't time."

"All right, Cloud, just be patient. They should have enough 'shrooms cleared soon."

Rab got to his feet and looked around.

The croppers were moving as fast they could but being essentially ineffective. They had to think of something else—some other way to clear more of the spillage and clear it faster. Some way to use the track.

"It's no use," Fin said, catching Rab with his eyes trained on a partly visible section of ruined track. "When the cart tipped, its wheels caught under the track and wrenched this side of it out of the ground all the way back past the trailing cart."

"But we could get a cart up to where it's wrecked, right?"

Fin shook his head. "Yes, but it won't help. The croppers will still have to carry each load from the tunnel to the cart. It won't save us any time."

"Having them stack it into those piles isn't working, Fin. They're too unstable."

"Don't you think I know that?" Fin shrieked.

"What if we brought one of the big carts right *up* to the tunnel?" Ruby shouted. She was lying on her belly on top of the trailing cart, head dangling over the side.

"But the track is ruined, Ruby," Rab called up to her. "That's what Fin just—"

"Forget the track," Ruby snapped. "Bring the cart up by itself. Lift it off the track and carry it." She pointed around the side of the trailing cart, towards the crowd of bystanders behind them. "There's enough of them to do it."

Rab glanced back at Fin, seeking confirmation. He had no idea about the weight of one of those big wood and metal carts and, if he was remembering correctly, the nearest undamaged cart was still some distance back in the 'shroom field.

"It's possible," Fin said. "We wouldn't have to lift it all the way. We could roll it until we got to the damaged section of track. But we'd still need to clear an area right beside the tunnel. And a free path through this part of the field to carry the cart."

"Then let's do it. You get a place cleared and I'll get that cart up to it somehow."

Rab leapt and more through fortune than skill, landed clear of the spilled 'shrooms, with his feet wedged between two of the boards that formed the side of the trailing cart and Ruby's hand reaching down to steady him.

***

Rab trained his eyes on the back of the cropper who was sweating and straining in front of him. Of all the croppers Rab had enlisted, he'd been the most sceptical, swearing blind that twenty people couldn't lift and carry a field cart. Thirty could have accomplished the task just that bit easier and faster, but twenty was all there was room for, ten either side of the cart. Nothing happened fast enough for Rab. It seemed to take forever to uncouple the closest of the big transport carts from the one behind it. And all the while they were doing that, Rab and the remaining croppers were emptying the load, tossing it into the field on either side of the track where, later, it could be regathered. They were badly bruising the crop; Rab could see that, and it must have sorely pained these tunnel-dwellers to do that. But none complained, not even the cropper who'd sworn blind, and kept swearing it, that they'd never even manage to lift the cart off the track.

When someone shouted 'Abby', Rab's immediate thought was that another incident had occurred up at the accident site. He looked up quickly, realised that the shout hadn't come from there at all but from the opposite tunnel, the one leading from 'the house' to the huge domed cavern of the 'shroom field. A woman appeared at the mouth of the tunnel and, during the short time he was watching, another two emerged from the tunnel behind her. Rab guessed the woman at the front was Lilly Benson. Word travelled fast in the tunnel city. Just before he lowered his head again, he saw Lilly stumble. She must have rolled all the way down because the next time Rab looked up, she was at the bottom of the slope, on her feet again and running for the track. The two women were chasing after her, shouting for her to pull up. They were making better time than Lilly and managed to overtake her before she reached Rab's cart. The last Rab saw of her, she was still some way down on the track, being held back by the two women who each had a grip on her arms. The women couldn't stop her ear-piercing screaming though. Rab and the croppers just worked on, ignoring her.

Once the 'shrooms were cleared, the nineteen croppers and Rab set about rolling the cart up to the ruined section of track. That was the easy part; the heavy draught harnesses were already in place and the croppers had rolled these carts backwards and forwards so many times through the tunnel, it was second nature. The crowd of bystanders, depleted to the number of Rab's workers, had been moved off by Fin or maybe Ruby to a small patch of crop-free ground on the other side of the tunnel entrance. Now they just had to lift.

And they did—although it nearly broke twenty backs to do it. Rab's position was near the middle, but all in all it probably didn't make a lot of difference where he was stationed. The croppers in front, behind, and on the other side were all bearing a load heavier than anything they had ever borne before. But the hardest part of all was to move forwards when the mass of the cart wanted to drive them into the ground. With each staggering step, Rab tried not to think about the fact that the same amount of weight was now resting on top of Stitch. Maybe Cloud as well. She'd said she was all right, but Cloud would say anything to save the cursed crop.

One more step forwards and the entrance to the tunnel grew a little closer. Another step and it would be closer still. Rab couldn't see much for the sweat pouring into his eyes and the broad back of the cropper in front of him, but every now and then he caught a glimpse of the large team frantically working to one side of the tunnel entrance. During one of those brief glimpses, he'd seen Ruby down on her knees as well. It was her; he could tell from that distinctive fuzzy head of hair.

The groans from his fellow lifters and the crunch, crunch, crunch of their heavy boots against unforgiving ground weren't enough to mask the sound of the bystanders' persistent whispering "They won't make it."

They'd make it!

Rab wouldn't accept anything less.

Sometimes he heard Fin bellowing out commands, ordering someone from his team this way, another that.

Maybe Rab hadn't ever got to know Fin as well as he could have—or should have—but he knew enough to know that Fin's team would make it, too, and have a place cleared for them before they got there with the cart. Fin wouldn't accept anything less, either—not where Stitch was concerned. It seemed such a long time ago now, when the four of them had recklessly ventured inside the old ruined factory by the river—Fin, Stitch, Gift and him. Fin had risked his life to save Stitch that day. No matter that the lad had fallen from the old catwalk and broken his leg anyway. It had still been Fin who had rushed forwards to try to abort the fall. And Fin wouldn't let a simple thing like half a harvest's worth of scattered 'shrooms beat him now.

Almost there. One more step. Another. Soon it would all be over. They'd have the path between the overturned carts and the tunnel wall cleared enough for a team of croppers to squeeze through and right the middle cart. Cloud would get herself out. Sure, she'd be fine just like she had said. And Stitch? Well, maybe he'd broken an arm. That gaudily clad arm certainly looked bent wrong way round. But that would be the worst of it. Stitch and his broken bones! Ruby could fix it. She'd fixed his leg and now Stitch could walk almost as well as everyone else. She'd fix his arm until it worked nearly as well as everyone else's, too. Worst that could happen was Stitch would lose the use of one arm. He could still get by that way. Fin would see to it that he did.

Rab's mind was racing as he staggered closer, ever closer, to the cleared patch of ground near the tunnel entrance. The thoughts were all that kept him moving. God knew what kept the croppers ahead and behind him moving, but move they did and soon the clearing was maybe forty hard-won steps away, now thirty, twenty, a meagre ten until at last there were no more steps that needed to be wrenched from muscles that were threatening to tear, bones that were threatening to snap, and twenty hearts ready to burst.

Around the shoulder of the cropper in front of him, Rab saw Fin rush to grab hold of the front end of the cart. When the cart began to swing, Rab nearly lost his footing. That's all this crowd of tunnel-dwellers needed. . .another body trapped beneath another one of their carts. Shuffle. Shuffle. The cart edged to the right as Fin called instructions on exactly where the cart needed to be positioned.

"Here! Here!" Fin shouted. "Stop! Feet clear now! And drop!"

The tail end of his shout was lost to a tremendous thud as the cart hit the ground, showering dust over the boots of the croppers who two and sometimes three at a time, crumpled down beside it.

Rab's muscles burned and spasmed. The cropper in front of him toppled right into his lap, while Rab tumbled into the lap of the cropper behind him. From somewhere he heard a cheer. The disbelieving bystanders? Fin's own exhausted team? *Who the hell cared!* Rab couldn't believe it either, and he was too exhausted to take a moment to marvel at what they had managed to accomplish. But the job wasn't over. They'd barely scratched its surface. All they'd managed to do was possibly save most of the harvest. They'd made no progress at all in righting the overturned cart or in freeing Cloud and Stitch.

By the time Rab had recovered enough to stagger to his feet, Fin's team had made a good start on loading the gathered 'shrooms into the cart. One by one, Rab's team rose to join them. But Fin was nowhere in sight and, Rab realised, a good number of his team were missing. He couldn't find Ruby, either, then realised they'd have left most of the croppers loading the 'shrooms while the rest began making their way to the overturned cart.

Rab was relieved not to have to scramble over the lopsided trailing cart again; the way was clear now for him to get between it and the wall of the tunnel. Two people could walk abreast there now. It would make getting an injured Stitch out of the tunnel a relatively easy task—once the cart was lifted off him—and that posed another problem. How were they going to lift the cart and hold it there long enough for someone to crawl underneath and drag Stitch out? Well, they'd done the impossible once. It was time to do it again.

Rab found Fin, belly-down on the floor, at just about the same spot as before, only this time his face was turned sideways into the dirt and his arms, up to the elbows, had disappeared underneath the tipped-up end of the cart. He started to inch backwards—not exactly easily, but it was clear that whatever he was dragging with him was trying to help. Fin's wrists appeared—his hands—then someone else's hands. There was no mistaking whose—Cloud's. When Fin had her dragged out to the waist, he let go and Cloud hauled herself the rest of the way out from under the cart. Rab darted forwards and got her onto her feet; when Ruby pushed him away, Rab turned his attention to Fin. The boy was already up and running towards the crumpled front end of the cart.

Rab's gaze flicked from Fin's back to a filthy Cloud, who was dusting herself off and animatedly protesting Ruby's ministrations.

She caught Rab's eye and nodded; his signal to chase after Fin.

The croppers were already in position by the time Fin arrived with Rab close on his heels. If there'd been some sort of plan devised, Rab had missed it.

Fin called once loudly to Stitch; no reply came back to break the silence.

When Rab stepped up, about to take up a position, Fin raised a hand to stop him.

"You've done enough lifting. You could drop it."

Reluctantly, Rab conceded that Fin was probably right. He stepped back and no sooner had he found a place to stand, out of the way, although still close enough to help drag Stitch free if he was needed, than Cloud and Ruby hurried up to join him.

His hand went out automatically and clasped Cloud's. Either his muscles were still spasming or she was trembling; perhaps both. Beside her, Ruby dropped to the floor and set to rummaging about in her medicine bag.

"On the count of three," Fin called. "One."

Cloud leaned her head into Rab's shoulder.

"Two."

He dipped his head to hers.

"Three!"

There was a unified groan from the croppers—then a kind of squeal—and slowly the cart began to move. Someone's foot slipped and, for a moment, Rab thought they were going to lose control of the lift, but the cropper managed to right himself and still bear his share of the weight. Higher and higher it rose until Rab could finally see Stitch's body, part of it anyway because most of him was buried beneath 'shrooms. Rab and Cloud rushed forwards and, together with the remainder of the croppers, those that weren't holding up the cart, began to frantically drag Stitch free. 'Shrooms fell and rolled to either side of him and the moment they had his feet clear, Rab called for Fin and his team to drop the cart. Sure it would wreck the 'shrooms lying in the drop zone but the first priority now was Stitch, who hadn't spoken a word or twitched, even in the slightest, one muscle.

As one, Fin and his team dropped the cart. It crashed loudly to the floor of the tunnel with a horrendous noise and a billow of 'shroom dust that must have sent the bystanders outside the tunnel into another panic.

Ruby shoved Rab aside, though Cloud was still left on the ground, kneeling by Stitch's head. Reluctantly Rab made way for Fin; he was the boy's true family after all. Rab pressed himself hard up against the wall of the tunnel. It was strange to be feeling nothing. It seemed he'd suddenly become an observer, who was looking down on this frenzied scene from somewhere far, far away. Just a watcher with no part to play, no stake in the outcome. Someone who, when it was all over, would simply walk away, unmoved by whatever transpired.

Fin had a hold of Stitch's arm, the one that wasn't all unnaturally twisted up and bent. Cloud was holding his head and Ruby was using some sort of scissor-like thing to cut away at the boy's new sweater. The area where Ruby was cutting was a uniform kind of red now, its once gaudy colour masked entirely in blood. It was that large and awful red stain that finally settled Rab's mind. There was no need to rush now. Whatever urgency there had been had passed.

Cloud glanced up at him and he looked down into her dirt-smeared face. She'd said Stitch could wait and she'd been right. There was no saving him; she'd known it all along. The girl was tough, tougher than Rab could ever be. She'd saved as much of the crop as she could and Rab didn't doubt for one moment that if it had been her instead of Stitch pinned so badly beneath the crumbled end of the cart, she'd have wanted it exactly the same way.

When she shook her head at him, slowly, so very very slowly, Rab turned and walked away. This was tunnel-dweller business now and he'd forfeited any place as a tunnel-dweller a long time ago. And now, too, his pledge to Gift, the thread that kept drawing him back to the tunnels over and over again, was broken. Stitch was dead.

Rab had a recollection that he might have passed Lilly Benson on the tracks on his way back to his empty space on Braham Street. He wasn't really sure. In fact, he wasn't really sure how he'd got there at all. He must have scrambled back through the tunnel, come down from 'the house'. If anyone along the way had tried to stop him and ask about the accident, Rab simply couldn't remember.

Had it been a cowardly thing to do? To leave Fin, Cloud and the others to clean up the mess? Fin wouldn't have wanted him there. And the croppers knew better than he did how to set the 'shroom field back to rights; they didn't need his interference. And Cloud? Yes, what about Cloud? Whether she liked it or not, Ruby would have dragged her off to the hospital, where Rab would have only got in the way. Rab had only ever had one significant contribution to make to these tunnel-dwellers: to keep his mouth shut. And now he could add to his worth a little bit of brute force when it was needed. The former would never be recognised; the latter soon forgotten.

Just as it should be.

Chapter 3

THE little Top-sider girl died that night not long after Stitch. They were to be buried together the next day. It made sense. Two bodies to be disposed of. One journey top-side to do it.

As it was with his own people, tunnel-dwellers were customarily buried naked. Though a tunnel-dweller's hair was generally left untouched, their clothes were usually salvaged for re-use. Fin hadn't wanted it that way and Rab hadn't wanted to see the boy laid into the ground in Cloud's ruined and bloodied sweater. They'd reached a compromise. Rab still had the coat Blaze had given him when he'd left the village, reluctantly carting three children behind him. The coat had seen better days and, last year, Rab had given up wearing it top-side anymore. Fin had accepted the old coat for Stitch. The Top-sider girl would be buried in the clothes she'd been wearing when the Pigeon Brothers had brought her into the tunnels; they weren't good for much else.

And so Rab found himself sitting on the floor of the space he now shared with Fin alone, ripping out the last of the padding from inside Blaze's old coat before handing it over to Ruby, who was readying Stitch and the girl child for burial. Despite the agony it caused him to use his ruined muscles even for this small task, Rab knew Cloud could use the padding and Stitch certainly didn't need it. Fin was off somewhere, maybe helping Ruby. Rab had begun to ask where he was going when he'd left their shared space early that morning, but then thought better of it. It was the young man's right to mourn as he chose. Besides, neither had slept that night; and another bout in their traditional run of confrontations wasn't going to help anyone.

"Can I come in?"

Rab didn't need to look up to know it was Cloud.

He nodded and the next moment she dropped down onto the aging carpet beside him.

"These are for you," he said, reaching out to touch the little mound of wadding he had made.

"I have something for you, too," Cloud replied.

At that, Rab did look up. He couldn't imagine what she could mean until she placed a pair of boots on the floor in front of him. Stitch's boots!

Well, why not? It's how things worked. He and Stitch were roughly the same size. He could make good use of those boots.

"Ruby said it was all right for me to give them to you," Cloud said hesitantly.

She'd obviously been apprehensive about Rab's reaction. She needn't have been.

As chief and only mortician, Ruby had first right of say on any item the recently deceased happened to be wearing at the time of their death. That used to be Sunny's purview but with her passing, the responsibility for that, too, had fallen on Ruby's broad shoulders.

Rab accepted the boots with a quiet thanks.

"Will you take this down to Ruby when I'm finished?"

"Of course I will, Rab. Fin told us to expect it."

So Fin *had* gone to help in the preparation of Stitch's body. Cloud, too, by the sound of it. Rab didn't ask why. He didn't know how close Stitch and Cloud might have become during his long absences. Or how close Fin and Cloud might have grown for that matter. Fin was nearer in age to Cloud than he was. Strange, he'd never actually thought about that before. And now that he had, Rab wasn't sure how he felt about it. But then, he supposed, he had no right to any opinion at all.

Beside him, Cloud shifted position a little.

"You're coming to the funeral, aren't you?"

What sort of question was that? A great reputation he must have gained down here in these tunnels if there had been even a suspicion that he might not go.

He dropped the coat and turned to stare directly into Cloud's dark brown eyes.

"Did you think I *wouldn't?*"

"Not me, no," Cloud replied, some hesitancy still evident in her voice, "but no one else really knows you, Rab. They don't know what to expect."

"Fin does," he said, refusing to release his lock on her eyes.

"And he said you'd go. It was some others who—"

Rab cut her off. "I don't care what anyone else thinks," he said and, looking away, resumed pulling out the last of the padding. "Except maybe for Ruby," he added.

Cloud was silent for a long time before she spoke again.

"Are you all right?"

She touched his shoulder just as Rab had finished with the coat.

"I'll be fine," he said, twisting his head to look at Cloud again. "I've buried my parents. My brother. Seen more people from my village die than I can even remember. It's Fin you need to worry about. Hell, I even buried John Braham and Sunny."

Technically, the latter wasn't exactly true, but no one in the tunnels, not even Cloud, needed to know the precise details.

"I just thought, well, you brought Stitch here, after all, and—"

Again Rab cut her off. "And he had ten good years here, didn't he? He'd have been dead inside one if he'd stayed back in our village."

Perhaps Rab was exaggerating a little, but Stitch certainly wouldn't have seen another *ten* years. None of them would have. Perhaps ten years was enough. Gift wouldn't have thought so. He'd broken his promise to her and maybe that failure might just have hurt him worse than the loss of Stitch, itself. And what sort of self-absorbed thinking was that? One that would see him out of this tunnel within the week. That much was certain. He'd see Fin settled first, as settled as he ever could be without Stitch, and when he left maybe he wouldn't bother coming back. Maybe he would just hook up with some Top-sider band instead and, unfettered by the need to husband his food supplies for the journey back, trek farther than he had ever dared trek before. Maybe. . .

"You're still going to leave, aren't you?" Cloud said, snapping Rab back to the moment.

In his head, he was already gone.

"Why not." It wasn't a question. He placed the stripped coat into Cloud's hands. "This is ready," he said, rising. "You can take it to Ruby now."

He expected Cloud to get up from the floor too, but she didn't. She just sat there, crossed-legged, looking down at her fingers that were pulling at the loose threads Rab had left behind.

"Fin and I are going, too."

Rab didn't think he could be shocked or surprised by anything or anyone ever again. He'd been wrong.

"What? Oh no, you're not!" He glared down at the top of Cloud's head. "You are not coming with me."

Cloud stopped fidgeting and glanced up.

"We're not going with you, Rab. We're going to take Stitch home. That's what Fin wants to do." She did rise then and looked Rab resolutely in the eyes. "And I can't, and I won't let him go alone."

Cloud wasn't making any sense. He must have heard wrong. He hadn't been giving her much of his attention. They were *burying* Stitch today.

"We're going to bury his body first. . ."

There, she'd said it.

". . . and carry his heart home."

What? That couldn't be! That wasn't right!

"What are you talking about?" he asked.

"Fin intends to bury Stitch's heart in his own village. I thought he told you."

No. Fin hadn't told him any such thing and he simply couldn't believe it was true. Only a monster would cut out a dead boy's heart. Why would Cloud say something so evil? What did she hope to achieve, lying to him that way?

Suddenly Rab felt very cold. On the surface and in the tunnels, he had experienced many different kinds of cold: there was the kind of cold that froze your mind and wouldn't let you think straight; the kind that could snap off your fingers and toes; the kind that made your breath frost and your teeth ache. And then there was the kind of cold Rab had only ever felt inside that spaceship with Sunny. It was that kind of cold he felt now.

He wrenched the coat from Cloud's hands. "I'll take this to Ruby myself. She'll tell me what's going on."

"But. . ."

Rab wasn't interested in anything else Cloud had to say. He left her there, standing in the middle of his space, and hurried away from her down Braham Street. Didn't matter if she was lying or telling him the truth. He simply *had* to get away from the bitter coldness of her and for the sake of his reason at that moment, as far away as possible.

Fin wasn't in the hospital when he got there and the bed where the little Top-sider girl had been lying was now conspicuously empty. Ruby, as usual, was sitting at her desk.

Rab let the door bang behind him and strode across the room.

"Did Stitch have a last name?" Ruby asked, glancing up. "Funny it's never come up before and I forgot to ask Fin." She pointed to a book of some sort lying open on the desk in front of her. "I'll have to register the girl as unknown, but I thought Stitch should have—" she didn't finish, but sprang out of her seat, clearly troubled. The look on Rab's face had finally registered. "What's wrong? Has something else happened?"

Rab flung the stripped coat on top of the open book.

"Depends. I've just come from talking to Cloud."

"Oh." Ruby slumped back into her chair, her face slowly draining of colour. "She's told you then."

"Told me! Then you know?"

"Of course I know. I did it. If I hadn't, then Fin would have—"

Rab raised a hand to ward off the gruesome details. "Don't say it. Just tell me *why*? How could you do that, Ruby? How *could* you?"

Ruby gathered the coat onto her lap and closed the book in front of her. "How could I not, Rab?" she said, folding her hands on top of the battered old cover. "Better I should do it than. . .well. . ." she hesitated a moment then hurried on. "It's what Fin wanted."

"So I've heard! Just how many people were in on this madness?"

"Just Fin, Abby, and me, Rab. No one else."

"Why Abby?"

Ruby shrugged. "She was standing there when Fin asked."

Rab simply couldn't believe the woman could behave so calmly, considering what she'd done. That was more Sunny's way. But even Sunny wouldn't have done *this*. Oh, not on account of some high moral principle, but because she simply wouldn't have bothered.

"I don't suppose he gave you an explanation for why he wanted to do such a despicable thing?" Rab demanded.

"No. And I didn't press him about it, Rab. For all I knew, it could have been a tradition in your village. Besides, I didn't think it was a despicable thing to do." She was looking Rab right in the eye. Not a flinch. Not a blink. Clearly at total peace with the unspeakable decision she'd made.

"Stitch couldn't be hurt any longer," she went on to say. "It's been done in the past, you know. Fin isn't the first to want that." She even had the gall to try and rationalise what she'd done. "I've read about it. In those books down in the library, there are stories—"

He *had* been wrong about Ruby; she was just like Sunny after all.

"I don't want to hear about any stories in any books, Ruby."

"Well, anyway, that's why when he asked me, I didn't think it was all that strange a request."

Rab ran a shaking hand through his hair. This place. These people. They were the stuff of nightmares.

"How can you possibly *not* think it was strange?" he said at last.

"Look, Rab, everyone grieves in their own way," Ruby said. She rose to her feet and, folding Blaze's old coat, laid it on top of the closed book. "You must know that. And I've worked down here in this hospital long enough to learn not to question why one person grieves this way and another that." She came around the side of her desk to face him. "I'd drive myself mad trying to find an answer. Me? I'd cry for days but sooner or later, I'd gather up the shreds of my life and move on. Someone else might grieve quietly to themselves and never say a word to anyone for a long, long time. Others grieve by refusing to grieve at all. This is Fin's way and I'm not the person to question it."

"And I'm too late."

"I'm afraid you are," Ruby agreed.

"They didn't even ask me."

"No. And they should have. And I should have thought to make them."

There was a hint of fatigue in Ruby's voice. It was hard work. . .racing through tunnels. . .tending to the dead and dying. . .cutting out hearts.

Rab didn't feel even a shred of sympathy.

"That was an oversight," she admitted.

"An oversight! I'd call it more than an oversight!"

Oh how so very much Rab wanted to reach out, grab Ruby by the neck and squeeze.

"Are you sure? You're hardly ever here, Rab, and Stitch was Fin's brother."

He wouldn't do it. Couldn't. It wasn't in him. Not because of this. He'd killed only once and then only because he'd had to. The fantasy now was enough.

"But I'm the one who brought them here, Ruby. Doesn't that give me some sort of say?"

"You'd have to ask Fin that," she said, leaning back against her desk. "But if you want my advice, I'd suggest that you don't."

"Like your advice is worth much. Did you even try to advise Fin not to do it?"

"I told you, Rab, everyone grieves differently. It wasn't my place."

It came again. . .that urge to just squeeze and squeeze.

"It wasn't your *place* to cut out a dead boy's heart," Rab snarled instead. "Do you know what they are going to do with it now?"

"No. I didn't—"

"You didn't ask," Rab interrupted. "Well, perhaps that's the one thing you *should* have done, Ruby. They're going to take it home."

"Well, it's not something I'd do," Ruby said after a moment's hesitation, "but if Fin wants to keep Stitch's heart in his space, then—"

"Not in his space here, Ruby. Home! Cloud and him. They're going to take it back to the village where Stitch was born."

Ruby's mouth dropped open, her eyes shot wide and she jumped up from her desk.

Rab allowed himself a second to revel in the triumph. So Fin's decision wasn't quite as rational and ordinary as she'd thought. *Imagine that!*

"But that's just crazy," she cried, lunging forwards to grasp Rab's arm. "Why?"

Rab shrugged, shook off her hold, then turned his back on the startled woman.

"I guess you *should* have asked *them*."

He wanted to leave feeling confident that he'd at least won this confrontation with Ruby. He couldn't change what she'd done. There was no going back. But he could make her pay and, for a moment, just at the end, he knew he had done just that. It should have been his cue to get out of there. But during his exit, he made the mistake of glancing towards that now empty bed. He hadn't meant to look. It just sort of happened and suddenly the victory he'd had over poor Ruby felt such a very, very hollow thing indeed.

Cloud wasn't there when he arrived back in his space, nor was the little mound of padding.

The bowl Fin had used for his meagre breakfast that morning had also disappeared from the floor and someone, probably Cloud, had made a small fire in the hearth. He walked to the stack of tinder and threw another piece of the broken-up table onto the fire. It was only then that he noticed Fin, back turned, lying on his low bed in the small niche he called his own. He must have come back while Rab was down in the hospital. Maybe he, not Cloud, had set the fire. Briefly it crossed Rab's mind to challenge him then and there, but the young man appeared to be asleep. Besides, what good would it do? Over the years, he and Fin had disagreed more times than they had ever agreed. It was a conflict that had begun the very moment they'd left their old village and very likely a conflict that would continue, in one form or another, until one of them went to their grave.

Rab wandered into Stitch's space instead. He lowered himself to sit on the boy's bed, realising that he'd actually never come into the boy's space before. There wasn't much in it. But then, who did have much? In the far corner, there was a neatly stacked pile of clothes; Cloud's or maybe Fin's doing again. Those clothes would be passed on to someone else now. But what of the stones that lined the perimeter of the wall? They were absolutely of no use to anyone. Rab had never thought to ask what the boy had done with the small gifts he had never once failed to bring back with him. Shouldn't that have meant something? Didn't that give him some right of say in what should or shouldn't be done with the boy's body? But Fin had never given him credit for that, had he? Never stopped to think how, by the end of each and every one of his journeys, those small and utterly useless stones had become such an unnecessarily heavy burden.

Rab eased himself off the bed and, from his own space, retrieved the smallest of his packs. Returning to Stitch's space, he began to wend his way along the wall. Every so often, he stopped, collected a stone, and dropped it into the pack. He figured around forty was enough.

It was a stupid idea—pointless—but maybe this was *his* way of grieving.

***

Tunnel-dweller funerals were small affairs conducted briefly at the far end of the plateau above the city. Graves were prepared ahead of time and the dead placed inside, ready for the mourners. It was the practical way to do things. Few tunnel-dwellers had the right clothes to weather the cold top-side for any length of time. And the plateau could only be reached by first traversing the wide, smooth platform of rock outside the city gates and then ascending a steep and narrowly incised set of stairs. Better the grievers didn't witness how the deceased were bundled up those steps. Once at the top of the stairs, the deceased was carried in a weaving, though comparatively more dignified manner through the shifting smoke field, that area along the top of the plateau where the exhaust from every hearth in the underground city was vented.

This day the mourners totalled ten in all: beside Rab, there were the two diggers, who were making fast progress filling in Stitch's open hole; Ruby, who was there to oversee the legality of the burials; Benjamin Caine, who with the passing of Elias Cooper last year had been elected chief magistrate, unlikely on account of his non-existent popularity but probably because no one else wanted the job. As senior official in such matters, Caine was obliged to be present. Then there was Cloud and Fin, of course, as well as two young tunnel-boys Rab didn't even recognise; friends of Stitch he guessed. Friends he probably should have known. And strangely there was Lilly Benson. Why she had decided to scramble top-side to see Stitch and the nameless Top-sider girl laid to rest, Rab couldn't imagine but didn't really care enough to ask. Perhaps Cloud had asked her to come; it was as good an explanation as any.

Cloud stood close beside Fin during the service. Rab hadn't spoken to the young man since he'd left their shared space early that morning. Even now, Fin seemed to be doing his level best to avoid Rab's eyes. In fact, he appeared almost disinterested in everything and everyone around him, as though this solemn procedure meant nothing to him at all. Was that how he truly felt? Or was it just some act of bravado? Rab had seen enough of those from Fin through the years but never when it came to Stitch.

On the other side of Stitch's grave, Lilly, Ruby and Benjamin Caine were huddled together against the cold. Rab stood alone by the grave of the little Top-sider girl. He didn't seem to have a place among either group by Stitch's grave and there was no one else to mourn the little girl. In fact, he would have felt more useful and comfortable assisting the diggers. But it wasn't the way of these tunnel-dwellers and either Fin had forgotten all about how things had always been done in their old village or he'd adapted to this strange and different society far better than Rab ever could. Aside from usually burying the dead naked, there was another practice that both the tunnel-dwellers and Rab's own people shared—the custom to leave a grave unmarked. Only a small proportion of the tunnel-dwellers could read and write and their cemetery was as inhospitable a place to visit as the cemetery outside Rab's small village had been. But scattered across the plateau were remnants of the odd attempt that had been made to mark a site. None were of wood, of course, but for an observant eye, it was possible to make out an irregularity here and there across the otherwise monotonously flat plateau. The first time he'd come upon one of those errant blocks of stone, Rab hadn't been able to interpret the strange scratching that marred its wind-etched and ice-cracked surface. He'd recognised it as writing and guessed it was likely to be a name. On his first trip top-side after Ruby had pounded a limited degree of literacy into him, enough to read letters at least and make a cursory job at sounding them out, Rab had returned to that stone to satisfy his curiosity. On his third attempt, he managed to painstakingly sound out a name. Bra—ham. He should have guessed it. One of Sunny's kin, of course, though Rab never did bother to ask who, even though the chief magistrate at the time could have consulted the official map of the cemetery and told him precisely who was buried there. Stitch's place would have been already marked on that map—and the little Top-sider girl's as well. Benjamin Caine would have seen to it.

Of all the tunnel-dwellers, Rab had a particular dislike of Benjamin Caine. He couldn't say why. Other tunnel-dwellers had lost their young daughters to Top-siders but, unlike Caine, most eventually put aside the burden that he seemed intent on carrying with him until he, too, was lying in the ground on the plateau above the tunnel city. Rab wasn't the only one who seemed to feel that way about the former cropper; more than once, he'd noticed a tunnel-dweller turn and hurry off in the other direction to avoid intercepting the big man. Even Ruby did it and Cloud seemed particularly uncomfortable around him. She had her reasons, Rab supposed. Deep down, maybe Benjamin Caine did resent her; after all, she had been brought home while his daughter would likely remain lost to him forever.

But today, Caine had his mind on other matters. Judging by the regular stamping of his feet and the way he had both arms wrapped tightly about him, his primary concern was the cold and getting this little unpleasantness completed as quickly as possible. As far as Rab had noticed, he hadn't even looked at Cloud, who never left Fin's side but glanced up every so often from under the hood of her heavy coat. Though her gaze was in Rab's general direction, she wasn't actually looking at him, but towards the ground at his feet. He was still wearing his old and tattered boots; though he'd toyed with the idea of wearing Stitch's, it just hadn't seemed right somehow. Maybe that's what she was looking at. Or perhaps it was the pack he had brought up to the surface with him that had her wondering—the pack with its cargo of forty small stones.

The two grave diggers worked fast; doubtless they were old hands at this. It wasn't easy to open up a hole above ground, as Rab knew only too well. On top of this thinly soiled plateau, it must have been especially difficult. The two must have spent a good part of the night top-side and were understandably anxious to get below ground once more.

It was Fin's duty to declare the ceremony completed, a state reached once the last of the soil was laid in place. That was the code of the tunnel-dwellers. No words were ever spoken, none that Rab had ever heard anyway in the three burials he'd witnessed since arriving in the underground city. As far as he could recall, Fin had never attended any of those ceremonies and it occurred to Rab now that he should have instructed the young man on what was expected of him. It appeared that someone must have spoken to Fin because no sooner had the diggers swept the grave site with their final load of soil, than the young man turned and began to walk away. His abrupt exit seemed to have caught Cloud by surprise. She hurried after him, leaving Lilly, Ruby, the tunnel-boys and Benjamin Caine following behind. Rab, as erstwhile kin but especially as kinsman, should have accompanied Fin every step of the way from the grave across the plateau to the steps.

But he lagged behind. The little Top-sider girl's grave wasn't finished and there was still something else he needed to do. With no one else to turn to, the diggers looked to him to declare her funeral complete when they'd finished filling in the hole. He nodded to each and watched as, tools in hand, they walked quickly away, heading for the steps and the comfort of their warm homes. It was then Rab noticed Cloud. She hadn't left with the others and was walking back towards him through the billowing plumes of the smoke field. The diggers hurried past her and Cloud just kept on coming. And so Rab waited. He was still angry with her but angrier with Fin. After all, it had been Fin's decision, not hers, and if she was prepared to sacrifice more of her comfort for his sake, then the least he could do was wait and satisfy her curiosity, which he assumed was what had prompted her return.

Rab had all the stones out of his pack by the time she came walking up. He'd been particular about size but hadn't placed too much emphasis on colour. Everything top-side eventually came to look the same monotonously dull grey. It was the stones themselves that mattered. With Cloud standing over him, Rab carefully and meticulously began to spell out letters with the stones in the disturbed soil above Stitch's grave. When he'd finished, he rose to consider the work. It was fine—as fine as any poor writer could do.

"What does it say?" Cloud asked, stepping forwards to link her arm through his.

"It says Stitch," Rab replied.

Yes, it had been a stupid thing to do. A year, two years from now if he were lucky, the stones would probably all be gone, ice, wind and rain taking them on a relentless, restless journey to some other place. But for now, it was what *Rab* wanted and Stitch *would* have wanted. At least, Rab hoped so.

Rab felt a tug on his arm.

"Come on, Rab. It's cold. There's nothing more we can do up here."

She tugged again, but Rab was reluctant to leave. It seemed there was something more that needed doing, so Rab, ignorant of what that something might be, allowed Cloud to lead him away. He didn't get very far. Breaking free of her light hold, he hurried back to the grave of the little Top-sider girl. Bending, he began to write in the soil with the tip of a gloved finger. And that had been an even more stupid thing to do; the next wind or rain would strip every vestige of those pitiful words away.

As he walked back to her, he recognised the look on Cloud's face. She was easy to read, when she allowed it, and today seemed to be one of those days when she put no effort at all into concealing her thoughts. Her brown eyes were narrowed beneath the heavy hood of her coat; her head was tilted just that little to the left. She was thinking he might just have lost another little bit of his mind. Maybe he had.

Still she linked her arm through his again when he neared, then walked beside him all the way through the smoke field. She seemed reluctant to let go of him in order to descend the stairs to the platform below and to home. Her home anyway. But the steep and narrow stairs only allowed one person to descend at a time. Once John Braham and Rab had coaxed, cajoled, and shoved a horse up those stairs onto the plateau; thinking back on it now, he wasn't sure how they'd done it. Better for the horse if they had failed. Poor Kix. Rab had come across his bones a couple of times during his search for Gift. And each time he did, Rab heard again in his mind the awful, sudden crack Sunny's gun had made when she'd shot the dying horse—the same terrible sound of his own shot inside the crashed spaceship. Each time, his abject anger at Sunny was refuelled. Though Rab had finally been able to reconcile that if anyone other than Sunny had killed Kix, the act would have been done in kindness. But it was Sunny, not someone else who had done it, and it was Sunny, not someone else, who had made him do what he had done inside the spaceship. For that, there was no reconciliation.

They found Benjamin Caine waiting for them just inside the city gate. There was little doubt he'd have been pacing, anxious for them to return so he could secure their city once more. He'd obviously forgotten that

Rab had his own set of keys, the ones he had taken from Sunny's pack, making it possible for him to come and go as he chose. There'd been some debate about whether he should be allowed to keep the keys when the tunnel-dwellers first found out he had them. He was, after all, a Top-sider. It had been Ruby who had settled the matter with her usual brand of simple logic. He'd come back alone the first time, hadn't he? If he'd had some act of sabotage against the city in mind, he would have orchestrated it then, wouldn't he? And the next time he wanted to leave, his intention was to go without Stitch and Fin, wasn't it? The boys were his security. He wouldn't do anything to compromise the safety of the city as long as they were inside. Though it had taken some convincing, Ruby had finally turned the mood of the tunnel-dwellers and, as the years wore on, it only became clearer still that betrayal had never been his agenda. The only objection that was occasionally still voiced focused upon the likelihood of his death out there on the surface and the possibility that the keys he carried with him would fall into the wrong hands. Ruby had had an answer for that, too. He was so obviously a Top-sider, himself, there'd be no reason to connect him to the city. The keys would be dismissed as some keepsake, perhaps, or something he'd happened on during his journeying. And so Rab had been permitted to keep Sunny's keys and all the talk and concern about his intentions and the dire consequences of him possessing them had eventually ended.

Everything moves on, even people. And it was time for Rab to move on again. Only this time he'd leave the keys behind as just that little bit of unnecessary insurance that he wouldn't be tempted into coming back. Better yet, he'd give the keys to Fin. There was no doubt in his mind that Fin and Cloud would make good on their vow to take Stitch's heart home and even less doubt that he had any chance of convincing them not to. By giving them the keys, he was at least ensuring that they could return should ever, or more likely whenever, the need arose without having to wait shivering on the surface before Ruby noticed the hanging chain.

"Nice service," Caine muttered, back turned to Rab and Cloud as he fumbled with clearly numbed fingers to fix the chain and its lock back into place.

The chain looked as shiny and untarnished as it had the first day Rab had seen it; he never had asked what it was made of. He no longer cared. A good-sized rock could still have broken it though. In the long run, giving Fin and Cloud the keys wasn't really such a selfless act at all; they could easily smash their way through the gate and Ruby wasn't likely to forget to check on the chain. Seemed there was no such thing as the righteous path. Fine words. Fine intentions. In the end, they meant nothing at all.

Cloud kept a tight hold on Rab's hand as they followed the magistrate through the dark twists and turns of the upper tunnel. Once at 'the house', the magistrate hurried on ahead of them down the shimmerer-lit lower tunnel. Rab was glad to be rid of him. As was Cloud evidently; the pressure of her hand on his relaxed a little.

"Nice service!" she mocked. "He couldn't wait to get off the plateau."

Rab shrugged. "Looked to me like Fin was just as anxious. Where's he gone anyway?"

"Don't know," she replied hesitantly. "Rab, what did you write on the Top-sider's grave?"

"Little Fawn," he said.

"Little Fawn." Cloud lingered over the unfamiliar words. "What does it mean?"

"Just that. A little fawn. A fawn is an animal, Cloud. A deer. It's like a. . .well, a deer is just a deer. I saw a picture of one once down in the library. When I saw the Top-sider, the little girl, lying on the bed in the hospital, she kind of reminded me of that picture. That's all."

"Oh," Cloud replied. "I thought you might have known her and Little Fawn was her name."

"No." Rab ushered her ahead of him through the exit of the tunnel. "Never seen her before, but Little Fawn's her name now."

Well, until the elements took even that away.

There were more customers in Market Square than Rab had seen for a long time and, tellingly, the vast majority of them were shoving and shouldering their fellows in an attempt to gain the front positions at one or other of the diminished number of food stalls.

"Food panic," Cloud sneered. "In the end, only a small percentage of the harvest was ruined, but you can't tell *them* that." She waved her free hand. "Look at them! I'll be glad to leave this place with its dark awful caves and its even darker, more awful people."

Rab stopped walking, bringing Cloud to a halt by his side.

"You can't mean that, Cloud," he challenged her.

"Sure I do." Her chin jutted upward in the direction of the surface high above them. "Top-side, that's where I belong. I was happier there."

Rab smiled thinly. "Now I know you don't mean *that*."

"No." Cloud's chin dropped ever so slightly. "I don't suppose I do." She turned to look at him directly. "But I do want something better than this, Rab. There's nothing here for me. Not really."

Rab started walking again.

"And that's why you decided to go with Fin?" he asked.

She shrugged. "Maybe."

"But what about your reweaving? The mushroom harvest? You're needed here, Cloud. So is Fin."

"There is always another reweaver. And as for the harvest? Well, they'll manage. Some of the younger croppers are pretty good now. They know what to do and what not to do. This city can get on without me. Same goes for Fin. Besides, there'll be two less mouths to feed." She elbowed a young woman who, having spotted an opening in the crush by the nearest food stall, barrelled right into her. "They should like that," she snapped, eyeing the woman.

Rab shook his head. "It's a long time since you've been top-side, Cloud," he reminded her.

"Umm." She hesitated. "Yes, I know. In fact," she continued, freeing her hand from his. "I wanted to talk to you about that. But not here. Let's go back to your space. There's something I need to ask you."

When Rab opened his mouth to speak, Cloud raised her hand and put a finger to his lips.

"Not yet."

They walked the rest of the way in silence with Rab having a terrible suspicion that, when it finally came, he wasn't going to like whatever it was Cloud needed to ask.

On reaching his space, Rab glanced around, noted that Fin was nowhere in sight, and then located two of Braham's old cushions. He shied one into the middle of the floor and grabbed the last one for himself.

"Well," he said, waving at Cloud to join him. "Sit down."

Cloud dipped her head, a tell-tale little gesture Rab knew well, and stepped inside.

"Before you ask me anything," he said, seating himself. "I want to know where Fin is."

"I told you before. I don't know." Cloud shrugged off her outer coat, then lowered herself into the opposite cushion. "I guess he's making preparations somewhere, but I really don't know. He didn't make me do this, if that's what you're thinking. This was all my idea."

"I wasn't thinking anything, Cloud. In fact, I don't even know what you're talking about. I just want to know about Fin."

Cloud lowered her eyes. "I'd tell you if I knew."

Rab relented. "All right, I guess you would."

He rose and moved towards the hearth. The fire had almost completely died during the brief time they'd been top-side. He threw another piece of the broken table onto the miserable flame. It spat, fluttered ominously, then began to build once more.

"It's not like he'd go off without supplies," Rab eventually conceded, sloughing off his heavy coat.

"Or me," Cloud countered.

"Yes, you. I'd almost forgotten about *you*."

Cloud shook her head. "No, you hadn't. You're really mad at Fin, aren't you?"

"Now why should I be mad?" Rab asked, lowering himself back onto the cushion. "He only got Ruby to cut out his brother's *heart!*"

"And I guess you're still mad at me, too," Cloud replied in such a small voice, Rab was momentarily startled.

"You let him," he said at last.

"Then I suppose you won't be happy about what I have to ask you, either."

"I doubt it," Rab agreed, "but go on."

"It's about the top-side."

"I figured that."

"Well, it's like you said before, Rab, you know better than we do how to survive top-side. Neither Fin nor I have been top-side for a long time. Things may have changed."

They had.

"We could lose our way."

They probably would.

"We need help."

Oh no! She wasn't saying that! She couldn't possibly be saying that!

"I want you to come with us, Rab. *We* want you to. Both of us." She inched forwards on her seat. "Will you at least think about it?"

"Go with you? Back to the village? With Stitch's. . ."

No. He just couldn't bring himself to say those dreadful words again.

Gently Cloud placed the palms of her hands on Rab's thighs. Her eyes in the glow of the firelight kind of sparkled. She looked very young to Rab in that moment. But she wasn't really. The young didn't stay young very long in this world. She knew full well what they'd be up against.

"We might not make it there without you," she said.

Or even with him.

Each time he stepped outside the city gates, Rab was taking a chance. But he had a purpose in doing it. A real one. Not this! A journey back where he, Fin, Gift and Stitch had come from to do what? To find what? Fin's grief had taken a turn Rab had never anticipated. Hadn't Fin found a home here? A purpose of his own? Why would he give it all up? And force Cloud into giving it all up as well? Fin's venture was entirely senseless. And likely Fin was at the core of Cloud's declaration of discontent; Rab had never heard her say anything even remotely like that before.

"Look, Cloud," Rab said at last. "I can't understand why Fin wants to go back home at all. There's nothing there. Everyone is dead."

"Fin said you'd say that."

Yes, Fin would.

"He also said that you can't be sure."

"Is that what this is all about? Hoping to find our people back at the village still alive."

"No, I don't really think so, Rab. I suspect Fin knows they are dead as well as you do. I think. . .well, I think he just wants to take Stitch home and—"

"That's a stupid reason to risk your life, Cloud. And that's what Fin is doing. Risking your life as well as his own."

"You didn't let me finish. You *never* let me finish. Once, just once in your life could you allow that other people have hopes and wishes, too? Yours is to find Gift. We know that. Believe me, we *all* know that. So it may come as a shock for you to know that Stitch had one, too. If you'd stayed around long enough, you might have known what it was. He wanted to go home, Rab."

"No, he didn't. If that's what Fin told you, then—"

"That's what *Stitch* told me. He knew he wasn't old enough to go just yet, but he did intend to go, Rab."

"I'm sorry but if that is true than Stitch was being foolish."

"Oh? Taking off top-side is foolish, is it? Just who do you think gave him the idea?"

"Me, I guess, but yes, it is foolish. Unless you have a damn good reason to do it."

"And Stitch's reason just isn't good enough for you."

"No, it isn't."

"But yours is." Cloud leapt to her feet and snatched her coat from the floor. "That's just the sort of self-centred response I should have expected from you. Well, I'm sorry to tell you, Rab, Fin is going. *I* am going. And so is Stitch's heart." She sped off towards the doorway, but stopped before launching herself into Braham Street. "And if you ever had any intention of being some sort of father to those boys then and any sort of friend to me now, you'd come, too. We need your help. I can't put it any plainer than that."

With that, she was gone.

Why was it, he wondered, that his life had *never* been his own? First Blaze had forced him into taking three little children with him on a perilous journey, one that came to an abrupt end the moment Stitch broke his leg. Something again that had had absolutely nothing to do with him. If Fin had only listened to his warning, Stitch wouldn't have been up on that catwalk in the first place. Then old John Braham had latched himself on. Stupid old man should have known better than to traipse about top-side seeking some mythical launch pad that Rab, himself, had been just as naive and idiotic to have believed in. . .once. But the person who had had and still had the most control of his life was Sunny. Damn that woman! Damn the promise she had him make to keep his mouth shut! And of course there was Gift and his seemingly endless search for her. Sunny was probably responsible for that, too. And now Cloud was bent on stealing just another little piece of him.

How had it come to this? He should have just stayed in the village and died along with the rest of them. At least then, it would all be over.

Just as that very thought surfaced inside his head, Fin, with arms laden, came walking through the doorway. The young man executed a little stop-start dance on seeing Rab, but continued on past the spot where he was still sitting and disappeared into his own niche. A moment later, he emerged, arms free.

"You just missed Abby," Rab said.

Fin had an infuriating talent for wearing Rab down, nudging and needling him to the point where he simply gave up on any given difference of opinion. But Fin used to send Stitch in to do his dirty work. With that option no longer available to him, he'd sent Cloud instead. The young man was angling to set a precedent. And Rab wasn't about to let that happen so easily.

"I passed her coming in."

Fin was making a bit of a performance out of stacking another piece of busted-up table into the hearth, obliging Rab to address his turned back.

"I understand you're going on a little trip together."

Fin didn't reply; he was still toying with that same piece of wood.

"And it's come to my attention that not quite all of Stitch is buried in that hole up there," Rab added.

So maybe it was a callous way to put it, but it had the desired effect.

Fin spun around, looking stunned.

"I—" he stammered.

"Yeah, you!" Rab cut him off. "You could have asked, Fin. You could have come to me, told me what you wanted to do. And *why!*"

Fin's initial shock was waning. Rab could see it in the young man's eyes.

"It's what Stitch would have wanted me to do. You didn't even know him. Not really." He was fairly spitting the words out now. "And you don't know *me*. You thought you could just dump us here and that would be the end of your responsibility. I told Blaze you didn't want to take us right from the start—that we'd have been better off staying where we were."

Rab jumped to his feet.

"Really? Would you mind explaining how that might be?"

"You don't know as much as you think you do, Rab. You say everyone in the village is dead. But you don't *know* that. You've never gone back to find out. You say Gift is still alive. But you don't know *that* either, and yet you go top-side time after time, trying to off-load your guilt for letting her get lost in the first place."

It was a good shot, Rab conceded. But if Fin thought he could get to him that way, he was sadly mistaken. Rab had been walking with that old demon for a long time. Guilt was nothing but a shadow to him; he wouldn't know what to do without it.

"They're dead," Rab said calmly. "Gift isn't. It's as simple as that."

Fin jabbed a finger in the air towards Rab. "For *you!* And maybe they are all dead. Maybe that isn't what matters."

"Then what does matter, Fin? You've done a terrible thing. Not just to Stitch, but to Ruby and Abby, as well."

"What have I done that's any worse than the things you've done? Tell me. Just what did happen to that old man and Sunny up there? How is it you came back alone?"

Fin couldn't know. This was just another of his barbs, an old one, and Rab would answer with the same old answer he gave every time.

"Like I've told you before, the old man wore out and Sunny died from blood-poisoning."

At least, she would have—eventually—if he hadn't shot her.

"Blood-poisoning!" Fin snapped back. "No such thing!"

Rab shrugged. "Have it your way. I don't really care anymore, Fin. I'm very tired of you trying to turn everything back onto me. Not everything that goes wrong is *my* fault."

Fin lunged forwards a step. "You're blaming *me*? Yeah, well, why not? You always have. All right, maybe I *should* have stopped Stitch from coming with me into that old factory. And maybe I should have been watching him more closely down in the 'shroom field. I'll just bet you're thinking it should have been me trapped under that cart—"

"Don't be ridiculous, Fin."

"Just stating the obvious, Rab. Like how convenient it is for you to forget that I was hardly more than a kid myself when Stitch followed me onto that catwalk. What was your excuse for putting us there in the first place? You were a grown man when you took Gift, Stitch, and me away from our village. You knew our chances weren't good but you did it just the same. And you blamed Blaze for making you take us instead of blaming yourself for giving in to her. Yeah, you're wishing it had been me trapped under that cart instead of Stitch all right. But you can't know how often croppers walk safely beside that cart and how unlikely an accident like that is, because you're *never* here to know. Just like you weren't there to know what really happened to our people."

Just at that moment, the piece of busted-up table Fin had placed in the fire tumbled out onto the floor. Fin jumped, startled, but it was Rab who took the time to resettle it. He dawdled, poking about among the embers for a while before he turned to face Fin again.

"Abby says you think they're all dead," he said, challenging Fin to deny it.

"Probably are," Fin conceded.

"Then what's the point, Fin? I'd really like to know."

"If Abby told you what I think, then she's told you what Stitch wanted, too," Fin replied.

"She said he wanted to go home."

"That's the truth."

"Then how come I'd never heard it before?"

"Maybe you just didn't listen, Rab. Neither of us ever wanted to stay here. We—"

Stepping forwards, Rab grasped the young man by the shoulder. "But you made a life for yourself here, Fin. Stitch, too. Didn't you?"

"Obviously *you* thought so," Fin replied, shrugging off Rab's light hold. "And you must think Abby has too, or you wouldn't be saying that I've done a terrible thing to her. I didn't force her, you know. She wants to go. She got by here. That's all. But you wouldn't know that because you're not here for her to talk to. Even when the snow forces you to stay, you spend all your time in that library, teaching yourself to read. What for? What use is it? It won't tell you what happened to our people and it won't tell you where Gift is now. You seem to think you're the only one who wanted Gift back, but Stitch and me, we did, too. But it's like I said before. In all your time top-side, you never went back to find out what happened to our people and you never even looked for Gift in that direction."

"Because things are clearly worse south of us, Fin. There is no one alive there. No reason to go that way."

Fin just shook his head. "That's just what these tunnel-dwellers say. You don't know that for sure. And now it's time to find out. So with or without you, Abby and me are leaving."

"Snow time is coming. Have you given any thought at all to that? Maybe you don't care what happens to you anymore, Fin, but what about Abby?"

"You've left it a bit late to start worrying about Abby, haven't you? You're not going to have it both ways, Rab. Not anymore. So maybe you can start blaming her now as well, for making a better choice."

Better choice? In leaving the tunnels? Or in him?

Fin wasn't making things exactly clear.

"Anyway," Fin was saying, "we'll be home long before snow time and, if we have to, we'll wait it out there."

Fin made to push past Rab as he headed for his space, but Rab reached out and grasped the young man's elbow to prevent him.

"Without food?"

"There'll be food. There was before. It's no use trying to argue with me, Rab," Fin replied, slipping his arm free. "We're going to take Stitch home and then we're going to go on. Maybe we'll find food. Maybe we won't. Maybe we'll even find Gift. Who knows? But we're not staying here. Not any longer. Stitch died in a hole in the ground. I don't want to.

And neither does Abby. You can argue all you like, but you can't change my mind because as often as you've taken your chances up there on the surface, I'm guessing you feel the same way."

Chapter 4

RAB left Fin to his preparations and retired to the comparative seclusion of his own, small space. Fin was right; there was no use arguing with him, not because he couldn't be swayed, although it was highly unlikely, but because his reasoning was entirely sound. Rab *didn't* want to die in a hole in the ground. So when it came to a choice. . .a *better* choice. . .

Maybe that was all Fin had meant when he'd spoken about Cloud's decision.

He had argued Cloud's case in the same way she'd argued his. It left Rab without much of a leg to stand on. They were the only 'family' he had and, even by their own admission, they needed him. He couldn't let them go alone. Come what may, their course, and his, was set. South it would be.

Rab soon grew restless, just sitting there on his bed, running Cloud's and Fin's astute reproaches over and over in his mind. He didn't know them. Not really. And he hadn't known Stitch, either. It was no use talking to Fin. Besides, after what Fin had done, Rab would never apologise to him for anything ever again. Let him seethe. But now that he'd had some time to reflect, Rab could see that Cloud was fundamentally innocent. Maybe she should have tried to stop Fin; maybe she had even tried to stop him. But Rab knew, perhaps better than anyone else, there was no stopping Fin once his mind was made up.

He left quietly without telling Fin where he was going. Cloud had a small space of her own down one of the minor tunnels that broke off roughly perpendicular to Braham Street. If he found her there, he'd try his best to make some sort of amends. If he didn't, well, they had a long journey ahead of them. It would be better to start out on agreeable terms, but it wouldn't be the first time he'd taken off top-side in the company of an angry woman.

Braham Street was empty as was the narrower minor tunnel that soon took him to Cloud's home. Evidently, the panic buying hadn't slackened any down in Market Square. Fin had set himself a difficult task. How, in light of the current shortage, was he going to secure enough supplies for the journey ahead? For once in his life, it was a problem Rab could delegate to someone else.

He suspected he might not find Cloud in her space, but it never occurred to him that he'd find Lilly there instead. Rab lingered in the doorway a moment, uncertain what to do or say. The woman was ransacking Cloud's belongings. At least that's how it looked. She hadn't seen him yet or evidently heard him coming, but something must have told her he was there. A shadow on the opposite wall perhaps. Whatever it was made her drop the clothes she had bundled up in her hands and spin around.

A look of relief washed over her face the moment she recognised Rab.

"Oh," she said, bringing the palm of one hand up to her chest. "You gave me a fright. I thought it was Abby."

"Pity it wasn't," Rab replied and stepped, uninvited, into Cloud's space. "Just what are you doing?"

There was a pile of clothes on the floor by Lilly's feet and a pair of boots lying on their side just inside the entrance.

Lilly's gaze flitted from the pile to the boots, then back to Rab. "What does it look like? I'm taking Abby's clothes."

"Why?"

"It's simple, Rab. If Abby has no warm clothes, then she can't leave, can she? She'll have to stay here with me."

Lilly's mind seemed uncommonly focused today because that did make a warped sort of sense. It also raised a matter Rab hadn't even considered. Exactly what would happen to Lilly once Cloud was gone? He wondered if Cloud had stopped to think about it.

When Lilly suddenly rushed towards him, Rab inched back a step.

"You'll talk to her, won't you?" she said, grasping one of his hands and clutching it to her chest. "Convince her this is a silly idea. She'll listen to you."

She hadn't so far and that wasn't going to change. Rab knew it even if Lilly didn't. He'd accepted it. . .grudgingly. Lilly never would, grudgingly or otherwise.

"Lilly, she's going," Rab said as sympathetically as he could. It wasn't easy with Lilly wringing his hand that way. "I couldn't change her mind. But if it's any consolation, I'll be going with them. I know the surface better than anyone here, Lilly. Even better than the Pigeon Brothers."

It was poor comfort, Rab knew. He could have lied. Told Lilly that Cloud *had* changed her mind, then let her wake up the next morning to find her 'daughter' gone. But that was something only a miserable excuse for a human like Sunny would do. As far as compassion went, maybe Rab wasn't much good either, but he was better than that.

Lilly flung his hand away.

"You don't even care."

Her, too!

Perhaps getting Fin and Cloud permanently out of this place wasn't such a bad thing after all. Top-side, they could reach a different understanding together, one that wasn't limited by the too tight walls of this underground prison. It was a wonder all the tunnel-dwellers weren't crazy. People weren't meant to live this way. Maybe they should never have tried.

Rab could feel himself begin to snap. Another time, he'd have walked away. Another time, he'd have let Cloud solve her own problems. Not this time. He'd had enough.

"Put everything back where you found it, Lilly. Now! If Abby comes back and—"

"Abby *has* come back."

Rab spun around to find Cloud standing in the doorway.

Her focus shifted from the pile of clothes in the middle of the floor and settled keenly on Rab. There was a storm brewing in those brown eyes of hers but it ebbed away quickly. Rightly, she'd judged him innocent of collusion in such a pitiful attempt at sabotage.

"I'll fix it," she said, directing those heart-breakingly calm words solely at Rab.

"I came to tell you. . .to say. . ."

Rab didn't know how to finish. Behind him, he could hear Lilly softly sobbing. How could Cloud possibly fix that?

As he passed Cloud still standing in the entrance, he briefly touched her shoulder.

"In case you didn't hear," he said quietly, "I'm in."

He left before she could reply.

***

Piece by piece, Rab went through the supplies Fin had gathered. The young man had asked him to do it; in years past, it would have been a very different situation. But Rab was the expert on the surface, so it fell to him not only to approve every item they would take on their journey, but to identify what had been overlooked. He dearly hoped he wouldn't come upon the vessel in which Fin was keeping Stitch's heart. He didn't; Fin was guarding it somewhere and that suited Rab just fine.

On the whole, Fin had prepared well, though he had had to trade-off most of what remained in John Braham's former space to do it. Even the tattered old cushions were gone, as were the ageing carpets that had covered the hard rock floors. But Sunny's gun and a few straggler pieces of the busted-up table still lay in the corner near the now cold hearth. Rab could put those to good use as well. Wood was wood after all.

Leaving Fin behind to restow their supplies, Rab tucked Sunny's gun under one arm and the last of the wood under the other and headed off for Market Square. The crowds weren't quite as bad today, although there was still that almost palpable smell of panic in the air. He was looking for a couple of extra canteens and a tough but lightweight container in which to carry his binoculars. Over the years, the constant banging around in the bottom of his pack had scratched up the glass. He carefully avoided Lilly Benson's stall, although he might have been able to find a canteen or two among the clutter of reclaimed pots and pans. In truth it surprised him a little to see that she was there, barely visible as usual behind her precariously stacked jumble of cooking wares. Whatever Cloud had done to appease her, she'd done well. Cloud had a way with the woman and, once again, Rab found himself wondering what would become of the wretched soul once Cloud was gone.

He pressed on, past Joe Dodson's stall with its tangle of used and re-crafted tools that never seemed to change over the years. The old wooden table out front was beginning to sag under the weight of its load. Old Joe would have to find himself a new one soon and consign 'old dependable' to the fire. Rab wished him luck.

Rab lingered at one of the used clothes stalls, momentarily tempted to sacrifice the container he wanted for his binoculars for the comfort of a sturdier pair of gloves. It was a fine balancing act, this business of trekking top-side. In the end, Rab forfeited the gloves. The loss was still on his mind when purely by chance, he found himself across the aisle from Lilly's pots and pans. He hurried on but not before noticing a young woman standing to Lilly's right directly behind an over-stacked tower of saucepans. He knew the woman's face although he couldn't name her.

Like Cloud, she, too, was a returned captive. In fact, she was one of the two younger girls who had been brought back to the tunnels on the very same day as Cloud. As far as Rab could recall, he'd never once heard her say a word since that day. Perhaps she couldn't. He'd never bothered to find out. Well, it seemed Cloud had come up with a potential distraction for Lilly as well as a quasi-guardian. Rab should have anticipated something like that. Cloud wasn't the type to leave a matter like Lilly's welfare unresolved. She'd be around somewhere now, monitoring the success of her plan. It took a while to spot her, but finally he saw Cloud standing sentinel at the far end of Market Square, shoulder propped against the tilted support of the last of the stalls. She didn't appear to have noticed him, so Rab slipped into the crowd and retraced his way back down the opposite aisle.

At one of the reweaver's stalls, Rab traded a length of wood for a short but tough piece of string and a small swatch of threadbare carpet. It wasn't the best solution but would protect his binoculars at least a little. He still had those canteens to find though. The boxes and baskets stall was an odd and unlikely place to find a couple of used canteens, but the oddest things turned up in the strangest places in Market Square and so Rab headed in that direction.

***

"That's it then," Cloud said, straightening.

She'd been rummaging through the contents of her packs, checking that everything Rab told her should be there was indeed accounted for.

He'd managed to find those elusive canteens, though not in the boxes and baskets stall, but back in old Joe Dodson's recrafted tool stall when, on another impulse, he'd retraced his steps to better inspect old Joe's wares and eventually traded Sunny's useless gun for what he'd found. Old Joe could melt the gun down. One of the canteens was now in Cloud's largest pack; the second and last in one of Fin's. Rab had three battered canteens of his own. Altogether, that made seven. It wasn't enough if the old, forgotten well he was depending on had gone dry. They'd had some good rains this last year, so Rab had some reasonable hopes that they'd be all right at least until they reached that well. From then on, they were at the mercy of the surface. Rab had never tracked farther south than that old well, so the last time he had seen any of the terrain beyond was during the journey he, Fin, Stitch and Gift had taken after leaving their village. But like he'd told Fin, there was no one alive in the south anymore. Still Fin wouldn't have it and Rab hadn't bothered to pursue the argument further. He'd find out when the time came and there'd be a change of heart and direction when the time came. To what and to where, Rab didn't yet know, but it wouldn't be south. It wouldn't be back to the city, either. That seemed clear. Cloud had cut her ties and, with the death of Stitch, Fin's ties had been cut for him.

"Well," Fin said, stepping out from his niche for the last time, packs tucked neatly into position on his back, "maybe you'll get to find that launch pad after all."

And that was just another topic Rab wouldn't bother to pursue because Fin couldn't know that he had given up looking for that launch pad a very long time ago.

"Maybe," Rab replied with a shrug and, stooping, gathered his own two well-worn packs. He glanced at Cloud and was almost overwhelmed by the same awful rush of sadness that had come over him the moment he'd finally accepted her decision. It was fair, perhaps even right, that he and Fin should leave. But not Cloud. Here, underground, she could go on being Abby with no one the wiser that she wasn't Lilly Benson's daughter. The tunnel-dwellers didn't have a lot of time left, but it was more than the three of them would have on the surface.

"Something wrong," Cloud said, becoming aware of his stare.

"Nothing," Rab said with a shake of his head. "If you're ready. . ."

He didn't get to finish what he started to say because Lilly Benson suddenly appeared in his doorway. At first Rab didn't notice that there was someone else there until the young woman stepped out from Lilly's shadow.

"We've come to say good bye," the young woman said. "Lilly and me."

Ah. So she could speak after all.

Rab looked again towards Cloud. She'd been caught midbend, hand extended to gather the first of her packs. There was a long awkward moment before she finally stood up.

"You didn't have to do that, Button," Cloud said at last.

Button! That was her name.

Rab motioned for Fin.

"We'll meet you up at 'the house'," he told Cloud as he passed.

As Button stepped aside for Rab, Lilly seized the opportunity to grab his sleeve.

"You'll bring my daughter back safely, won't you, Rab?"

She was looking up at him with a stabbing focus in her eyes, her mind as a sharp as any knife down in Market Square.

Rab didn't know what to say. He just assumed Cloud would have told her they wouldn't be coming back. Thankfully Fin was smart enough to keep his mouth shut. He pushed past Rab and started off down Braham Street alone.

"We'll be careful," Rab finally replied. "Every step of the way."

It was the best, least committal thing he could think of to say. For an instant, he thought Lilly had seen through his little ploy. She blinked but when her eyes opened again, Rab recognised that same old lack of clarity. Her mind had drifted off again, signalling his chance to break free. As he moved off, Lilly's hand slipped from his sleeve and though he glanced at Button as he brushed past her, she had her head down, busy retrieving something from inside the fold of her skirt and didn't notice.

Rab caught up with Fin halfway down Braham Street.

"Why didn't Abby tell her?" he asked, assuming Cloud would have shared her intentions with Fin.

The young man shrugged. He seemed to be struggling with the heavy and unfamiliar load on his back. "I thought she did," he said. "Maybe Lilly forgot."

Maybe she had, but Rab didn't think so. Well, it wasn't his place to question Cloud. Lilly wasn't his problem, thank God.

Cloud didn't catch up with them until they were almost through Market Square. Rab heard the fast-paced pounding of her boots on the hard stone floor long before she reached them. No one ran in Market Square unless they had good reason. She didn't offer a single word of explanation when she fell in beside Rab.

"Everything all right?" he asked, glancing her way.

"Fine," she answered, smiling weakly. "Everything is completely fine."

Nothing was ever completely fine when it came to Lilly Benson, but whatever Cloud had said to her back there must have appeased Lilly enough to stop her from chasing after them. It was beginning to dawn on Rab that *no one* in the city knew they weren't coming back. Apparently neither Fin nor Cloud had shared their plan with anyone. Perhaps not even Ruby. For some reason Rab had just assumed everyone knew. He glanced at the last of the stalls as they passed them. Maybe there were a few more clients than usual and admittedly there was a conspicuous reduction in stock available for trade, but for the most part, business in the Square had returned to normal. The initial panic was over and the tunnel-dwellers had set about doing what they did best: adapting.

No one paid them any particular attention, which seemed to confirm that not a single tunnel-dweller was aware of Fin's real intentions. Had they known their best reweaver and horticultural magician was on her way out of the tunnel forever, Rab would have expected some sort of reaction. For all the interest they were shown, they could have been on one of those excursions the younger tunnel-dwellers took to collect oil from the seep in the valley below.

Rab turned his attention to Fin, hoping the young man's expression might give something away, but there was no clue to be had there. Fin just kept looking forwards, past the last stall towards the tunnel ahead.

"Wait," someone called.

Rab stopped and turned around. Ruby was hurrying towards them through the Square. If it hadn't been for the accident down in the 'shroom field, he might never have noticed just how old Ruby had grown. She ran a little lopsidedly, favouring the left, and by the time she caught up with them, she could barely speak. Her face was kind of flushed, too, as though she'd been standing for some time over a very hot fire.

"I've brought. . ." she began, then gasped another lung-full of air, ". . . this for you." Grabbing Fin's hand, she slapped a largish pouch into his palm. "There's sulfur," she said. "And purple mushroom extract."

"We've—"

Cloud would have said more had Rab not prevented it by firmly grasping her arm. Ruby didn't appear to notice; she was still too busy catching the rest of her breath.

"If it's too bad," she wheezed, bunching the front of her heavy blouse up with a clenched hand, "you'll come back, won't you."

It didn't seem to be a question.

She knew. Whether she'd been told by Fin or Cloud or not, she knew.

Rab didn't know what prompted him to slough the packs off his back and reach out to embrace the little woman. Maybe because he'd never see her again. Maybe because Ruby was one of those people whose thousand and one acts of kindness never seemed to go acknowledged. Maybe it was the only way he could tell her that he forgave her for what she had done to Stitch.

"You take care of yourself, Ruby," Rab said, releasing her, then bent to gather his discarded packs. He made sure to turn around quickly, so Ruby couldn't see the flash of indecision in his eyes. "Get going." He gave Cloud a less than gentle nudge in the back.

Fin was already on his way and reached the lower tunnel ahead of them. At the entrance, Rab glanced quickly back towards Market Square, half expecting to see Ruby still standing where they had left her, but she had already melted back into the crowd of stall keepers and clients who, long after he, Cloud and Fin were gone, would continue to go about their business, picking through wares that were recycled, then recycled again. As long as the 'shrooms in the field still grew, they'd be there. As long as light glowed from the shimmerers, they'd be there, wandering from stall to stall beneath a ceiling speckled in brightworms, whose shine would, for as long as he lived, ever remind Rab of what a heaven full of stars must look like.

***

It didn't make a lot of sense but all Rab could think Fin was trying to do by retracing, exactly, the route they had taken to reach the tunnel city was undo the last ten years. There was probably a shorter and quicker way to return to their village, although Rab had never investigated it. He'd never even thought about it and Fin wasn't prepared to discuss it now. He was determined to return through the deserted village where the factory workers had lived and where they had first met up with Sunny, to pass by the factory itself, and skirt the river towards home. It was a bad idea. The river was a bad place to be and Rab would never have taken that route the first time if he'd had a clue where he was going, other than north. The fouled river was the one landmark he had back then. But during the years he'd spent trekking top-side, Rab had learned to read the subtle changes of light in the monotonously grey sky. No matter the season, he could pinpoint north, south, east and west with uncanny accuracy. He could get them home much faster if Fin would only allow it or he could rely on Cloud to support his argument. But Cloud deferred wholly to Fin. If it was only a matter of loyalty, Rab could understand that. Fin was their leader; it was his expedition and Rab was only along because of his particular talent on the surface, which, so far, Fin had assiduously elected to ignore. Sooner or later, they'd have to turn to him. The question was: would it then be too late? So for now, at least, that became Rab's job: to stay one step ahead of the weather, the terrain, and Fin; to make sure that he recognised that moment well before it came.

"Will this weather hold all the way there?" Cloud asked.

She was following close on Rab's heels, trudging almost step for step behind him.

"Depends where 'there' is," he replied.

She'd meant to their village, of course, but Rab couldn't resist the urge to needle her. Maybe if she'd worked a little harder to dissuade Fin, they wouldn't have to be worrying about how long the comparatively good weather would last. If, as Fin had implied, the better choice she had made was *in* him as opposed to simply leaving the tunnels, then maybe, just maybe, she would have had influence enough to have done it.

"But we'll get to your village before snow time?"

Rab glanced over his shoulder. "Fine time to worry about that, Cloud. But yes, I think we will."

She quickened her pace and was soon walking beside him.

"What's it like? Your village?"

Rab shrugged. "Empty, I'd say. Fin is wrong. There'll be no one left."

"And if there is?"

"What are you getting at?"

The way she had the hood of her coat, he couldn't see much of her face. She sounded anxious about something.

"Well," she began, "what if they don't want us there? What if they send us away?"

"I think that's the least of our concerns, Cloud." He nodded towards Fin who had taken the lead. "If there are people alive the way he hopes, they'll let us stay at least until snow time is over. That's all the time you intended to spend there, anyway, isn't it?"

Cloud hesitated a moment before answering.

"Yes, of course it is."

Second thoughts! It was a simple matter to plan while in the comparative comfort of the underground where there was always a fire somewhere to keep you warm, food whenever you felt hungry, company when you wanted it, seclusion when you didn't. They could turn back now; Rab had kept the keys for just this possible eventuality. He'd thought about turning them over to Ruby, but reconsidered. Still he hadn't anticipated Cloud cracking quite so soon.

He waited, but Cloud said nothing more.

Fin pulled up a little way ahead of them.

"Which way?" he asked once Rab came within earshot.

South. Always south. Should he deceive Fin now? Seize the opportunity to take them on a more direct route? How long would it take Fin to work it out? And what would he do once he did? Have them backtracking, probably. The young man was as stubborn as they came.

Rab pointed due south. "That way. We'll be on level ground for a while yet, then it's a downhill walk to the road. Easy really if the weather holds."

"What road?" Cloud asked. She stopped beside Rab and, dropping her packs to the ground, bent to adjust the straps.

"There's an old road that leads to the deserted village. That's the way we came before."

"Where does it come from?"

"I don't really know. I run across it sometimes, but I've never found the northern end of it. The southern end stops at the brick factory."

"Oh yes," Cloud said. She heaved her packs up from the ground and resettled them on her back. "Fin has told me about that place. He says it's a ruin."

"A dangerous ruin," Rab corrected her. "We won't be going in."

He looked at Fin, anticipating some retort, but the young man had nothing to say about it.

"Ready?" he asked of Cloud instead.

She waved Fin forwards. This time Rab lingered behind. He wanted to keep an eye on Cloud. She'd already had to stop to adjust her packs. She was fit for the tunnels and at one time, fit for the surface, but she'd become pampered underground.

"I'm not going to fall down, if that's what you're waiting for," she called back to him.

"We all do," Rab shouted ahead, "sooner or later."

He swore he heard Cloud laugh.

Fin kept moving due south, just as Rab had directed. There was little in the way of landmarks to guide him, which meant Fin possessed a pretty good sense of direction, something Rab noted with some relief. If anything happened to him, Fin might just manage alone with Cloud. It was half a day's walk to the village, so Rab hadn't bothered to estimate the time until they began the slow descent from the plateau. It looked like today's trek might take marginally longer. No surprise. He'd intended to start them out slowly. The temperature was just that little bit warmer than usual, about the same as it had been the last time he'd been top-side for any length of time. If it stayed that way, they would easily reach their old village before snow time. Fin had been right about that. But the weather on this planet was something Rab never ever trusted; tomorrow they would have to walk a little faster.

When Fin stopped walking suddenly, Rab's first thought was that something was wrong. He hurried past Cloud to find out.

"I see it," Fin called. "The road."

Reaching Fin, Rab halted and looked down the gentle hill. They weren't quite where he'd expected. Perhaps a little farther north than he'd have liked, so tomorrow he'd have to take the lead. Still it wasn't a problem; they would still reach the deserted village well before nightfall.

He waited for Cloud to catch up.

"So that's what a road looks like," she said, throwing back the hood of her coat.

Rab had never stopped to consider that she'd never seen a road before, not even during her time as a Top-sider.

"What were you expecting?" he asked with a smile.

"Something better than that. It looks wrecked."

"It is," Rab replied and started downhill after Fin.

Cloud soon caught up with them, but not without sending a shower of loose rock ahead of her.

Rab shot her a cautioning look. "Keep that up and we'll all fall down."

"Sorry," she said. "I lost my footing."

"My point exactly, Cloud. There's no Ruby here to take care of you."

"Hey. I can take care of myself, thanks," she snapped and stomped off, reaching the road ahead of them both. "That way?" she called, pointing south.

"Yes, we stay on the road now," Fin replied before turning to Rab. "We're too far north, aren't we? This doesn't look quite like I remember it."

"A little," Rab said, joining Cloud on the road. "But it's all right."

Fin snatched a hold of his arm. "Why didn't you tell me?"

"I wasn't paying attention," Rab replied with a shrug then started off after Cloud, whose head snapped around to glance back at him.

***

"It's no better than the road," Cloud observed.

They had arrived at the edge of the village and it, too, was evidently not quite what Cloud was expecting.

"Of course it is," Rab replied, slinging his arm over her packs and urging her forwards. "There's shelter. And if it hasn't gone dry, there's a well."

"What well?" Fin asked, trailing a pace behind. "I don't remember a well."

"No. Sunny neglected to tell us about that. I found it a long time ago. The water is a bit muddy but drinkable. Well, at least it hasn't killed me yet." He sneaked a sideways glance at Cloud. "Changed your mind yet?" he asked.

"What?" she snapped. "Over a bit of muddy water?" She cast a quick look at Fin. "Would either of you like to know what we drank when I lived top-side? What's a little muddy water!" she snorted, striking out ahead of them. "You boys are spoiled."

Rab caught Fin almost smiling; it was the first time since Stitch's death that Fin had worn anything but a look of cold determination on his face.

"I think you might have underestimated her, Rab."

"Never," Rab replied with a shake of his head. "Just misunderstood."

"Do you think she remembers much about her life top-side?" Fin asked. Cloud was well out of earshot; there was no chance of her overhearing.

"Most of it, I'd say. Why?"

"She never talks about it. I've told her everything about our village, but she's never said a word about her life or the Top-siders who took her. The others do, but not Abby. Every time I ask her, she changes the subject."

"Then I wouldn't go asking her anymore, Fin."

"She's never told you anything, either?"

"Not much," Rab replied. "Nothing really, now that I think about it."

Suddenly Fin stopped walking, bringing Rab to a halt.

"You don't suppose she only agreed to come so she could find them, do you?"

Of all the. . .

"Find them?" Rab barked. "What for?" He pushed Fin forwards with a firm hand to his shoulder. "What happened to the 'better choice' she'd made, Fin? Having doubts? *You* wanted out of the city. She said she wanted the same. Personally, I think you're both mad. But then who on this planet isn't?"

Cloud was getting too far ahead of them.

"There's a lot of debris ahead of you, Cloud," Rab shouted over Fin's head.

"I see it," she called, swinging around. "Which way should I go?"

"Just wait until we get there." Rab turned to Fin. "We're going to stay here the night. Move on early tomorrow."

"But there's a lot of daylight left."

"This is the last shelter we'll have for a while, Fin. Remember? It's better we start off fresh tomorrow."

Fin seemed to be considering the logic.

"All right," he agreed at last and set off after Cloud.

Rab took them first to the old well. It hadn't gone dry and the rope he had replaced a few years ago had weathered the rains, snow and wind better than he had expected.

"The Top-siders sometimes dig wells like this," Cloud said.

She was leaning over the side of the low stone wall. Fin made himself useful restowing the canteens as Rab filled them.

"A Top-sider dug this one," Rab said, pulling on the rope. He hadn't had to lower the battered bucket very far at all to reach water.

Cloud straightened, then turned to look at him.

"What do you mean?"

"Village people are Top-siders, too."

"Oh, yes. I know the people in the city think that way but I never really have," she said, dusting off her gloves. "There's tunnel-dwellers, villagers, and Top-siders. But we're really all the same, aren't we?"

"Which are you?" Fin asked as he stowed the canteen Rab just handed him.

"Fair question," Cloud replied. "Which are *you?*"

"Villager," Fin answered, rising. "Always. But Rab here seems to be a bit of everything."

Rab upturned the old bucket and returned it to the spot where he'd found it, which fortunately happened to be the spot where he'd last left it, well concealed under a pile of brick and rubble.

"Pity it doesn't make me any smarter," Rab said, then motioned for Fin and Cloud to follow.

He threaded an easy path through the rubble-filled lanes and passage-ways. The abandoned village was familiar territory to him, but Fin and Cloud were obliged to tread more carefully. A simple thing like a trip over a fallen brick could twist an ankle or break an arm and there were a lot of fallen bricks to worry about.

"Who built all this, do you think?" Cloud asked.

"The same people who built the factory we'll pass by tomorrow," Rab replied. "They were probably abandoned about the same time."

"Then where did all the people go?" she pressed him. "They can't have just disappeared."

"Don't know." He waited for Fin and Cloud to catch up, then pointed through the jumbled wreckage towards a ruined structure on the opposite side of the lane. "We'll stay there the night. It's a safe place. Good shelter. And we can build a fire."

"In that?" Cloud grasped Rab's arm to avert a little stumble. "But it's all fallen down."

"It's all right inside. I've used it before."

Cloud looked at Fin, openly seeking his opinion.

"If he says so," Fin declared, then began to head off through the rubble.

"I hope you know what you're doing," Cloud remarked before starting off after Fin.

"You invited me," Rab called after her.

"And that might just have been a mistake."

They'd made a mistake all right. Starting out at all.

"You'll have to duck your head to get in, Fin," Rab said, then realised he was stating the obvious.

"Never would have thought of that," Fin replied before disappearing inside the ruined doorway.

Cloud followed close behind, leaving Rab alone in the open. He took advantage of that moment alone to look up and down the abandoned street. The bucket was exactly where he had left it; no one had come this way recently. Still Rab was always a little wary whenever it came to stopping overnight in this village. Bounty hunters were known to use this place and not all bounty hunters were as comparatively harmless as the Pigeon Brothers who had one agenda and one agenda only—profit—pure and simple. They were traders, scavengers, and opportunists. No more. No less. Rab knew of bounty hunters with far more disturbing natures and methods, although so far he'd been lucky enough never to have encountered any firsthand—except maybe for Sunny.

"Someone's here," Fin shouted from inside the ruin.

Rab leapt over the rubble in front of the doorway and, heart pounding, rushed inside. He blundered right into Cloud.

"There's wood piled in the corner."

Fin was still shouting.

Was that all?

The pounding in Rab's chest began to subside and his eyes slowly adapted to the dark.

"That was me, Fin. I stacked it there. Take it easy, will you. You scared the hell out of me."

"*You?* What about us?" Cloud gave him a powerful shove. "You could have warned us."

"I did. I said I used this place before."

Cloud sloughed off her packs and flung first them, then herself onto the floor.

"There's a hole in the roof," she said, pointing up.

"I know," Rab replied, shrugging his own two packs to the floor. "That's why the fire you're going to make goes directly under it."

"Me?" Cloud snapped, turning the upraised finger on herself.

"I already know how to make a fire top-side. You've probably forgotten."

Cloud pointed towards Fin, who was bent over gathering wood from the top of the pile. "What about him?"

"His turn comes tomorrow."

Fin straightened, length of wood in hand, and glanced at Rab.

"I remember how to start a fire top-side."

"That's good, then you won't mind doing it," Rab replied and folded himself onto the floor beside Cloud. "Well," he said, turning to face her, "what's holding you up?"

Cloud sprung to her feet. "You're enjoying this, aren't you?"

Rab shrugged and reached for his packs. Once Cloud had the fire started, they would eat. There'd be little left to do after that but sleep. Whether Cloud and Fin recognised it, a good, long sleep was exactly what they'd be needing now. Even Rab felt a little tired, although he supposed his current state of weariness had little, if anything, to do with the short journey they'd just completed. He toyed with the idea of having them sleep in shifts, but decided against it. Had the well looked disturbed, that's exactly what he'd have done. But it didn't and nothing else about the abandoned village suggested that there'd been any recent traffic. Chances were good they wouldn't have any unwelcome visitors during the night.

"So, Sir, is this satisfactory?"

Rab had been lost in thought and, when he looked up, was surprised to find that Cloud had the fire going already.

Good. She remembered better than he had hoped.

"Perfect," he said distractedly.

Fun was over; now they needed to eat. His two young companions were going to have to adjust to one substantial meal a day, substantial while the stores held out anyway, and there was no time like the present to start adjusting. Rab doled out a generous portion of 'shrooms for each of them.

"That's an awful lot, isn't it?" Cloud said, taking her share from his hands.

"That's how we did it before," Fin interrupted before Rab had the chance to speak. He accepted his share and seated himself close by the fire. "We eat something very small before we start out, maybe something in the middle of the day, maybe not, and then eat as well as possible at night."

Cloud twitched a shoulder. "All right," she said. "But that's not how the Top-siders I know do it."

"Maybe they don't walk as far in a day, Abby."

Cloud settled herself down between Rab and Fin. "Guess not." She turned to Rab. "Just how far *will* we walk tomorrow?"

"I don't know how to measure distance any better than you do, Cloud. How far is it from your space to the mushroom fields?"

Cloud stopped chewing to think a moment. "I don't know that, either. Funny how everything becomes bigger top-side. I'd forgotten about that. I really have been in those tunnels too long. I like it better up here. . ." she glanced towards her dusty boots, ". . . despite my sore feet."

"There'll be more than sore feet to worry about before long," Rab told her, getting up from the floor, "and then we'll see how well you like it. Finish up. Get some sleep. We rise when the sun does."

"If we could see it," Fin muttered, then stood and walked to the pile of wood. He had another length of splintered wood in his hand when he came back. "Who's going to stoke the fire?" he asked of Rab.

"Whoever wakes up first and finds it's going out."

Cloud's brow was deeply furrowed when she looked up.

"Believe me, one of us will get cold enough to notice," Rab told her.

"Just so you both know, I'm going to be right here," Fin said, clearing a space on the floor and laying out one pack for his head.

Somehow Rab doubted the pack he intended to lay his head on was the one that contained Stitch's heart; it had to be in the other one, a guess confirmed when Fin carefully placed his second pack to one side. All day long Rab had managed to keep his mind occupied enough not to think about what Fin was carrying around on his back. Now the best he could do was look away as Fin lowered himself down and turned his back to the fire.

"Whichever one of you does get up," Fin mumbled, "don't step on me."

"There's someone with the right idea," Rab said, finding himself a spot closer to Cloud and the fire.

"Won't be far behind," Cloud replied. "Just *have* to get these boots off first."

Rab watched as she began to work on the lacing. On the other side of the fire, Fin's breathing sounded very soft and shallow. He was already asleep.

Rab pitched his voice at a whisper for fear of waking him. "Fin is starting to suspect you're hiding something."

"Can't imagine what."

"Your motives for going with him."

"Oh, that. Told you before. I'm tired of living underground. I'd rather take my chances top-side. Never went before because I didn't want to try it alone and going with you was no use. You kept coming back." She had one boot off and was starting on the other. "I'd forgotten how hard it is walking on loose stones, though. My feet are really sore."

"I don't suppose Fin ever explained why he is so determined to revisit every place we passed to get home again."

"No," Cloud replied with a half-hearted shake of her head as she stripped off the remaining boot. "And I never asked. I think it's something he feels he has to do."

Rab poked at the fire with a wayward stick. "Seems none of us here are too good about sharing."

Cloud's head snapped up. "What do you mean?"

"Well, for one thing, why didn't you tell Lilly the truth? You left letting her believe you had every intention of coming back."

Cloud shrugged. "I thought it would be easier."

"On who?"

"I don't think I deserve that," she replied after an uncomfortable pause.

No, she didn't.

"I've looked after Lilly for years, Rab," she continued, scooting closer, "when I didn't have to do a single thing for her. But it doesn't seem to make a lot of difference anymore. I thought it would be less of a shock if I just disappeared. Besides, it's easier for Button that way, too. Could you imagine how difficult Lilly would be to handle now if she knew I wasn't coming back?"

Rab hadn't thought about that.

"Better she comes to the realisation slowly. I was the one who took care of her, not you. So I think it's pretty poor of you to judge how and when I stop."

Rab flung the skinny stick into the fire. "You're right. On both counts, Cloud. It probably is better this way."

"Thank you! So what's your story then?"

It was Rab's turn to be surprised.

"My story?"

"Yeah. What haven't you shared with the rest of us?"

"Nothing I can immediately think of."

"Like I believe that," Cloud said, pointing past him. "Pass me that pack. No, the other one. I've got to do something about this pain in my feet if I'm ever going to get any sleep."

Taking the pack, she rummaged around for a moment and at last drew out a brownish-coloured vial that measured about as wide as her palm and as long as her hand from wrist to fingertip. After a brief fumble with the cap, she managed to unscrew the lid, then tipped the vial upright, blocking the opening with the index finger of her right hand. She must have collected something on her finger because she immediately thrust the tip of that finger into her mouth.

"What's that?"

Cloud withdrew her finger from her mouth. "Purple mushroom extract. I only used a couple of grains," she said guiltily. "Hardly any at all." Recapping the vial, she stashed it back into her pack, then nodded towards Fin. "I think that's the first real sleep he's got in days. You look like you could do with some, too, Rab. Maybe this idea of his isn't as stupid as you think."

"How is that?" Rab asked with a glance towards their sleeping companion.

"Well," Cloud said, brightening. "We could just find somewhere, you know. Somewhere we could stay. Somewhere better than the tunnels."

Rab couldn't hold back a sigh. Not tonight. He really was just too tired. "The three of us? How cosy. Anyway, Cloud, I keep telling you—"

"Yes. Yes. There's no one alive in the south. Things are much worse in the south. But you can't *know* that for sure, Rab. Don't shake your head at me like that."

"You *really* believe that, don't you?"

"Sometimes."

***

Rab woke to find Fin sleeping soundly and Cloud gone. She'd spent the entire night lying on his shoulder, sleepily settling herself back in every time he returned from stoking the fire. He'd expected her to have selected Fin's company over his and, in some respects, kind of wished she had. His muscles when he tried to flex them felt stiff and sore.

He found Cloud outside, propped on a large chunk of building waste, staring up at the sky.

"Fin is still asleep," he said, startling her so badly she nearly fell off her perch.

"Did you hear anything earlier this morning?" she said, swivelling around to face him. "Kind of a 'whoosh' sound?"

That wasn't what he needed to hear first thing in the morning. "Land-slip," he suggested. "Up in the hills. Sometimes I hear them."

Cloud shook her head. "No. It sounded like it came from overhead." She pointed to the sky. "From up there."

Rab began to relax. "Sounds get turned around out here, Cloud. Could even have been the wind."

"Maybe," Cloud replied as she came to her feet. "But it didn't sound like any wind I've ever heard before. And look at that," she said, pointing skyward again.

Rab glanced overhead, already anticipating what Cloud could have seen. Sometimes he saw something in the sky, too—like a tear in the fabric of the clouds. And that's exactly what he discovered when he looked up. This rip was larger than most he'd seen before and coloured a very watery shade of blue.

"It's just a break in the clouds," he told her, glancing down. "I've been seeing them for the last year or so."

The expression on her face betrayed a little of her excitement. "I've heard the bounty hunters talk about such things, but I never thought I'd see it for myself."

Rab motioned for her to follow him back into the shelter. "And now you have. But as far as what you heard, I wouldn't worry about it."

But *he* would. At least he'd be just that little bit extra alert until they were well out of the village and on their way.

Fin was awake and moving around. He looked over when he saw them, gaze lingering a while.

"I've laid out a little food," he said at last.

There was just enough light from the dying fire for Rab to notice the wary expression on his face. Was he wondering what he and Cloud had been up to out there together? Or was it something else? Rab settled on the something else. Fin seemed to be anticipating some sort of argument.

Rab smiled to himself. Fin had a long memory. If Fin, the boy, had taken it on himself to distribute the food, Rab would have had something to say about it. But Fin was a young man now, not a boy. Rab trusted him; at least he'd vowed to trust him until Fin gave him cause not to.

"I'll just go refill the canteens then," Fin said hesitantly.

"Fine," Rab replied, bending to collect his share of the food Fin had laid on a brushed-off chunk of rubble by the fire. "Just stay alert. Cloud heard something this morning. Probably the wind, but it wouldn't hurt to pay extra attention."

"Why don't you look up at the sky while you're out there," Cloud called, beaming him a smile.

Rab straightened and caught the fleeting look of uncertainty on Fin's face.

"All right," the young man replied and started about collecting all the used canteens. He had them bundled up in his arms when he left.

Cloud stuffed her mouth with the last of her share of the food, then slipped to the ground to put on her boots. It was only then Rab realised that she'd gone outside without them on.

"Aren't your feet cold?" he asked.

Cloud paused with the first boot halfway back on her foot. "No," she said, eyeing Rab suspiciously. "Oh no!" She dropped the boot, then stripped off two layers of socks to expose the bare skin of her feet.

Chapter 5

"WELL?" Rab prompted.

"They're all right," Cloud said with a loud sigh as she inspected her feet. "I shouldn't have been able to do that, should I?" she asked, looking back at Rab. "Walk out there without my boots?"

Rab handed her a discarded sock. "Maybe you don't feel the cold as much as the rest of us."

"I don't know," she said, turning her attention to the task of replacing her socks. "It just didn't seem that cold to me, but I hadn't stopped to think about it."

Rab hadn't either, but now that he did, he realised Cloud was right. He'd been more concerned with working out the stiffness in his shoulder and hadn't registered the absence of the hard and bracing slap he ordinarily received every time he stepped out into the morning air top-side.

"Odd," he said, now passing Cloud her boot. "It *wasn't* as cold as usual."

"Is that good or bad?" she asked, lacing.

"Interesting question." Rab rose and tapped Cloud's shoulder. "Pack up your stuff. When Fin gets back, we'll start out."

By the time Fin returned with the canteens, Rab had the fire out, Cloud had her boots on and her packs sorted.

"Well?" Cloud prompted. "Did you see it?"

"Yes, I saw it," Fin replied, glancing at Rab. "The weather is changing."

"Well, I wouldn't feel too encouraged by it, Fin. It could change back just as easily and quickly."

Rab didn't bother to ask if Fin had come across anything else unusual; Fin would have told them instead of wordlessly distributing the filled canteens and retrieving his own gear.

A moment before they stepped through the low and ruined doorway, Rab caught the young man by the arm, hoping to receive a different answer to the question he just had to ask.

"The factory?"

Fin nodded.

"Why? There's nothing for us there."

Fin shrugged Rab off. "I want to go. If you and Abby would prefer to start off to the village ahead of me, then do that and I'll catch up."

Rab shook his head. "We are not going to split up, Fin. Anyway, Cloud wouldn't go on without you."

"No, I wouldn't," Cloud agreed. "Besides, I'd like to see that factory for myself. I can't even imagine what it looks like."

"A mess," Rab said. "Just picture this place, only taller."

Cloud graced him with a smile. "Don't believe you," she said, then, ducking, led the way outside.

Rab was the last to leave.

"Fin says there's a river nearby," Cloud observed, glancing back at Rab.

"The factory is right on it."

"I've never seen a river, either. Not a real one anyway. Once, when I was with the Top-siders, we came across a little stream. I remember being disappointed."

Rab adjusted his packs. Tonight, Cloud would have to find herself some other pillow besides his shoulder.

"Well, don't get your hopes up about the river. It's filthy."

"Oh," Cloud said, sounding a little crestfallen. "Fin didn't tell me that."

"I did," Fin objected. He'd moved to take the lead. "You've forgotten."

"Doesn't matter, I suppose," she said, brightening. "I still want to see it."

"You're not going to get to step in," Rab warned her. "Or stay too long. The air there is really bad."

"Why?"

"I don't know. Look, are you going to keep up these questions all the way? Can't you just wait until we get there?"

Cloud shot him another quick glance.

He'd snapped at her; he hadn't meant to do that. It was this business about going to the factory. They were taking a stupid risk for absolutely no reason at all.

Cloud fell silent after that. Rab doubted he'd hurt her feelings; she wasn't that fragile, just smart. At the edge of the village, Fin and Cloud stopped walking, waiting for Rab to catch up. Despite yesterday's resolve to take the lead from Fin, he'd been lagging behind, allowing his lack of enthusiasm to influence his pace. Bad idea. Better to get there, quickly accomplish whatever it was Fin wanted to do, see or otherwise, and move on. They'd be in the open after that but at least they'd have some reasonable direction in mind. They could wait out snow time in their old village. Rab was counting on something having survived: one of their shanties; better still the old storeroom. With luck maybe a little of their stores might have survived as well. Perhaps a few holdouts from the colony of grubs they tended.

Who was he trying to kid?

The stockpile of 'shrooms would be all gone; the grubs would all be dead. No, their best hope in the village was shelter and tinder from the ruin of it for fire. Once the supplies they'd brought with them were exhausted, finding food would be an altogether different problem. There was a chance that the old 'shroom fields were still yielding something. It was a lot easier to feed three people than an entire village. A little might do. If they found the fields entirely barren, then that was pretty much it, wasn't it?

"I see it."

Rab had lost track of time. When Fin called out, he was surprised that they were almost at the factory and must have been walking close by the river for some time. Although he wasn't aware of it, a gentle breeze had to be blowing in the opposite direction because Rab hadn't noticed much of a stench at all.

"There," Fin said, pointing.

"Where?" Cloud asked, grasping Rab's arm. "Oh, that's not what I was expecting," she said, glancing at Fin.

Rab, either.

Something about the place looked different. The two spindly towers! They were gone.

"All right, Fin," Rab snapped. "That's it. We're not going in. The towers have collapsed. And the rest of the smaller buildings have probably collapsed, too. If you have it in your mind to go foraging about in the brick piles again, you can forget it."

"You can stay outside if you want. Keep Abby with you. But you won't stop me, Rab." Fin moved off, heading straight for the factory. "You couldn't before and you can't now."

Rab was about to remind Fin what had happened the last time he'd wandered off into the factory but he'd have been wasting his time. That experience would have been at the forefront of Fin's mind as he hurried off down the road.

"That's where Stitch broke his leg, isn't it?" Cloud asked, snaring Rab's attention.

He pointed. "Somewhere over there. Stitch had followed Fin up into the roof structure. It was unstable and he fell through."

Cloud shook her head. "Well, he won't get me to follow him. I'll be staying on open ground." She tugged on Rab's arm. "We'd better not let him get too far ahead."

Fin was at the gates by the time they caught up with him. The wire gates were lying exactly where they had fallen when Fin had broken them down, frames twisted up and rusted.

"It doesn't look like anyone has been here," Rab said, glancing around the empty site.

"Like who were you expecting?" Cloud asked, sounding suspicious.

"No one. But the bounty hunters who use the village we were in last night might come here."

"South?" Fin said, glancing back. He was starting to make his way cautiously around the fallen gates. "There's no one alive in the south, remember. Why would they come in this direction?"

Typical of Fin to use Rab's own argument against him.

When Cloud made a move to follow Fin, Rab caught her arm.

"One at a time around the gates."

"So here we are again. There's something you're not telling us," she said. "You're always looking around as though there's been someone ahead or behind us."

"There could be, Cloud."

"Like bounty hunters?"

"Or Top-siders."

"So? I think we're all a little too old for the bounties hunters to pass us off as returned captives. And what if we do run into Top-siders? They don't want us, either. Me maybe, but a grown woman's a bit too much trouble to deal with. That's why they take kids in the first place. Besides they're not all bad, you know, Rab. You're one yourself."

"There's Top-siders and then there's Top-siders," Rab said, hoping to finish the matter. He released Cloud's arm with the intention of starting after Fin but Cloud quickly grasped the back of one of his packs to prevent him.

"Care to explain that a little better," she said.

Rab sighed. He'd been avoiding this for a long time.

"In the tunnels, they cultivate food. My village cultivated food. Not so well, but we tried. The roving Top-siders have to rely on what they find. Take food wherever they can get it." He wrenched himself free of Cloud's hold. "You figure it out."

He'd just made it around the gates when he heard Cloud clattering after him.

"Slow down and get off there," he shouted, swinging around.

She didn't and it was only a stroke of good fortune that she didn't get a boot caught along the way. She jumped the last section of gate and landed, breathless and heavily, in the dirt beside Rab.

"Are you trying to tell me," she whispered after glancing around to find Fin, "that when I lived top-side, I ate—"

Rab cut her off. "I don't know, Cloud. It's like I said, there's Top-siders and then there's Top-siders. And what does it matter now anyway?"

She seized the front of his coat with both hands and began to shake. "*What does it matter?*"

Rab took hold of her hands. "Look, Cloud. People do what they have to do to survive."

"No," she said with a vehement shake of her head. "Maybe some other Top-siders, but not *mine*. Not the ones *I* lived with."

"Good." Rab dropped one of her hands but kept a firm hold of the other. "Then you don't have to think about that anymore. Come on," he said, leading her off. "Fin is getting too far ahead of us."

Another illusion shattered! There were so few left. But doing it made Rab even more determined never to shatter the last. He'd take Sunny's cursed secret to the grave just the way she wanted. That same old bitter resolve prompted him to tighten his hold on Cloud's hand. He could feel it tremor. She wouldn't say another word about the way her Top-siders might have survived. And nor would he. That damage was done.

"Fin," he called, obliged to hurry Cloud along. "Wait up."

The young man stopped at the leading edge of a broad expanse of debris.

"I'm not going much further," he called back, pointing behind him. "Just here."

What in God's name for? Rab wondered.

If memory served him correctly, Fin had zeroed in on the same mound of old bricks he'd climbed up once before. Farther on was the ruined building where Stitch had fallen. . .what was left of it. And past that, the fouled river. But Rab still couldn't smell anything overpoweringly bad. Sure, there was an unpleasant odour in the air, but nothing as bad as the last time he'd been here when the inside of his nose and mouth had burned and his eyes had stung and watered. Something had changed at this site. And just like the change in temperature he and Cloud had discussed that morning, Rab wasn't sure if that was a good or a bad thing.

He turned to Cloud. "Still maintain you don't know what he's looking for?"

"I don't," Cloud replied flatly. "Is it possible to at least *see* the river?" she asked with a little shrug. "We're here after all."

Her enthusiasm to get her first sight of the river had waned a little. If he refused her, he had the impression that she wouldn't particularly care. Rab glanced around, hoping to uncover some safe way to at least give her a look at the water. The two towers had pretty well collapsed; there was little danger from them any longer. But Rab had no intention of allowing either Fin or Cloud back into the building where Stitch had fallen. He'd stop them; if he had to knock them out cold to do it.

"Maybe here isn't the best place, Cloud," he said, accepting defeat. "The river's not all that far from my village. Just a place it wasn't safe to go." He'd learned that for himself the hard way. "But the river doesn't seem to be as bad as it used to be. Last time I was here, I could hardly breathe. Could be it's better downstream as well. We'll just have to wait and see."

"There *is* an odd smell around here," she said, breaking away from Rab to find a perch on a low pile of broken bricks. "Kind of a stale smell." She shrugged out of her packs and dumped them to the ground.

"Fin doesn't mind. The kids from my village weren't able to smell or, if they could, didn't seem to care too much about *what* they smelled."

Cloud rubbed her nose with a gloved hand. "Could be an advantage."

Rab settled in beside her to wait and watch. Fin was down on his hands and knees now, rummaging among the same mound of old bricks. First he'd pick one up, examine it, toss it aside, then pick up another to repeat the process all over again. Cloud's eyes were downcast, looking at a little patch of light on the ground by her feet.

"Sunlight," Rab told her. "Coming through that break in the clouds. It's still there. See?" he said, directing her attention skyward.

"It's beautiful," she exclaimed, turning back to Rab. "I knew we were right to leave."

Rab didn't reply but watched Cloud as she shifted her boot in and out of the weak patch of brighter light over and over again.

"What can he be doing?" she asked at last, looking up.

They weren't left wondering long. Whatever he'd been seeking, Fin appeared to have found it. He got up from the ground and, with a single brick in hand, made his way over to Cloud and Rab.

"Here," he said, offering the brick to Rab. "Read that. You couldn't before."

Rab glanced down at the broken brick in his hand. He turned it over to find the same worn and indistinct inscription gouged into the surface of both sides. It wasn't easy to read, but possible, even for someone with his meagre skills. How was he going to tell Fin?

Rab looked up. "What are you hoping to find, Fin?"

Fin hesitated for a moment before replying. "Something about the people who used to be here. Where they came from. Where they went."

Rab added the broken brick to the ruined pile he was sitting on. "It's not on that brick, Fin. All that's there is a couple of letters and then some numbers."

"Are they the same as the bricks back in that village?" He pointed back the way they had come.

Rab shrugged. "Could be, but I didn't look too closely at any of the bricks there, Fin. A lot of the buildings in the village were made of brick. This brick factory is nearby. I don't understand what you're getting at."

"There were a lot of bricks in our village, too, Rab. Where did *they* come from?"

"I wouldn't know, but I doubt very much they were from here. It's a long way to haul—"

Fin interrupted him. "But they didn't just appear out of nowhere."

"Fin, our village has been there a long time."

"Like the bricks. Is that what you're saying?"

"That's what I'm saying. It's more likely our people made them themselves." Rab glanced around. "Not on such a large scale. But it's not that hard to make a brick, Fin."

For a long time, Fin stood, eyes downcast, considering the brick Rab had discarded to the mound.

"What were the letters?" he asked.

"Two 'B's'."

"Could be Braham," Cloud suggested, drawing both Rab's and Fin's attention.

"I know my letters," she said defensively. "Just can't string it all together. Ruby was helping me, too," she added, looking at Rab.

"Could also be anything else," Rab said. "Even Benson begins with a 'B'."

"Yeah," Cloud agreed, coming to her feet. "I could own this heap of trash." She began to brush off the seat of her pants, then stopped to glance at Rab. "Lilly could," she mumbled.

"Maybe there's something else," Fin suggested. "Just let me look a while longer."

He struck off and Cloud dropped back down onto the mound.

"This is a waste of time," she said with a loud sigh.

"Finally something we agree on."

Cloud rubbed at her nose again. "I also agree that this isn't a great place to be. It does stink, Rab."

"Told you."

Fin was on his way past the mound where he'd found the inscribed brick. The mound didn't appear to interest him any longer. Instead he began what promised to be a slow steady transit of every part of the ground he could get to. He kept his head bowed down, looking.

Rab glanced away from him towards Cloud, who was reaching down to retrieve one of her packs.

"Just a little," she said, noticing Rab's attention wander to the vial she withdrew, the one containing her personal supply of purple mushroom extract.

In the daylight, Rab could see that the colour of the vial wasn't uniformly brown as he'd thought last night in the fire light, but a messy blend of dirty green streaks and deep reddish-brown blotches.

"Do you want some?"

Rab shook his head. "Where'd you get that vial anyway?"

"Lilly gave it to me just before we left. Remember?"

"There's something on the side of it," Rab replied.

"Yeah, it's a figure of some sort. But it's just a piece of junk. Been lying around Lilly's store for years." She hefted it once into the air. "Kind of lighter than you'd expect. Here," she said, passing the vial to Rab.

Rab turned the vial over in his hands, then twisted the illustrated side around so it faced Cloud. "Did you see the stones? Up here?" He pointed to a spot near the top of the vial. "On what looks like the head of some sort of animal?"

"I never paid much attention. They're kind of like its eyes, aren't they?"

"Do they look blue to you?"

Cloud leaned in, looked intently at the vial for a long moment, then shrugged. "Hard to say. They're all cracked and dirty. Maybe. But what animal is that supposed to be?"

"It looks a bit like a bird to me," Rab replied. He took one last look before handing back the vial. "But I've never seen one quite like that."

Cloud smiled as she worked on unscrewing the cap. "We've never seen a bird at all, Rab, so how would you know it looks like a bird?"

"I meant like the pictures I've seen of birds. In books. In the library."

"Oh, those," she said dismissively.

"I wonder where it came from."

"The bounty hunters bring in a lot of strange things and trade them with Lilly. But," she said, placing the loosened cap on the mound of broken bricks beside her, "this is one of the strangest I've seen. Pretty though, if it wasn't all beaten up and rusty looking." In a repeat of last night's procedure, Cloud tipped a little of the powder onto her finger and placed it in her mouth.

"As pretty as this?" Rab asked, digging deep into his pocket to retrieve his small draw-string bag. Opening it, he tipped Gift's little stone out into the palm of his glove.

Laying the vial on the bricks between them, Cloud took the stone between her thumb and forefinger, then held it up to the sky.

"Hold up the vial so I can see it in that bit of brighter light," she said.

Rab picked up the vial and turned the illustrated side of it towards Cloud again.

"They could be the same stone, Rab," she said, flicking a glance from the stone to the vial, then back again. "Except this one is all kind of rough and those on the vial are smooth and round. Is that supposed to mean something?" she asked, lowering her hand.

"That's Gift's stone." Rab accepted the stone from her outstretched hand and passed her the vial. "A Top-sider boy gave it to her."

"I see," she said, breaking a brief silence during which she returned the vial to her pack. "But even if you'd seen that vial and noticed those stones while we were still in the tunnels, it wouldn't make any difference. I doubt Lilly would remember where she got it."

"The bounty hunter who gave it to her might."

"Lilly wouldn't remember him, either. Besides, she's had it a long time. I told you. And it's not a Top-sider thing any way. Who knows where she got it."

"I suppose you're right," Rab said and reluctantly returned the stone to the pouch and the pouch to his pocket.

He could feel Cloud's eyes on his every move.

"Maybe we should help Fin look," she suggested.

"For what?"

"Something. Anything that will satisfy him and get us out of here."

"I'm afraid there's nothing here that's going to give him the answer *he* is looking for, either."

Cloud leapt back onto her feet. "Well, I can't even understand the question. If we can't go and look at the river, then I don't see the point of hanging around here fretting about a few silly stones and looking for something when we don't even know what it is." She snatched up her discarded packs. "I'm going to go and get him."

"Good luck," Rab muttered to her as she strode away, heading for Fin. "And be careful!"

What would Cloud say and Fin do, Rab wondered, if he gave them both the question and its answer right there and then? It was a surprise to discover that Fin was still even looking!

He eased himself off the mound. Cloud didn't appear to be making much progress with Fin. He could hear them arguing but didn't pay much attention to what either one of them was saying. One or other of them would win; he was betting on Cloud. Sooner would be better than later and any interference from him would ensure it would be later. Every so often as he made his way back to the broken gates, Rab glanced over his shoulder. The first time he glanced back, Fin was still down on his hands and knees with Cloud standing over him. The next, Fin was on his feet, although neither he nor Cloud had moved away from the pile of rubble Fin had been digging in. Rab was almost back at the gates, growing increasingly troubled that he'd be obliged to intervene after all, when, turning again, he saw them both walking slowly towards him. He stopped and waited for them outside the fallen gates.

"I'm sorry," he said to Fin when he passed.

If Fin heard, he didn't answer.

"He's all right," Cloud said, falling into step beside Rab. "Just disappointed, but I guess you know how that feels."

Disappointed? Was that the right word to describe how he felt every time he returned, empty-handed, to the tunnels? Maybe at first, but not so much any longer. Tired. Resigned. They were some of the right words. Determined? Maybe. Or had his search just become part of some endless routine? It wasn't smart to examine things like that too closely.

"Fin," Rab called. "Up and over the hill. Then wait for us please."

Fin waved a hand above his head.

There'd be no road from now on. It ended at the factory, so they'd be relying on memory, wind direction and Rab's ability to read the fickle sky.

"Hope your feet feel better," he said, turning to Cloud. "It's all open ground from here."

"Don't worry about me," she said.

He did. He always would. . .even if she, *and* Fin, didn't know it.

With Cloud beside him, Rab began his ascent of the hill. It wasn't exactly hard going, but it did call for some caution. A slip on loose stones could send any one of them tumbling downslope.

"Do you still believe it's out there somewhere?" Cloud asked.

"What? My village?"

"No, the launch pad, of course. I mean after all this time you've been top-side, you'd think you'd have come across something or at least someone who knew where to look."

So it was time for that part of his performance again, was it?

"It's out there, Cloud. It really is."

It wasn't a lie; just a big stretch on the meaning of 'out there'.

Give them a reason to go on.

More and more lately Rab found himself earnestly longing for the day when he could pass off that responsibility to someone else.

Let the believers go on believing. Let the rest go on making the best of this place. Thanks, Sunny.

"Fin thinks it is," Cloud said.

So Rab had just concluded from the young man's behaviour at the factory. He was looking for clues—only in the wrong places. But just when did Fin have a change of heart? Not that it mattered. The launch pads did exist but they'd never reach one.

"He says that's why you never went south," Cloud was saying. "He says you don't want to find the launch pad—not until you find Gift. But I'm not so sure they ever existed."

"That's the way of it," Rab said with a little shrug. "You believe one thing. I believe another. Brand me guilty of back-thinking nonsense if it makes you happy. Wouldn't be the first time."

"You see that's what I don't understand about you, Rab. You want us all to jump on these spaceships, so we can zoom off and find a better place. But it doesn't bother you one little bit that most of us believe those spaceships are a myth and don't waste a second even thinking about them."

"Why should it? If I said that coat you're wearing was green instead of brown, what difference would that make?"

Cloud glanced down at her coat.

"That's not the same thing. It is brown, and brown is brown."

"So you say."

"You know," Cloud said after a moment. "I'm sorry I even asked you. I should have known better. It always ends up this way. Some day you're going to make sense to me, but it isn't going to be today. What with you and your little blue stones and him. . ." she gestured towards Fin, who had just reached the crest of the hill, ". . . scavenging in brick piles, I'm over it."

She took off, racing as best she could up the hill after Fin.

"At least until tomorrow," Rab called after her.

"Yeah! Yeah!" she sang without glancing back.

There was a time when Fin would have ignored his instructions entirely and just kept on going, guided by his own instincts, but when Rab glanced down from the top of the hill, he saw Fin seated on the ground, waiting for them, directly at the base of the rise.

Cloud reached him first but Rab wasn't far behind.

"Just keep the wind at your back, Fin, and we'll track due south. You'll know it if it begins to turn."

Even encumbered with his overstuffed packs, Fin rose effortlessly to his feet; a far cry from how he'd managed the last time. Cloud was faring all right as well, despite the minor discomfort of her ill-fitting boots. If the gentle wind and comparatively milder weather held, they might reach the village sooner than Rab was anticipating. They didn't have two small children in tow this time and they knew exactly where they were going.

"We won't have any shelter tonight, I'm afraid," Rab said, turning to Cloud. "And it's going to be some days before we can have a fire."

Beneath the hood of her coat, Cloud was looking at him askance. "How can we ever have a fire? There's no tinder out here!"

Rab was taken aback; he'd have thought Fin would have regaled her over and over again with the tale of his discovery. Fin was just full of surprises.

"He's talking about the fallen forest, Abby," Fin said, starting out ahead of them. "If it hasn't rotted out completely, we should be able to make a fire like last time."

Cloud snatched the sleeve of Rab's coat. "Is he joking?"

Rab couldn't help smiling. "Oh, there's a forest all right. At least there used to be. But it fell down a long time ago. A lot of it is rotten like Fin said." When Cloud's face began to brighten, Rab shook his head. "No grubs, Cloud. I looked last time. It's dead."

"Well, then," she said, settling her packs before she started out, "at least we'll have something to see along the way."

That was one way of looking at it, Rab supposed, because otherwise there was going to be precious little to break the monotony of their journey.

They didn't get very far before a long, low rumble pulled Cloud up.

"Now that," Rab said as she turned to him, "was a landslip."

She frowned. "And definitely *not* what I heard this morning."

***

No sooner had they eaten their meal that night than Fin fell into a dead sleep. Cloud was sitting quietly beside Rab, so quietly in fact that he jumped when she touched his arm.

"Hear something?" he whispered.

"See something," she whispered back. "Up there."

Rab glanced skyward and discovered, with little surprise, that Cloud had spotted the star. It was the first and the only one Rab had ever seen and, by his reckoning, he'd seen this same star at least three times before. Always directly overhead. And always around this time of year.

"Star," he told her. "Must be a really clear night. I never see it otherwise."

He sensed Cloud turn to him. "You've seen them before then?"

"Not them," Rab replied with a shake of his head. "*It.* There's only one. . .well, the only one that's visible anyway."

"But it's so tiny! Nothing but a little speck. Are you sure it's a star?"

"What else could it be?"

"Huh," Cloud murmured.

"It's a long way away," Rab reminded her.

"Yeah," she agreed, looking skyward once more. "I guess it must be. Makes you wonder how they *could* make it to another planet though, doesn't it? It seems so distant. So impossible."

"They made it," Rab said.

He couldn't see her face, but Rab knew that Cloud was smiling at him.

"You never give up, do you?"

"What's going on?" Fin asked, speech slurred by sleep.

"Nothing. Cloud just saw a star," Rab told him.

"What do you mean she saw a star?" Fin sounded alert now.

"That little whitish dot overhead," Cloud said, slipping her head to the ground. "Rab said it's a star."

"That all!" Fin snapped irritably. "I've been wondering what that was. Thought I had grit in my eye. Not much to get excited about in my opinion."

Rab heard a bit of a rustle; Fin turning on his shoulder as he settled back down to sleep.

And Cloud, who had wisely elected to keep her uncomfortable boots on this time, was soon breathing shallowly beside him. Neither stirred again until morning. Rab was certain that he'd remained awake for the rest of the night, watching that one small and lonely star until, just before dawn, he thought he heard the strange, whooshing sound Cloud claimed to have heard before. But no, he decided almost immediately; he must have only dreamed it.

When they started out, he let Fin take the lead again. Overall he was doing a good job of keeping them on target with Rab only occasionally obliged to sing out a course correction. Cloud walked beside him all the way. She had little to say but by the way she kept glancing at him from under the heavy folds of her coat, Rab was all too aware that something was running through her mind. It wasn't until late in the day that she revealed what it was.

"How can you keep doing this?" she asked, breaking the last in a series of long silences. "Over, and over, and over again."

"Funny question coming from you. The Top-siders you lived with did this, didn't they? Roamed from place to place."

"Not exactly," she snapped.

Cloud invariably became defensive whenever *her* Top-siders were mentioned. Whatever had happened to her while she lived among them couldn't have been all bad.

"We only moved when we had to. When the food and shelter ran out. It's not like we traipsed around out in the cold and desolation day after day, year after year."

"Like me?"

"Yes, like you. Aren't you tired yet, Rab? Haven't you had enough?"

"Long ago," he said. "But what alternative is there? Live underground?" He turned to smile down at her. "Even you couldn't stomach that."

Cloud shrugged. "I wish you were right. I wish there was a launch pad out here. I wish you could find it."

"Three wishes," Rab observed. "It's all you get."

"What?"

"Three wishes. It's an old. . .oh, never mind. Just something I came across in a book once."

"You and your books," Cloud muttered. "It must really bother you to have to leave them behind every time you go."

"Left them for good this time, haven't I, Cloud?"

"Not much of a loss," she said. "Hardly any left now. Last time I was down in the library. . .What?" She stubbornly returned Rab's stare. "I told you Ruby was trying to teach me to read. Never could get the hang of it. Pretty pictures though." She gave him a gentle shove. "I really liked the ones of rabbits."

"Prefer clouds myself."

"Then maybe you should start looking at them, instead of talking about them," Fin sang out.

Rab had thought Fin was too far ahead to hear their talk.

Fin's skills at judging the weather had suffered underground. Rab *had* been keeping an eye on the clouds. Rain was coming but it wouldn't be today; likely not even tomorrow. But they'd be out in the open when it did hit. There was no getting around it. They simply could not make it to the village in time. Rab had lost count of the number of times he'd trudged top-side in the rain. But Cloud and Fin? They'd grown soft underground. Once their boots filled with water, their feet would begin to blister. And if it was a cold rain, one or other of them, perhaps both, could come down in a fever. If the fever was minor, purple mushroom extract would suffice. If the fever became severe. . .

"Nothing to worry about, Fin," Rab said just the same. "There's days yet."

***

The rain caught them two days later out on the open plain. It was a light rain, milder than most Rab had experienced on the surface. Cloud with her ill-fitting boots fared the worst of them. She slipped and slid and once came down hard on her hip. She never complained but kept on trudging directly behind Rab.

The last time Rab had journeyed across this plain, the monotony of it had caused him to lose track of time. And he had been burdened by the weight of Stitch on and off his back. He knew that then it had taken them many days to cross the featureless landscape but, this time, he intended to keep a very careful account. After all, the odds were very high that they'd have to backtrack this way again on their return to the tunnels. Their supplies had to be managed accordingly.

"Do you think it'll be as bad as last time?" Fin asked.

It was their fourth night out from the factory and the light rain had degenerated into a fine kind of vapour that clung lightly in little beads to their clothing and the tops of their packs. Fin was sitting, huddled and miserable-looking, on the ground by his packs. Cloud was looking heavenwards, a habit she'd just recently developed, although she couldn't have seen much through the low-hanging ceiling of the sky.

"What?" she asked, glancing down from her study to question Fin. "The forest?"

"I think Fin's referring to the weather," Rab replied, swiping the latest thin smear of moisture from the top of his pack. "Not long after we left our village, we were caught in a snow storm and later had to walk for days and days through a dense mist."

"And what if the same thing happens again?" Cloud asked, turning to Rab. "I mean. . .how will you keep track of our direction in the middle of a mist?"

"I did before," Rab told her. "If I have to, I'll do it again."

Rab caught Fin's eye. The young man seemed to be considering if Rab was up to such a task.

"I think you should take the lead from here on," Fin said finally. "At least until we reach the forest."

"I agree," Cloud said, marking the end of any discussion.

Well, it was why they'd brought him, he supposed—to tap his skills on the surface. Once Rab had abjectly feared journeying blind top-side. Not any longer. He'd travelled blind more times now than he could remember. If by some peculiar coincidence they did come on that mist again, he knew he could bring them through—with much less angst and soul-searching than he'd had the last time. As for encountering another snow storm—they'd just have to take their chances.

Still Rab was pleased when he woke to discover that the rain had left them quietly during the night. It took five days in total to complete their traverse of the plain and come to the rise that, as Rab remembered, they'd climb for one full day and descend for another full day. In those five days, Cloud's gait had grown progressively more irregular; those boots of hers weren't anywhere near adequate for the rock-strewn surface of the plain. Still she made no complaint although Rab did notice that she'd taken to tipping a finger to the mouth of that stone-encrusted vial at least every other evening when they set about making camp. And twice again they'd seen that same star high, high up in the night sky and twice again heard that same odd and unexplained sound that came right around dawn. It was just like Cloud had described it. A whooshing, beating kind of sound coming from the air above.

Rab crested the rise ahead of Fin, who had dropped back to walk beside Cloud. He stopped and waited for them to catch up. Cloud had begun to limp a little and there was still a long way to go. The last thing they needed was to encounter another broad patch of mist or further rain. The latter was exactly what they got. As before, the rain wasn't particularly heavy, but it was enough to make it slick going down the gentle rise. When, halfway through the downward trek, someone came sliding down the slope, shooting right past him, Rab's immediate thought was that Cloud had lost her footing.

But it was Fin, not Cloud, who had fallen and gone sliding down the hill-side. Fortunately his packs had taken the brunt of the rough descent and, when Rab caught up with him, he found Fin, still seated on his rear on the sharp-edged stones, inspecting the damage. By the time Cloud had reached them, Fin was already up on his feet. There was tear in one of Fin's packs; not a bad tear but one that would require repair sooner rather than later.

"Why didn't one of us think to bring a needle?" Cloud muttered, frustrated when she could find nothing to serve inside her packs. "I might have been able to reweave it."

Fin had set to rummaging about inside his own packs and ultimately ended up sacrificing one of his sturdier spare shirts, securing it around the tear and using the arms to tie it off on the side of pack.

It would have to do until they found something better. At least nothing would fall out. They simply couldn't afford to have part of their food supply or, perhaps just as bad, the vessel that held Stitch's heart fall by the wayside. If either happened, they'd be obliged to backtrack to retrieve it.

And so they pressed on with Rab again in the lead, heading now towards the unknown—that stretch of terrain that, ten years ago, he and his young companions had traversed completely blind. It seemed they were to be spared a repeat encounter with the awful sound-deadening mist, but, on and off, the light rain still doggedly pursued them. As it turned out, the dense mist they'd faltered through all those years ago hadn't hidden much from them. There wasn't much to see. Boulders. The evidence of past drifts. And, when the clouds cleared enough to permit it, a blurry glimpse of hills in the distance.

But the wind was blowing constantly at their backs and, ever so often, Rab caught a whiff of the sour river—and that was all the guide he needed. Without it, he could probably have managed—his ability, acquired after years tramping the surface, to determine direction would have seen him through, but the confidence the south-blowing wind provided made the going just that little bit easier—both on his companions and on Rab's mind. There'd be no time lost due to error.

As they neared the end of that long, dreary stretch of country the rain that had relentlessly pursued them began to ebb, and Fin's confidence seemed to return. He started to edge a little farther ahead of Rab and Cloud again each day and, by the time they had passed into remembered territory, had taken the lead again. As a consequence he was the first to reach the outer perimeter of the fallen forest. His call to Rab came as a welcome relief. If any useable wood remained, they could build a fire, dry their clothes and rest. Maybe see if there was something that could be done about Cloud's boots and the tear in Fin's pack.

Fin had negotiated the ruins of the forest once before, and knew to keep alert for rotten trunks. Cloud could easily shove her boot through one and twist an ankle. She didn't resist when Rab began to guide her. In fact he wasn't quite sure she was aware of his hold. Her attention wandered this way and that, taking in the toppled and twisted landscape.

"I can't believe it," she muttered to herself over and over again. "Why didn't either of you ever tell us this was here?"

"Thought about it," Rab said, taking a long step over a prone limb. "But it would have been an enormous task to transport it back. Besides," he kicked at another limb lying across his path, "most of it is too rotten to be much use. See?" He toed the stringy bits of loosened bark. "You can get a good fire out of it for a couple of people. Not much more."

"What's the matter with you?" Cloud said, sounding incredulous. "I could have used stuff like this to feed the 'shrooms."

"I suppose you could. . .*if* you could get it back to the tunnels."

Breaking free of Rab, Cloud dropped to her knees. With a gloved hand, she scooped up a palm-full of the crumbly bark. "There must be a way," she said, glancing up.

Rab reached down and dragged her upright. "Maybe. But you're not going back to the tunnels. Remember? Anyway, this isn't the place to stop, Cloud."

"Oh yes it is," Fin called out unexpectedly.

Rab dropped Cloud's arm and hurried up to Fin, anticipating. . .well, he didn't know quite what. Cloud quickly came up beside him.

"Not Top-siders," she said, kicking at the remnants of the recent fire Fin had stumbled across. "Too small."

Fin bent to his knees and prodded at the ashes with a burned stick. "Bounty hunters maybe?" He glanced up. "It's been out a while by the looks of it."

"Rain could have done that," Rab said. "No way of knowing now."

Fin tossed the stick aside and rose. "Well, someone's been here and not too long ago. Could be the Pigeon Brothers."

As usual Rab cringed at the mention of the name. "As far as I'm aware, they were still in the city when we left. They couldn't have come this far south. Never have before. It's got to be someone else but I've never known any other bounty hunters to travel this way, either. They've no reason to."

Cloud toed absently at the dead fire. "They did this time," she said. "Anyway. . ." she looked up at Rab, ". . . how sure are you that bounty hunters *never* go south? You keep saying that but. . ."

She ended with a shrug. It was the same old argument and Rab concluded that her feet must have hurt too badly for her to bother pursuing it.

"Should we stay here or move further on?" Fin asked.

When all was said and done, bounty hunters were actually more nomadic than Top-siders. If bounty hunters had made this fire, then they had travelled south for *some* reason and it was unlikely they'd be coming back this way anytime soon. And if they did? Well, most bounty hunters were of the opportunist breed and Rab and his two young companions had little of value except food. There was a kind of code top-side with regard to food; most adhered to it, some didn't. If Cloud were younger, Rab would have had more reservations about staying put, but she'd said it herself: a grown woman was too much trouble to deal with.

"We stay," he said at last. "Might as well take advantage of what they left behind."

Fin didn't protest but, instead, dropped his packs and set off through the remains of the ruined forest. Gathering enough useful tinder was going to be a more difficult task this time; the last of the fallen trees had almost entirely rotted out. There was a kind of stink to the place; not a bad stink really, just a pervasive one.

"My turn to cook," Cloud said, sloughing off her packs. "It's a pity we didn't bring one of Lilly's pans. We could have sacrificed a little water to make something hot. Lilly makes this mushroom paste that doesn't taste too bad." She dropped to her knees and began sifting the worst of the ash from the fire. "Better than eating this dry stuff all the time. But," she said with a shrug, "we didn't, so dry mushrooms it is."

"Don't be too critical of mushrooms, Cloud," Rab said, dropping his own packs to the ground. "They've saved us from rickets."

"Rickets?" Cloud asked, glancing up. "What's rickets?"

"Bone deformity from a lack of vitamin D."

"Oh thanks, that explains it. Now what is vitamin D?"

Rab flipped back the hood of his coat. "Don't know exactly. All I know is, without it, your bones don't grow right and our mushrooms have it."

"Really," Cloud said, rising. "And just how do you know that?"

"Simple. I read the part about rickets." He reached out and bared Cloud's perfectly formed arm. "And our bones have grown straight. See?" He rotated her arm. "Has to be the mushrooms. It's basically all we eat."

Cloud glanced down at her arm, rotated it twice again. "Hmm." She drew her sleeve down and looked back at Rab. "What you don't know, you make up, don't you? Rickets!" she scoffed and returned to her task sifting ashes. "I'll bet there's no such thing. I always wondered what you thought about when you're alone top-side."

"Well, it's not rickets," Rab replied.

"Stupid name," Cloud muttered, flinging ash down-wind.

Fin returned, arms laden with strips of wood.

"It's still kind of wet. These are the driest bits I could find," he said, dumping the load beside Cloud, who reached out and began to sort.

"I'll manage."

Rab left Cloud to build the fire and Fin to collect more wood. If there had been other visitors to the forest, he wanted to know about it, so started off on a slow circuit of their immediate surroundings. On the off-chance there were some grubs, he smashed a few of the fallen limbs as he walked. But just like last time, there wasn't a grub to be found or evidence that any other Top-sider or bounty hunter had passed this way, either. That one small camp fire was it, although maybe the rain had just washed all other signs away. Rab had become an expert at dancing around the truth, but he tried to never out and out lie about anything. When he told Cloud that there was no one alive in the south and that he'd never known a bounty hunter to travel in that direction, he'd thought he was telling the truth. But now it was obvious that someone had travelled south before them. . .or come north. Neither explanation made any sense.

"Food," Cloud called.

He returned to their camp to find that Cloud had a fire started and his rations neatly laid out waiting for him.

"Nice fire," he said, bending to retrieve his food.

"Thanks," Cloud replied absently. "I hope it's enough to dry us out." When she began to fuss with her boots, Rab set the remainder of his food aside to help her.

"Blisters?" he asked.

Cloud shook her head. "No." She upended one of her boots. "There's a hole in the bottom. See?"

Rab fell back on his haunches. "Well, how do you expect to keep walking on that?"

"Been doing it," Cloud replied. "But my socks get wet."

"Really?" Rab snapped.

"There's no need to get nasty." Cloud stripped off her socks and stretched them and her bare feet out towards the fire. "They're my boots, my socks and my feet."

"But they'll be our problem if any of them get worse," Fin said.

Fin was looking at her over the fire and Cloud's face when she glanced up to meet his eyes revealed just what she thought of his observation. Long before she ever said anything, Rab could always tell when Cloud was about to get angry. As soon as that little line appeared above the bridge of her nose, there'd be trouble.

"You, too?" She flung up her hand, wet sock and all, in Rab's direction. "I thought he was the only one allowed to criticise."

"I'm not criticising, Abby," Fin replied defensively. "Just pointing out a fact."

"Well pardon me. But doesn't one of us also have an unfortunate rip in one of their packs? Now who could that be?" Cloud asked, feigning uncertainty for a moment. "Oh, I remember. That would be you!"

Rab went back to eating, content to leave them to it. Fin was right, of course. And Fin was in charge of this little expedition. Let him sort it out. Cloud was right, too, but although Rab had looked around he'd seen nothing in the vicinity to immediately fix either problem. Both would have to wait. But, all in all, their disagreement was a positive thing. If they were fit enough to argue instead of complain about how cold they felt or how wet, then they were fit enough to go on. When they stopped arguing with him or each other, then it would be time to worry.

Once he'd eaten his meal, Rab set about arranging his bedding, what there was of it—one pack for his head—another to shield him on one side from the cold. Tonight he intended to revel in the luxury of the fire. He settled himself on the ground beside Cloud; she was still arguing with Fin but Rab easily shut it out. The rain had cleared once more and, for this planet, it was a comparatively clear night. He squinted his eyes and found again that one same old star overhead.

The hard edge of Cloud's voice weakened and frayed and the broken threads of her words started to drift like frail snow flurries inside his head. Farther and farther the wisps drifted, higher and higher, until there was nothing at all.

***

Rab woke with a start. Some sound had woken him. Fin or Cloud moving about, tending the fire? A glance through the flames confirmed that Fin was still where he'd settled down for the night, but he was up on his knees now, looking skyward. Rab reached out, seeking Cloud who should have been beside him; all he found was cold ground and her abandoned packs.

Anxious and sleep-addled were a poor mix and Rab stumbled over his own packs as he got to his feet.

"Where's—" he began but Fin cut him off with a raised hand.

"Shhh. Can you hear it?" Fin whispered, coming slowly to his feet.

Rab listened. He'd heard something earlier that had woken him. Must have. And Fin must have heard it, too. He couldn't hear anything now though and right at the moment he was more concerned about Cloud's whereabouts than some phantom sound. It wasn't quite dawn yet but it was closing in, so there was adequate light to see by, but Cloud shouldn't have been up and about already. Rab glanced around and finally spotted her not too far away, standing, back turned to them, out in the wreckage of the fallen forest. Like Fin, she was looking up. Then, just as he was about to call to her, Rab heard the noise again, the one that must have lurched him awake. That whooshing kind of sound.

As quietly as he could Rab stepped around the fire to stand by Fin.

"Where's it coming from?"

Fin shook his still raised head.

"Can't tell. Overhead?"

Impossible.

Rab looked again towards Cloud. She hadn't moved, probably wasn't even aware that he and Fin were also awake and listening.

"What the. . ." Fin shrieked, then dropped to the ground, grabbing Rab's arm as he went down.

Rab landed on his knees with barely enough time to throw up both arms to shield himself from the down draught when an unidentifiable black something whizzed past. It was heading southward, a trajectory that was taking it directly for Cloud. Out of the corner of his eye, Rab saw Cloud duck as whatever it was hurtled right over her head. The thing was going so fast, it was gone from sight, lost in the grey light of the emerging dawn, long before Rab could get back onto his feet.

He jumped over the fire and, with Fin close on his heels, heedlessly smashed and pummelled rotten branches into ruined pulp as he raced towards Cloud. She was still crouching low to the ground when they got there, but she must have been aware of their approach because slowly she turned her head and looked up. Her gaze fell first on Fin, rested there a while before it shifted unhurriedly towards Rab.

"Will one of you please tell me you saw that?" she said before calmly rising from the ground.

Fin was evidently as lost for words as Rab. For someone who'd just missed having their head taken off, Cloud seemed remarkably composed until suddenly she began to list, jolting Rab out of his stupor. He caught hold of her shoulders just in time.

"I'm fine," she said, "fine," then pointed southward. "You saw it, didn't you? *You both saw it?*"

Now came the shock Rab had expected. When Cloud started to tremble in his arms, Rab, with a twinge of shame, felt infinitely grateful for the distraction. Otherwise he might have started shaking as well. In all his time top-side, he had never seen anything even remotely similar to what the three of them had just seen. Never heard tell of anything similar, either. . .although most bounty hunters and Top-siders he'd come across were disposed to tell a disturbing tale or two. Some were real, most invented in the hope of scaring the pants off some gullible fool, none had ever claimed an encounter with something that came streaking out of the sky like that.

"Yes, we saw it, Cloud," Rab said, finding his voice. "Maybe you'd better sit down."

"I don't need to sit down," she shouted, shaking him off. "I need someone to tell me what that was."

Rab glanced at Fin, who, looking noticeably paler than usual, only shook his head in reply.

"It flew!" Cloud grabbed the front of Rab's coat. "Flew!" she repeated, tightly bunching up the cloth in both hands. "You *knew* those things were out here."

"I didn't," Rab pleaded. "I've never seen anything like that before. I swear I haven't, Cloud. I can't explain it any better than you or Fin can."

As gently as he could he began to work Cloud's hands free and, as he did, watched an odd change come to her face. It was almost as though she was coming to understand something. Before Rab knew what was happening, she was gone.

"You nearly got me killed," she screamed, bearing down on Fin. Curling her fist, she delivered one mighty punch to the shoulder that sent Fin reeling backwards. She raised her fist, about to deliver a second.

Rab had just enough time to pin her around the waist and forestall it. She struggled, kicked him once in the shin, but Rab held on.

"You lied to me, Fin. I thought you wanted to get out of the city just as much as I did. That you wanted to take Stitch's heart home. But it was all just lies." She squirmed in Rab's arms, twisted and tried to duck free. "You wanted to come back here for *them*."

"*Them*? That flying thing? Abby, I don't understand what you're talking about," Fin declared as he backed out of range of Cloud's feet. "If you think I knew anything about that thing, you're wrong." His glance darted to Rab. "He knows more about top-side than I do. I haven't been up here for years."

All those years of reweaving and hauling crops had certainly paid off; Cloud was as strong as they came. Rab was having one hell of a time stopping her from getting at Fin. "He's telling you the truth, Cloud. And so am I. If we knew there was life in the south, why wouldn't we tell you? And if for some peculiar reason we did want to keep it a secret, why drag you here where you could find out about it? Think about it, Cloud. It doesn't make any sense."

Her squirming was becoming less frenzied, but Rab wasn't prepared to release her just yet.

"Besides it barely missed us, too," Fin said.

"Really?" Cloud spat the word out as though it was some unpleasant tasting brew. "Let me go." She twisted her head around to plead with Rab. "I won't hit him anymore. I promise."

Slowly Rab began to relax his hold. True to her word, Cloud kept both arms down by her sides as she took a step towards Fin.

"Barely missed you, did it?" she said, then touched her gloved hand to the top of her head and, bringing it back down, held out the wet and red-stained fingers for him to see. "Pity I can't say the same."

Rab had Fin bring his smallest pack and he tended to Cloud's wound right there out in the fallen forest. The cut wasn't deep, but still deep enough to sting when he sacrificed a little of his water and a shred of cloth from the lining of his coat to clean it.

"Sulfur," Cloud said, grimacing.

"What?" Rab stopped his dabbing to look at her.

"Use the sulfur. There's plenty. Ruby gave us extra."

"Right." He returned to his task.

"Sorry," she muttered, eyes downcast.

"Don't apologise to me. Talk to Fin there."

"Forget it," Fin said before Cloud had a chance to say anything. "I'd probably have done the same thing."

Yeah, Rab thought, *he would have.*

"Ouch!" Cloud grimaced. "It gave me a fright. That thing coming out of nowhere like that. Worked out what it is yet?"

"Not really." Rab was almost finished with the cleaning.

"Bird," Fin said. After he'd brought Rab the pack, Fin had honed in on a solitary rotten trunk that was lying on the ground nearby and settled himself on it to wait. "Some birds must have survived. . .just like us."

Rab stopped working and glanced back at Fin.

"Never seen a picture of one that big," Rab said, then looked away to fish out the sulfur from his pack.

"But," he began dabbing Cloud's wound with powder, "I can't imagine what else it could be."

"Then it's a bird," Fin said in a tone that clearly marked the end of discussion for him. "You're almost finished. I'll start packing."

As Rab was returning the container of sulfur to his pack, he accidently caught Cloud's eye.

"Well?" she prompted.

"Guess it was a bird."

"And you've never seen one before?"

"Never," Rab said with a shake of his head.

Cloud sighed. "Why is it," she said as she started out after Fin, "that I always end up not quite believing you?"

Rab just smiled and trailed her back to their camp site. She seemed over the shock of the strange encounter and her wound wasn't especially worrisome, although Rab intended to keep a close eye on it for the next few days. Even though Cloud's injury was minor, Sunny's experience weighed heavily on his mind.

"All right, my young friends," he said, dumping his pack by the fire. "You might as well put that down, Fin."

Fin was caught with his second pack half on, half off his back. He let it slip to the ground.

"We need to agree on what just happened and we're going to sit right here until we do." Rab reached down, collected the few remaining strips of tinder and tossed them into the fire. A halo of bright, little embers danced for him in the morning air.

"I thought we all agreed already," Fin said.

"Hey, I never said it was a *bird*." Cloud lowered herself to the ground in front of the fire and began stirring it with the end of a salvaged stick.

"Then what was it?" Fin pressed her.

Cloud shrugged. "Could be one of Rab's spaceships for all I know."

"A *lit-tle* small, Cloud," Rab countered, smiling weakly.

"I can't see what difference it makes to us right now anyway." She broke the charred stick in two and tossed both pieces into the fire. "It went south. We're going south. Maybe we'll come across it again."

"My point exactly," Rab said and dropped to his haunches beside her. "If there's one of them, there's probably two. Or more."

"So?" Cloud turned to question him.

"How do we know that hitting you like that was just an accident?"

"No," she said after a moment's hesitation. "It had to be." She glanced towards Fin. "Didn't it?"

Fin raised his arms, beaten.

"Well, I say it was an accident. . ." she glanced at Fin again, under her lashes this time, ". . . now that I've had time to think about it. Besides it wasn't *that* big."

"Big enough it could have killed you," Rab reminded her.

"But we know to watch out for them now," she insisted.

"They come out of nowhere, Cloud. Besides if it's out there, maybe something else is out there, too."

Fin began to laugh. "Now that's a turn around," he said. "What happened to 'there's nothing alive in the south'?"

"Well, I guess I was wrong," Rab snapped, glancing darkly in Fin's direction.

"Yeah, I guess you were." Fin bent to gather his discarded packs. "Are you coming, Abby?"

Cloud jumped to her feet.

"No, I'm not. Not this minute anyway. I'm confused. My head hurts." She leaned down and retrieved one of her own packs. "And I'm hungry."

She was also not quite as fine as she claimed. Though it was barely noticeable, her hands were trembling slightly as she rummaged around inside her pack.

"Accident or not, I was the one who nearly had their head knocked off," she said, reseating herself beside Rab, slab of 'shroom loaf in her hand, "so I think it's my right to propose a compromise. First we eat." She held the loaf aloft, pointing it towards Fin, then turned to Rab again. "Then we go south just like we planned. At least until we get to your village. If we don't come across anymore of those things. Or *anything else*," she hastened to add when Rab made to interrupt, "then we continue going south."

Fin, evidently left without an immediate argument, stayed mute.

Seemed it was up to Rab to ask the obvious question.

"And what if we do come across one of those things again, Cloud? Or something else?"

"That would depend," she said between bites of 'shroom loaf.

"On?" Rab prompted.

"What it is."

Chapter 6

AS HE walked along between Cloud and Fin, Rab glanced repeatedly from the rocky ground at his feet to the grey sky above his head. The weather was holding and that was probably the only positive thing he could say about the day so far. The dirty grey clouds roiled. They wisped. They drew up and collapsed down again. It was a fairly typical day on the planet. Comparatively warm again, but still cold enough to numb anyone caught top-side unprepared. They'd make it through another day. No question. Unless conditions changed or something else Rab hadn't anticipated suddenly materialised. . .like more of those flying things or whoever it was that had made camp before them in the fallen forest. The flying thing had gone somewhere. Whoever had made camp before them in the fallen forest had gone somewhere. Was it the *same* somewhere? One was possibly tracking the other—but just which was tracking which? And what was that thing?

It wasn't a bird, as Fin thought. Rab had already decided that. Yes it was possible, perhaps even likely, that the refugees from Earth had carried birds on their ships to this planet, but there was no bird on Earth quite *that* big. None that Rab was aware of anyway and he'd looked at an awful lot of pictures in old John Braham's books. He could still be wrong, hoped he was, but he really didn't think so. There was still other life on this planet—life that didn't owe its presence to some failed mission from Earth. Not even Sunny had given much thought to that.

"It's long gone," Fin said, startling Rab.

While he had been watching the skies, Fin must have been watching him.

"Doesn't mean it won't come back."

"To make a meal out of Abby?"

"Yeah, well," Cloud snapped, "maybe I don't think you knew anything about it anymore, Fin, but that doesn't mean I think that's funny."

"Wasn't meant to be," Fin replied, then, without further word, struck out ahead.

Cloud made to hurry after him, but Rab called her back.

"Let him go, Cloud. You're lucky that's your only payback. I'd have flattened you."

"No, you wouldn't," Cloud said with a little smile. "You'd have ducked and I'd have landed flat on my face."

"Works just as well. Do you children always squabble this much when I'm gone?"

"*Children?*"

Rab shook his head. "You should have seen yourself."

"When a big bird tries to take *your* head off, we'll see how well you behave."

"That bird isn't our only mystery. Something *is* different top-side, Cloud. Just small things really. Like that star we see now and then. And how long it's been taking snow time to come these last few years. And how much shorter snow time lasts." He looked briefly skyward. "And the clouds. Sometimes they seem higher and show those narrow openings. Then the next day, they look as low and as dense as they always have."

Immediately Rab regretted having said anything at all to Cloud. If Sunny had ever had some knowledge about what to expect from this planet, she hadn't had time to share any of it with him and, had the business with the 'bird' not rattled him, Rab would have had enough wits about him not to mention the things he'd been noticing for some time now.

"Maybe you've just been top-side too long, Rab," Cloud suggested.

"Well, maybe so. Maybe I'm just imagining things," he said, hoping to put her off. "Maybe everything is the same as it always was."

"No, that can't be right, either," Cloud said with a shake of her head. "You're right about the star and the clouds. And those bird things. Where have they been all this time? And why are we only seeing them now? Maybe it really is better in the south. And that's got to be a good thing, doesn't it? I mean, despite the birds. . ."

"I don't know, Cloud."

It was true. Rab really didn't know if it was a good thing, just like he didn't know where those 'birds' had come from. Or why they had suddenly appeared. But he was beginning to suspect he knew where they *had* been a very long time ago. Sunny, Gift and he had sheltered in one of their houses once. Roosts, Sunny had called them. But the damn things hadn't built those houses themselves! And if at some point in that long ago they had survived and moved south. . .

"When are we stopping?" Fin called, interrupting Rab's thoughts.

Rab tallied up the days in his head. Barring any more unforeseen incidents, tomorrow night, they should arrive at their village. He could push them faster, farther. After all, this time he didn't have two small children to consider. Cloud wasn't badly injured, hadn't even complained much about her head—or her boots. She was walking fine now, although Rab couldn't imagine how that was possible.

"How are your boots?" he asked.

"What?"

"The hole in the bottom?"

"Oh, I fixed that with some strips off that wood back there. Works fine." She raised first one boot then the other to show him. "Put a strip inside each boot so I'm not lopsided. They were too big for me anyway. Fit just fine now."

Well, if that didn't. . .Rab couldn't help but smile.

"Keep going, Fin," he called ahead, still smiling.

***

Cloud wasn't boasting about her resourcefulness or the fine fit of her boots any longer. Last night, the weather had turned on them. They passed through the long, cold darkness huddled together for warmth and security. Rab had faced trials on the surface before, but he'd usually been able to anticipate when the weather was about to shift. Somehow he could tell from a particular way the clouds hung in the sky, a sharper than usual tang in the air, a subtle difference in sound as he tramped the ground. Those warnings allowed him to prepare. Most times he'd find a ledge or a depression of some sort; anything that provided him shelter. Sometimes, if the ground were soft enough, he'd dig himself in. But this shift had caught him by surprise without the luxury of a ledge or a depression in which to shelter and ground so hard and unforgiving, there was no opportunity to dig themselves in. If he'd been travelling with tunnel-dwellers completely devoid of any experience top-side, Rab suspected his company would number at least one less by now.

Cloud's feet were his biggest concern. She'd begun to hobble on those patched boots of hers. He'd never heard of anyone patching boots with tree bark before—for all he knew, it *could* have worked. She'd make it to his old village; he felt certain of that. But she could not go any farther.

Rab wouldn't allow it. In the short term, it didn't make a lot of difference. Rab had always known that the village was the end of their road. But, when snow time passed, how was he going to get her home?

Rab had taken to walking alongside Cloud full-time, uncomfortable with lagging behind or edging any distance ahead of her. As it turned out, Fin possessed a pretty good sense of direction after all; some inherent Top-sider gift perhaps. Rab didn't question it; he was just grateful that Fin's ability allowed him to dedicate most of his attention to Cloud. She'd have been incensed had she been aware that he was keenly watching her every step. Why hadn't he thought to check her boots before they'd left the tunnels? Not that there was much he could have done about it. A good and sturdy pair of boots were a luxury, even inside the tunnel city.

By evening they should reach the village and despite the cold it would bring, Rab kept wishing for the evening to hurry along. They'd come upon the old 'shroom field just shy of the village itself and, if they were very lucky, find the hardiest stands of the crop still alive. All they'd have was those 'shrooms and maybe some residue of the stores in the old warehouse to see them through snow time. If neither were still edible, he wouldn't have to worry one shred about the condition of Cloud's boots or how he was going to get her home. He had no doubts whatsoever that they would find no one left in the village, but he did have serious misgivings about where, and in what condition they would find their remains. If Fin had given any thought at all to such a grisly prospect, he hadn't voiced his concerns. When they'd left, both of Fin's parents had been alive. He'd better hope they'd been among the first to die, been fortunate enough to have been given a decent burial. One thing was certain: there would be someone's remains left to find. Rab would bury the bones; he'd already decided that. And maybe, just maybe, there'd be something to tell him which of his old friends he was burying.

He reached out and took Cloud's hand.

She glanced at him briefly from under the hood of her coat but said nothing. Fin had crept farther and farther ahead of them and, in the gloom, Rab couldn't see him any longer. He'd have called out but there didn't really seem a lot of point. They'd come on him soon enough.

This *was* the end of the road.

"Where's the river?" Cloud asked, breaking the long silence.

Rab pointed over her head. "That way."

"I can't smell it. I thought you said we could smell it."

"Depends on the wind," he told her. "There were times when the mist came in and shrouded the village completely. Couldn't see. Couldn't breathe. Couldn't even hear properly when it did."

"Seems a bit stupid to have stayed here then, doesn't it?"

Rab shrugged. "Where would we have gone? Most of the time, it wasn't too bad. Besides, there was a good 'shroom field nearby. Water. I don't know. Maybe we just stayed out of habit."

Cloud turned to look at him. "Except for you."

"Except for me," Rab agreed.

Something was moving towards them out of the gloom. Looked like Fin but Rab wasn't entirely sure until he heard the young man call.

"Some of the field is still alive. It's just up ahead. I've been there. I've seen it. Hurry up."

Rab was close enough by then to make out Fin's raised arm, waving them on.

"The mushroom field?" Cloud asked.

"Must be."

"Then we'll have food to go on."

"Maybe."

"What do you mean 'maybe'? You know, Rab, it never ceases to amaze me that you left your village in the first place. You're the biggest pessimist I've ever met. If you had faith then that there was a launch pad out here somewhere and faith enough that someday you'd find it, why can't you show some faith now?"

Rab wished she wouldn't bandy the word 'faith' around like that. It was a word he'd intentionally put away from him many years ago. Faith was Sunny's real name, something he'd discovered shortly before her death. Whether the irony of her name had ever registered with Sunny Rab was never to know. It hadn't escaped him though.

"Come on," Cloud said eagerly and began to drag Rab forwards. "Let's see what Fin has found."

As it turned out, Fin had indeed found the field with much of its crop still thriving. The thought struck Rab immediately that someone must be tending it. A closer inspection revealed it wasn't so. The crop had gone wild. Another little irony. For as long as he could remember, the people in his village had fretted and slaved over the 'shroom field, battled insipid disease, hard snow times, drought that promised no end, and just plain bad luck. But though diminished in size, now the crop itself was the healthiest Rab had ever seen it. The 'shrooms were of the larger variety, bigger than those that grew naturally in the tunnel city and much bigger than those Cloud had started to cultivate when disease had threatened the entire underground crop.

It was obvious she was anxious to join Fin in the field and the moment Rab released her hand, she darted off. As she hurried up and down between the row upon row of 'shrooms, bending every so often to inspect a stalk or a particularly large cap, she laughed. Fin was studying the field a little more assiduously. He'd be estimating the yield. Rab wasn't going to interfere. The crop looked fine; from where he was standing, he could see enough of the stalks and caps to feel certain that the 'shrooms were unlikely to be diseased. At least superficially; how much toxin had seeped underground from the river over the years was something he simply couldn't evaluate. If the 'shrooms were healthy, they'd survive. If eventually some ground-absorbed toxin gradually poisoned their systems, so be it. Either way, they were stuck with eating the 'shrooms. Very soon, it would be all they had.

"There's plenty of food here," Cloud called to Rab over the tops of the sturdy caps. "A mountain of it!"

Hardly! But Rab wasn't about to ruin Cloud's moment. At least she'd forgotten all about her feet and pestering him about every little thing.

"Come look!"

Rab waved her on. "I can see it from here."

It was good to have a little time to himself. He'd grown accustomed to his own company over the years but had never realised before just how much he actually craved it.

The time was over too soon.

"Told you it would be all right," Fin said, making his way out of the field towards Rab. "Maybe there is someone alive here after all. I mean. . ." he glanced around, ". . . if this has survived—"

"I wouldn't count on it, Fin," Rab said, interrupting him. "It's a fluke. That's all. A good year."

With a little jump, Fin resettled his sliding packs. "We'll see," he said and started off towards their village and home.

They *would* see. Rab could be wrong, but he doubted it. And if he wasn't, was Fin truly ready to accept what they saw?

"Where's Fin?" Cloud called.

She was weaving a watchful path through the rows of 'shrooms, heading back to Rab.

"He's gone on ahead. Come on, Cloud. It's going to be dark soon. I'd like us to have found some shelter before then."

"Just how *small* is your village, Rab? There's got to be something left. Even if everyone is. . .even if it's empty."

"There'll be something," Rab replied, urging her forwards with a hand to her back, "but it's not much use sheltering in something if it hasn't got a roof. We might as well be out in the open still."

Cloud shrugged and stepped out in front of him.

They would come to the cemetery soon, a place Fin was very likely to stop. Rab was a little anxious to get there now himself. The 'shroom field hadn't divulged much about the fate of his people, but the cemetery might. He hurried Cloud along. It was best to be with Fin when he got there. Best they, the last people of this village, be together when they found out.

He caught up with Fin just before the cemetery. Fin had turned very quiet and Rab had more or less anticipated that he would. This was the place where he intended to lay Stitch's heart to rest. This was the place where, if they had been among the first to die, his parents had already been laid to rest.

Fin stopped at the bottom of the little hill that led up to the cemetery ground.

"Together," he said, turning to Rab.

"Together."

Rab glanced back, looking for Cloud. She was making slow progress towards them. "You stay here," he called and waited until he saw her nod.

Side by side, Rab and Fin began to climb the rise. Rab didn't know what to expect. He knew less about what Fin expected. There would be no markers; their people did not read or write. But there was a chance they might spot a disturbance here and there on the ground. And if they did, it wouldn't tell them who was buried there. Maybe not even how many.

Rab remembered perfectly where the graves that mattered most to him were located. His parents lay together near the top of the hill, his brother, Bird, lay beside them. The unrequited love of his naive youth, Shy, the wife of another, was buried closer to the bottom of the hill. They'd pass her grave first and he wouldn't stop. What point? They hadn't come to grieve the long-lost. Instead, they'd brought a new fresh grief to bury among the others. In time, Stitch would become just like them. . .a name, a memory, someone with whom a brief moment in time was shared until those who shared it, too, were gone.

"It all looks the same," Fin said. "Just as I remember it."

And so it did to Rab, too. There was nothing here to find. If any of their people had been buried here during the time they had been away, there was nothing left now to show it. And maybe, Rab wondered, maybe that's just how it should be.

They walked the cemetery nonetheless, past graves they knew absolutely were there beneath their feet and past graves they could easily imagine. But real or imagined, all were merely spectres now.

"Come on, Fin," Rab said at last, stopping at the crest of the hill. "We'll learn nothing here."

"I thought. . ." Fin began as he came up to stand beside Rab. "I thought. . ."

Rab put his arm lightly over the top of Fin's pack, around the young man's shoulder.

"Abby's waiting," he said in an attempt to urge Fin down the hill.

He didn't know why he'd called Cloud, Abby; it just seemed the right thing to do.

Cloud was usually an astute judge of a person's mood and Rab was relieved to discover her running true to form when they reached the base of the hill. She said nothing to Fin, but fell into step behind them as they set off together on the last part of their journey to the village.

One of the first spaces they would come across would be Jep's. Rab held out no hope at all of finding his old childhood friend still alive. The baby, Shy's baby, would be dead, too; she'd have died long, long before her father. Rab should have been there to comfort him. He should have been there to comfort them all.

Unlike him, Jep had been a dedicated caretaker and the condition of his home would tell Rab much about what to expect when they entered the village proper. When they came upon the ruin Rab wasn't surprised, only saddened, by what he saw. The walls that Jep was forever patching had finally tumbled, leaving scattered piles of crumbled mortar upon the ground. The roof was leaning askew off the structure. There were large ragged holes in what was left of the roofing iron, testifying to years of corrosion and rot.

"I'm sorry, Fin," Cloud whispered so faintly Rab could barely hear her. "I think it's going to be like Rab said."

Out of the corner of his eye, Rab saw Fin's answering shrug.

"I know," the young man said. "But I had to find out for myself."

Briefly it crossed Rab's mind to look inside Jep's ruined space but he quickly decided against it. Later. He'd find out later if Jep's bones numbered among those he'd be obliged to bury.

They continued on and with Fin again in the lead, Cloud stepped up to walk by Rab.

"Do you think he'll be all right?" Cloud asked in that same muted voice Rab had to struggle to hear.

"What other choice does he have, Cloud?"

One after another, they came on more empty and deserted spaces and, as they passed, Rab put a name to each ruin. He remembered them all although he wished he hadn't. Better that the years had stripped their names and their faces from his memory. Gone. All gone now. Probably long ago. Stitch, as Fin wanted, was truly coming home.

"Are *you* all right?"

Rab was surprised to hear Cloud ask it.

"Yes."

A one word answer was all he had to offer. But it was the truth. He was all right and he'd continue to be all right. Fin might have hoped and wished for something different, but the narrow lanes littered with the waste of what had once been their homes had come as no surprise to Rab. What did come as a surprise was the absence of any obvious human remains. It wasn't possible for every last one of his fellow villagers to have been buried. Just because the ground in the cemetery wasn't prepared to give up its secrets didn't mean it didn't have some. But at least one unlucky soul had to be the last left alive. And the bones of that last unlucky soul had to be lying somewhere, waiting to be found. He hadn't anticipated how powerful the silence would be, either. Rab was accustomed to silence, lived with it day in, day out as he walked the top-side looking for Gift. But here was a different kind of silence. . .like echoes deprived of voice.

Rab tried not to think about those quiet echoes as he followed behind Fin, peering through broken doorways, seeking the best of the ruins. They needed to find one with walls that wouldn't topple over on them during the night, a roof that offered some sort of shelter, a floor with the least amount of debris. When they found it he hadn't expected it would be his own space, the one place in their village that, as long as it had been in his care, had never benefited from a moment's worth of repair.

Rab stopped outside his old space. He could sense Cloud looking up at him, anxious for an explanation, but was momentarily lost for words.

Whoever had lived in his space after his departure had patched its crumbling doorway and tended to the many yawning holes in its roof. Whoever it was must have been among the last to die. Whoever it was must have been a master at his craft. Rab simply couldn't imagine who it could possibly have been.

"It's your space, isn't it?"

Rab turned to find Fin standing behind him. He'd thought Fin was still walking on but the young man must turned back to find them.

"Yes it is. But something isn't right here, Fin."

"What's not right?" Cloud said. "It looks fine." She made to step through the doorway but Rab pulled her back.

"This is my space, Cloud, and it should be lying in a flattened heap by now. It's been repaired."

"So? Someone fixed it after you left."

"Take a *good* look, Cloud. And then compare it with the rest of the spaces in the village."

Cloud took her time, looking around.

"I see what you mean," she said at last. "Someone's living here."

Rab shook his head. "No, I don't think so. I can't smell fire. But someone *did* live here. And maybe not all *that* long ago."

"Bounty hunters," Fin suggested.

"Here? Why here?"

Fin shrugged. "I wouldn't know. But they've been in the forest, haven't they? Why *not* here?"

"We don't know for sure it was bounty hunters who made that fire in the forest, Fin."

"Does it matter *who* made it? They're not here now. If they were, we would have seen some evidence of them. And you said yourself you can't smell the remains of any fire."

Fin stepped around Rab. "There's only one way to find out," he said. "Abby can stay out here while we go in together."

"I'm not staying out here," Cloud snapped and, before Rab could prevent her, pushed past Fin and slipped through the open doorway, muttering. "Frightened of your own shadows."

Rab hurried in after Cloud and Fin followed close behind.

It took a moment for his eyes to adjust and when they did, Rab found Cloud standing by the remains of a generous but dead fire in an otherwise empty room; he'd already sensed as much with his blindsight.

"No one here but me," she said, flinging out both arms. "All right, there *was* someone here." She pointed to the long cold fire. "But they're gone. And they won't be coming back."

"Thanks for your insight, Cloud. Now would you mind telling us how you arrived at that conclusion?" Rab asked.

"If they were coming back, Rab, don't you think they'd have left *something* behind." She kicked out her boot and sent a little puff of ash into the air. "Everything but this is gone. Anyway," she added as she began to wriggle out of her packs. "They should be more worried about us than we should be worried about them. We're following *them* after all."

It was a fair observation.

"I'm staying right here," Cloud declared. "I'm going to eat something and then get some sleep. You two can do what you like." She folded herself into a neat little package on the bare floor and set about undoing her packs.

"If we're staying here, we need a fire," Fin said behind Rab. "I want to look around some more anyway. I'll bring back whatever I find."

With that, Fin ducked back through the doorway, leaving Rab alone with Cloud.

She glanced up from her fussing the moment Fin was gone. "Well?"

"Well what?" Rab asked, shrugging his own packs to the floor.

"Admit I'm right."

Rab declined to answer because Cloud could just as easily be wrong. Anyone travelling the top-side usually travelled light; she should know that as well as he did.

"I'll take that as an admission," Cloud said and turned back to her packs.

She had her food out long before Rab concluded he should be doing the same. They were stuck there for the night and at least it was familiar territory to him. But the last place he ever thought he'd be resting his head again was in his old space back at their village. He set about making himself a meal.

"What do you think he's going to find out there?" Cloud asked between mouthfuls.

"Something to burn I hope," Rab replied as, food in hand, he seated himself on the ground by Cloud.

"That isn't what I mean."

"I know what you mean," Rab replied without raising his head.

When he looked at the food in his hand, he sighed. Years and years eating the same old thing. Years and years *doing* the same old thing. Sometimes he truly did wish for the end.

Cloud stopped chewing for a moment. "Should one of us have gone with him?"

Rab shrugged and began to eat. "Fin's not a child anymore. He knows what to expect now."

"I don't think there's anything to find," Cloud observed. "Oh, don't give me that look. You're thinking the same thing I am. This seems more like a place that was abandoned than a place where everybody died."

"We haven't been everywhere yet," Rab reminded her.

"Could they have moved on?"

"Where?"

"Yeah. Where?" Cloud answered thoughtfully. "Could be they joined up with some roaming Top-siders."

Rab shook his head. "Top-siders never came this way."

Cloud slapped the ground with her free hand, snatching Rab's attention. "There you go again. *We're* coming this way." She kicked out with the toe of her boot and disturbed the dead fire once more. "Whoever built this fire came this way."

"All right, Cloud." Rab reached out and gently touched her knee. "Top-siders never came this way *before*."

"Thank you. You know, if I were you I'd be hoping that my people did join up with some Top-siders. They're not all bad."

Rab tried but failed to repress another sigh. "Haven't we been down that road already?"

Cloud had finished eating. She got to her knees and set about resorting her pack.

"Yes, we have. Of course, we have. And we'll keep going down it until I get you to admit that some Top-siders *are* better than others." The pack retied, she began punching at it with a fist. "You're not far removed from one yourself, Rab, but you're probably the only person who hates Top-siders worse than my father does."

Rab's head snapped up and Cloud's fist was left hanging in midair for a long time before she finally brought it slowly down.

"I beg your pardon," Rab said at last. "Your *what?*"

Cloud began to tidy her mass of unruly hair. She seemed to be intentionally avoiding Rab's eyes.

"Shouldn't have said that, should I?" she muttered.

"Maybe you should have said it a long time ago, Cloud. Care to explain?"

"Oh, it doesn't matter now, because whatever you say, I am not going back." She fell back on her haunches and turned to look directly at Rab. "Ever wondered why the Top-siders called me Cloud?"

"No. Why would I? Villagers. Top-siders. They both use those kinds of names."

"Yeah. They do, don't they?" Cloud replied. The corners of her mouth had turned up into a little smile.

"Just something else Top-siders and villagers have in common?" Rab prompted.

"I hadn't thought much about that, but yes, it is. Although that isn't what I was getting at." She edged closer to Rab on her knees. "They called me Cloud because they wouldn't use my real name. It was a tunnel-dweller name and I wasn't going to be a tunnel-dweller any longer. That's just something they do to all the captives."

Yes, that was true. Rab knew that. It was just what they had done to Faith Braham.

"My name was Claudia."

"Pretty," Rab observed half-heartedly. He was struggling to get that unwanted image of bright-haired Sunny out of his head. "But I think I like Cloud better."

Cloud tapped his leg, gathering his complete attention.

"Then how do you feel about Claudia Caine?" she asked.

Rab felt his face drain of colour. "Benjamin Caine is your father? Chief Magistrate Benjamin Caine? Your father?"

"He was only Cropper Caine when I was born. But that's him. I knew it the first moment I saw him."

"Cloud, are you sure?"

"Sure I'm sure," Cloud said, raising an unsteady hand to work on her wayward hair again. "You knew Lilly Benson wasn't my mother. You've always known it. Just like I've always known Benjamin Caine is my father."

Rab shook his head; this new and extraordinary piece of information didn't want to slot into place. "Then why didn't you say anything? You let

Caine live all those years, desperate to have his daughter back, while there you were, only a reach away all along."

"Simple. I didn't like him. I liked Lilly."

Rab raised an eyebrow. During their first meeting, Cloud had gifted Lilly Benson with one of the blackest eyes he'd ever seen.

"Well, I got to like Lilly then," Cloud conceded with another of those small brief smiles. "Besides, she needed me. He didn't. Not really."

"Cloud, that isn't true. He *did* need you."

"No," Cloud insisted with a vehement shake of her head. "He needed Claudia. And I wasn't Claudia anymore."

Rab jumped, partly in response to the things Cloud had just said but mostly on account of the crash coming from the direction of the doorway. He looked up and found Fin standing over a pile of tinder he'd just dumped on the floor.

"There's more," Fin said hesitantly. Rab's little start seemed to have him puzzled. "But this was all I could carry."

Rab certainly hoped there was more. What Fin had brought could get them through the night. No more. Whether his two companions were ready to accept the inevitable yet or not, they'd have to wait out snow time here and to survive it, they had to have fire.

"Did you see anything?" Rab asked, loathe to have an answer just the same.

Fin shook his head. "Nothing," he said, stooping to collect some of the tinder before bringing it to the dead fire. "It's like they all just got up and left."

Rab glanced at Cloud as he rose with the intention of helping Fin.

"Told you," she mouthed.

He frowned at her and she said no more.

"Tomorrow," Rab said. "We'll take a good look around tomorrow." He bent to gather more of Fin's tinder. "Cloud and I have already eaten. I'll do this. You get something to eat."

"I'll make the fire," Cloud said, jumping up. "You always make a mess of it."

Rab spun around, arms laden with tinder. "Really?" He opened his arms and let the tinder fall nosily back onto the untidy pile. "Then I guess you'd better carry it all, too."

***

Rab thought he might sleep more peacefully in his old space but it wasn't to be. When he wasn't watching the fire, he found his attention drifting through its dancing flames towards the open doorway. Fin and Cloud slept soundly; he heard their soft and shallow breathing beside him in the darkness throughout the night. He must have drifted off to sleep sometime before dawn though because he woke with a fright and just in time to spot Fin disappearing through the doorway. Fin hadn't made enough of a noise to stir Cloud; she was still asleep beside Rab.

Tendrils of wan light were seeping through the open doorway, tugging and towing him farther and farther into the daylight world. He didn't want to go. Today would be a bad day. Today they'd attempt to find out what had happened to their fellow villagers and today they'd bury Stitch's heart. Perhaps that was what Fin had gone to do but Rab doubted it. Cloud might be offered the opportunity to go with him. Rab suspected he wouldn't be receiving an invitation.

"Where's Fin?" Cloud's sluggish voice.

Rab turned to find her up on one elbow, glancing past him towards the doorway.

"Out," he said simply and rose reluctantly to his feet.

Cloud yawned. "Should we follow him?" she asked sleepily.

"Later. We'll eat something first."

As he set to sharing out a meagre meal for the three of them, Cloud scrambled to her feet and made her way to the doorway.

"Can't see him," she said to Rab.

Rab glanced up to find Cloud looking back at him. Even in the mean light from the spluttering fire, he couldn't miss the worried expression that had suddenly descended on her face.

Slowly Rab got to his feet. "What?"

"Listen," Cloud said softly, motioning for him to join her at the doorway. "Can you hear it?"

Rab listened but heard nothing unusual.

"It's that whooshing sound again," Cloud said after a moment.

Rab did hear it then.

"It's another of those bird things," she whispered.

Rab scanned the deserted village, looking for Fin but he was nowhere in sight. Perhaps he'd heard it, too, and taken shelter. He turned his attention skyward.

"Can you see it?" he asked of Cloud.

She shook her head. "Nothing. It seems to be getting further away."

"Don't tell me," Rab said, glancing down into her face. "It's moving southward."

"Fine," she replied and turned back into his space, leaving Rab alone in the doorway. "I won't."

"Did you see it?" Fin called, appearing on the opposite side of the lane. He was some spaces down, outside Blaze's old space.

"It went that way," he called again, making his way back towards Rab with his arm raised, pointing south.

"Heard it," Rab called back.

"Was it the same one, do you think?" Fin asked in less of a shout, drawing closer.

If there was one of them, then there were probably more. How could they possibly tell one of those things from another?

"Don't know," Rab said, latching a hold of Fin's arm to drag him back inside the relative safety of his space.

"They only seem to appear at first light," Fin said excitedly.

"Well, they're somewhere the rest of the time. And I personally don't want to find out where."

"They're flying," Cloud said. She had rekindled the fire and was sitting cross-legged in front of it, helping herself to the rations Rab had portioned out. She pointed to the roof of Rab's space. "They're up there. I think they're sleeping somewhere at night and then when dawn comes, they wake up and take off south again."

"Or the other way around," Rab suggested, following Fin towards the fire and Cloud.

"Huh?" Cloud mumbled.

"They move around at night and fly back to wherever they came from at dawn."

"Yes." Cloud glanced briefly at Fin. "I suppose they could," she said, then looked back at Rab. "But then why don't we hear them at night?"

Rab had no answer. He bent down and picked up his food.

"We'll find out when we go further south," Fin said, folding himself onto the ground beside Cloud.

Rab held his tongue. It wasn't the time.

"Eat," he said, pointing to the last of the food. "Then we'll look around. How far did you get just now, Fin?"

Fin reached forwards to collect his food. "Not far. The space next to us is completely empty. So is the one opposite."

"There's *nothing* at all?"

Fin shook his head. "Nothing. Not a thing on the floor or anywhere. Except—"

"Well, whoever was here, they took everything," Cloud declared, interrupting him, then pointed at Rab. "No matter what he says."

Clearly someone did, so Rab didn't argue. But neither Top-siders nor bounty hunters had much use for the bones of the dead. What had happened to them?

"Bring that with you, Fin. Let's go find some answers."

"What if that bird comes back?" Cloud asked, getting to her feet.

"Didn't we just agree that they only appear at dawn?" Rab replied.

Cloud glanced at Fin, who was in the process of rising.

"Seems so," he said with a shrug. "Besides, we can't just sit in here the rest of our lives."

"You've got the best ears, Cloud," Rab said, heading for the doorway. "Just keep listening."

"Oh, I'll do that all right," she replied, stepping around Fin to follow Rab.

The first thing Rab noticed was the temperature. It was just a touch colder than yesterday, not enough to concern him though. Looking skyward, he saw the same old familiar grey and nothing more. Not a single sign of Cloud's 'bird'.

"Just checking," Rab said when he noticed the direction of Cloud's stare. Her dark brown eyes had him pinned.

"Hmm," she crooned, glancing away before she struck out in front of him.

"I think we should split up," Fin suggested, emerging behind Rab. "I was going to tell you before that I've seen some tracks. Like cart tracks or something."

"Not bounty hunters then," Rab observed. "How old do you think they are?"

"No, not bounty hunters," Fin agreed. "But I can't tell how old they are and they're kind of scattered on account of all the rocks. If you want to search this side of the village", he said, then glanced towards Cloud.

"I'll go with Rab," Cloud announced and popped her head through the ruined doorway of the neighbouring space.

"Fin's already looked there," Rab called as Fin headed off alone, making for the other side of the village.

Her head reappeared. "Doesn't hurt to have another look. But he's right. There isn't a single thing anywhere."

Rab urged her ahead of him to the next space, keeping his eye alert for those tracks Fin had seen.

"Me first," he said and, pushing past her, ducked through the doorway. He could hear Cloud close on his heels.

Inside he discovered only more of what Fin had described. The floor almost looked as though it had been swept clean. In the next space they found pieces of a broken table; in the next, some scraps of frayed cloth lying in a pile in the far corner. The table they could burn and maybe Cloud could find a use for that cloth—but as finds went, it was pretty paltry.

"This can't be all there was. Where can it all have gone?" Cloud asked, scrambling after Rab over the ruin of the next doorway to gain entry. "I mean it's not *possible* for everything to have been taken away."

"Not quite everything is gone," Rab reminded her, "or Fin wouldn't have been able to find that tinder last night. And we found a broken table, that cloth." He'd just banged his knee on a jagged brick sticking out from the edge of the doorway. Rubbing at it, he stepped inside.

This space wasn't as thoroughly stripped as the others, although it was obvious it had been picked through. There was a mound of debris that looked as though it had been intentionally collected and left in the middle of the floor.

"I'm beginning to think you're right." He turned to Cloud in the close darkness. "Top-siders must have been here. All that's left is rubbish."

Cloud sighed. "Then I guess finding me another pair of boots is out of the question."

"I can fix the ones you've got, Cloud. Just have to find something."

Her shrug was barely noticeable in the gloom. "What? They've taken everything that's of any real use." She wandered into the room, bent to her knees and began to sift through the mound of debris. "More strips of cloth. Broken bricks. Bits of tin it looks like." She drew something out of the pile and held it high for Rab to see. "Piece of a cooking pot." She tossed the shard back onto the pile, raising dust, then got back onto her feet. "I wonder if some of Lilly's stuff didn't come from here," she said, dusting her hands off on her coat.

"Doubt it. We didn't have much worth trading. Bring those pieces of tin."

"Well," she said, coming towards him, jagged strips of tin in hand, "*someone* thought it was worth something."

Rab made his way back outside and as Cloud followed, he turned to her and said:

"Could be there isn't as much missing as we think."

She tilted her head, clearly puzzled.

"Could be they used it all up."

Judging by the expression on her face, she was giving that notion serious consideration.

"All right," she said at last. "I'll concede they might have used up a lot of it. But I seriously doubt they swept what was left into a nice little pile in the middle of the room. It's odd. . ." she glanced to the ground, hesitating, then raised her eyes again. "It's almost as though whoever did that cared about this place."

"The last survivors maybe," Rab said solemnly.

"Do you think they'd have had the strength to do that, Rab? I mean, if you're that close to death, would you. . ." She stopped midsentence. "Sorry. I wasn't thinking. These were your people."

"But you're right, Cloud. It doesn't make any sense. Come on." He tugged on her sleeve. "We should check the warehouse next."

Rab led the way to the largest space in the village, the old warehouse where all of their harvest used to be stored. On the way he noticed some of those tracks Fin was talking about and, like Fin, couldn't determine their age, either. But the tracks weren't his biggest concern. If they found the warehouse in complete ruin, as Rab suspected they would, then they'd be reliant on the remnant 'shroom crop alone to sustain them through snow time.

"This is where you come in," Rab said. "'Shrooms are your speciality, not mine."

The condition of the large double outer doors told Rab much about what they would find inside. One door was hanging off its hinges and largely broken. An enormous splinter projected into the warehouse. It looked to Rab as though someone had broken down the door, although there was no way of knowing when. It could have been yesterday; it could just as easily have been many snow times ago. With the door hanging loose and broken that way, if there had been any harvest left inside, the rain and savage winds that sometimes frequented this place would have spoiled it.

Rab gently nudged the broken door aside and then swung the other intact door back in the opposite direction, spilling light into the front third of the warehouse. If any of the last harvest remained unspoiled, then he'd repair the door. Rab had always found the warehouse a dark and troubling place, where it was easy to envisage that at any given moment the mound of dried 'shrooms would come tumbling down. There'd be no quick rescue for any unlucky soul trapped beneath it. But it had been the smell that usually assaulted him first and it was the same this time only now the smell was one of disappointment, not promise.

"Ugh." Cloud spluttered and coughed behind him. "What is that terrible smell? Surely that can't be mushrooms."

Rab turned and discovered her with a hand up and over her mouth and her brow deeply knitted.

"It's 'shrooms all right," Rab told her. "Ruined 'shrooms."

He pointed to the thin layer of blackened dust just inside the open doors. . .the ruin of the villagers' last harvest. For the most part, that thin layer of dust was all that was left of the 'shrooms, although in places here and there throughout the warehouse, small piles of the same black, horrible-smelling powder, some reaching calf height, lay scattered about the floor.

"Oh, shut the doors, Rab, please," Cloud pleaded. "We can't eat anything that came out of there."

As Rab struggled to shore up the broken door, Cloud swung the second and undamaged door into place.

"That's it then," Rab said, turning to Cloud. "We'll have to rely solely on the crop we passed coming in."

"There'll be enough," Cloud told him. "I'll make it enough," she added when Rab made to shake his head. "You just said it. Mushrooms. . .sorry, 'shrooms. . .*are* my specialty."

"We'll see," Rab replied half-heartedly. "There are still a few spaces left to check. Let's just get this finished and then see what Fin has found."

"I hope he has an eye out for some boots," she said, stumbling then righting herself.

They completed the remainder of the search together, mostly finding just more of the same: either complete emptiness or neatly gathered mounds of largely useless debris piled into the middle or corners of each space. Rab salvaged what he could, but it didn't amount to much. Some tables, chairs that were in such a ruined state, all they were good for was tinder. But that *was* useful. Some more broken pots and, in one space, lying just below the surface of a layer of dust, a perfectly good pair of gloves. They would fit Cloud well enough, so Rab handed them to her.

"Rab," Cloud asked, bending to finger the splintered pieces of a ruined chair. "Where did your people get all this furniture?"

"What furniture?" Rab glanced up. He was down on his hands and knees, picking through the same pile. It was the largest they had come across so far. The space had belonged to Gift's parents.

"The wooden stuff."

"Oh. It was always here." Rab glanced away and returned to his task. "Long as I remember."

"You mean it was passed down?"

"I guess."

"From whom?"

He glanced up again. "What do mean from whom? Parents to children. That's a stupid question."

Cloud came down onto her knee in front of him. "No, it's not. I mean who had it originally. You're just like the tunnel-dwellers, Rab. You've got no trees."

Rab shrugged. "Then I guess we *did* have some once."

"When?" Cloud pressed him.

Rab fell back on his haunches. "Just what are you getting at, Cloud?"

"Wood doesn't come out of nowhere. The tree has to grow, be cut down and then someone has to work it."

"So?"

"So where were the trees growing?"

"Here. Or maybe a long time ago my people had made it as far as that fallen forest. I never thought to ask."

"Pity."

"I'm not following you, Cloud. What difference does it make?"

"Well," she began, "say your people did get their wood from that forest, then that means they might not have always been *here*. They could have been roaming Top-siders, too. Top-siders who decided to stay here instead of going on."

"And?"

"And if that is so, then where is everyone else? The people who would have been here? I never did believe that the people in the north were the only survivors on Earth. But now it seems to me," she said deliberately, "that might be true after all. Maybe you and old John Braham were right. No one in the south survived and maybe your people were just a group that wandered a little further south than the rest. That's all. But even that doesn't make complete sense. If that's so, then wouldn't someone here have *known* that was what happened? Something isn't adding up."

"Or maybe there were trees here and what wasn't cut down, finally died."

Cloud shook her head. "Maybe but, even then, something is still wrong."

"What?"

"I don't know exactly but it takes too long. Either way. If your people had been in that fallen forest to get their wood, they'd have remembered. If there had been trees growing here once, they'd have remembered."

"Did you ever stop to think that maybe they did remember and I just never listened?"

"No," Cloud said with another shake of her head, more vehemently this time, "that's the one thing I'm sure couldn't have happened. Besides, there's the other things to consider, too. The cloth you used for your clothes." She held up her hand. "This tin."

"Sounds to me like you now think this whole idea of Fin's is a *bad* idea. And that south is the one place we *shouldn't* be going. Just like I've been trying to tell you all along."

"No. If I am right then south is where we need to go if we want an answer."

Rab got to his feet. "Then someone better explain the question to me first." It was quite an admission for someone who once thought he knew it.

He left Cloud kneeling there and made his way back into the lane.

"So?" he prompted, spotting Fin approaching from the opposite side.

"Same as before," Fin called to him. "Some empty. Some just full of rubbish."

"All neatly piled up, I'll bet," Cloud said over Rab's shoulder. She'd come out into the lane and stopped behind him.

Fin nodded as he joined them. "But there aren't any dead, Rab. And no sign that there ever were any. Just that rubbish all piled up inside and a few scattered tracks outside."

"Same on our side," Rab told him. "I can't understand it. Who would bother to do that? Bury the dead? Someone had to be the last to die and the dead can't bury themselves."

"South," Cloud said with a touch to Rab's shoulder as she began making her way back to his space. "That's where we'll find the answer."

"Top-siders," Fin said, looking after her. "Had to be, like she said before. They buried the bones and stripped the village. It's the only thing that makes any sense."

"Maybe."

"What about the warehouse?" Fin asked, almost as an afterthought.

"Ruined," Rab told him.

Fin shrugged. "Figured it would be. We'll just have to find our own food," he said and wandered off after Cloud.

He'd made it sound so simple.

Rab followed them back to his old space. The fire Cloud had rekindled was all but out again and she set to work stoking it. The pieces of tin she'd brought with her lay in a tidy pile to one side of the tinder. It wasn't all that cold, so the fire was something of a luxury. Rab almost chided her about the waste. They'd need every scrap of tinder left in the village to see them through snow time. Instead he said nothing about it. If anything, Fin and Cloud appeared even more determined to move south immediately and Rab wasn't up for another futile argument.

When Fin bent to his knees and began to sift through the stack of tinder, evidently looking for one strip of wood in particular, Rab was at the point of asking what he was doing until suddenly he suspected what the young man was up to. His guess was confirmed when Fin settled on a sturdy and sharp-ended stick. Cloud had been watching him, too. Fin, either oblivious or indifferent to the fact that he was being watched, got up from the ground and moved towards one of his packs.

Rab turned away but he could hear the young man rummaging around inside it.

"What's he doing?" Cloud whispered so low Fin couldn't possibly have heard her.

"I'll be back soon," Fin said as he walked past them.

Out of the corner of his eye, Rab noticed something clutched tightly to the young man's chest.

Cloud also saw it and made to rise but Rab jerked her back so smartly, she toppled onto her backside.

"He's going to the cemetery," she snapped at Rab once Fin was out of hearing. "Someone should go with him." With little effort, she broke Rab's hold and jumped to her feet.

"Sit down, Cloud, and enjoy the fire. If he'd wanted someone to go with him, he'd have asked."

She pointed towards the doorway. "But we can't just let him go alone like that. He's going to bury Stitch's heart."

"I know what he's going to do," Rab said, glancing up. "That's what he came here for, isn't it? So let him do it the way he wants."

"But. . ." Cloud stammered, then cropped back down beside the fire. "Is this some village ritual or something?"

"No ritual," Rab said with a shake of his head.

"Then I think we—"

"Take your boots off."

"What?"

Rab turned to look at her. She was regarding him with that old familiar look in her eyes.

"I said take your boots off. And pass me those pieces of tin."

She just kept staring at him.

"You want them fixed, don't you?" he asked with a smile.

***

To occupy her while Fin was gone, Rab had Cloud search the tinder for nails. He'd need something to fix the layers of tin to the bottom of her boots. When she found none, he loaned her his own boots and sent her back out into the village to scavenge what she could. She came back with an assortment of broken nails and small, sharp pieces of metal.

"Will this do?" she asked, tumbling the collection from her palm to the floor by Rab's feet.

"Should, if I can punch a hole through the metal and the rim of the boot. Should have brought a hammer or something," he said, glancing up. He'd been tearing off frayed bits of sole and was almost finished. "But who'd have thought I'd be needing one."

"A hammer?" Cloud fell silent a moment. "I can get that," she said at last.

"Bring back some of that cloth, too," Rab called to her as she disappeared once more through the doorway.

By the time she returned Rab had trimmed a neat hole in the sole of Cloud's boot using the sharp edge of one of the pieces of tin.

She folded herself onto the floor beside him and handed over a small flat-sided stone. "That should work," she said.

Rab hefted the stone in his hand. It was deceptively heavy for its size and fitted nicely into his palm.

"Did you bring the cloth?"

She raised her hand and let dangle a variety of coloured strips.

"You didn't tell me what size."

"That's your problem," he said and rose onto his knees. "You'll have to rip them to size and stuff them as tightly as you can into the hole on the inside of the boot. If it's not tight, they'll come loose and you'll get blisters. Now get one of those broken bricks. No, a flat one. Put it here." He pointed to a spot on the ground in front of him. "You're going to have to hold the boot while I hammer."

Cloud fixed him with a long stare.

"How good are you at this?" she asked at last. "If you miss, you could break my hand."

"Do you want to hammer then? Frankly I'd prefer that you didn't, but—"

"You do it," Cloud said, interrupting him. "But can we at least do this outside where you can see better?"

Rab gathered her boot, the nails and pieces of tin he'd selected and Cloud carried the brick and the flat-sided rock. The ground outside Rab's old space was nice and level and Cloud wasted little time choosing a place to drop the brick. Trading the flat-sided rock for the boot Rab was holding, she bent to her knees and set about positioning the rim of the boot firmly against the edge of the broken brick. Once she had the thin sheet of tin he had fashioned lined up over the sole, Rab slipped to the ground beside her. In his left hand, he held one of the nails and a thin sheath of tin to take the impact; in his right, their make-do hammer.

"Ready?" he asked, glancing briefly over at Cloud.

She shook her head. "I can't get a good grip," she said, then stripping off both gloves, flung them aside. With her hands now better able to grasp the boot, she closed her eyes tightly and yelled. "Go!"

Rab went and the first nail punched through both the tin and the rim of the boot perfectly.

Cloud's eyes popped open.

"Well?" she prompted.

"Just another nine to go," he told her, smiling broadly. "On this boot."

Rab worked as fast as he could. Cloud was bare-handed and he, save for a thick layer of socks, bare-footed. Outside was no place to linger. He managed to hammer in all twenty nails with little difficulty but the sharp points of them were left protruding from the top of the boots. Rab was loathe to hammer the nails flat for fear of tearing the thin rims of the boots.

"Makes for a good weapon," Cloud said, examining the lethal looking boots.

Rab rose up from his knees. "It's the best I can do."

He gathered the flat-sided rock and the remainder of the nails and tin, expecting Cloud to follow him back inside but when he turned around found her standing, repaired boots in one hand, retrieved gloves in the other, looking down the empty lane.

"He's been gone a long time," she said, glancing briefly in Rab's direction. "One of us should go and get him."

"Leave him alone," Rab replied. "He'll come back when he's ready."

No sooner had Rab said it than he noticed a lone figure walking towards them from the very edge of visibility at the farthest reach of the lane. He waved for Cloud.

"Come inside now. You've still got to fix the hole on the inside of that boot you know."

Cloud's eyes lingered on Fin for a moment longer before she turned and followed Rab through the doorway. She found her old spot by the fire, removed Rab's boots, then set to work tearing strips of cloth to size. Rab was still putting his boots back on when Fin came through the doorway. Neither he nor Cloud looked up, but he could see that the young man was still carrying that sharply pointed stick in his hand and nothing else. As he passed the fire, Fin snapped the stick and tossed the two broken ends into the flames.

Chapter 7

FIN sat silently, looking down, across the fire from Rab, while, beside him, Cloud was making the final adjustments to her boot repairs. Rab busied himself thinking and periodically poking at the fire. As he saw it they had two options. The first was to return to the tunnel city immediately while the weather was largely continuing to hold. The second was to wait out snow time at the village, the course of action Rab had originally envisioned would be the only choice open to them. To stay they'd need to prepare. The warehouse would have to be cleared and cleaned, the harvest gathered, the condition of the old well assessed. If the well was dry, then they'd be forced to resort to gathering their water from the river, something his people had never done before. The river was bad. For as long as he could remember, the river had always run bad.

Fin, and probably Cloud, would oppose him. The weather was conducive to travelling on, going south as they both intended. Rab had a hard task ahead of him: convincing them to change their minds. And the hard task was made even more difficult since Rab, himself, remained undecided about their best option. Should they take the chance that the weather would hold just that little bit longer and so make their way back to the tunnels or should they stay put, wait on the arrival of a snow time that was now overdue, and shelter where they were while it lasted?

He looked over at Cloud, trying to assess her mood now, since as far as the fate of the village was concerned, he had been proved right. Granted the whereabouts of the bones of the last of the survivors was a mystery, but it was a mystery that didn't beg solving. Knowing what had become of his people would do the three of them no good at all. Fin had achieved his chief goal; Stitch's heart now rested in home soil.

Undecided about Cloud's leanings, Rab's gaze drifted to Fin. The young man appeared lost in his own thoughts. What was running through his mind? What new purpose was he seeking?

Fin had seemed so preoccupied that it startled Rab when the young man looked up quickly and caught him watching.

"It's time to start making plans," Fin said, switching his focus to Cloud, who had just completed the repairs on her boot. "We'll be needing food, water, and we probably should go through all the spaces in the village again to see if there is anything else we can use like extra clothes, packs, things like that."

Rab could feel Cloud's eyes turn to him.

Fin hadn't strayed in the slightest from his original objective. He'd see them travelling south. But south to what?

Rab pitched the stick he'd been toying with into the fire.

"I said it was a bad idea to start with, Fin, and I haven't changed my mind. We should go back while we still can."

Rab was surprised to discover that he had actually settled on a decision.

Across the fire, Fin was shaking his head.

"I didn't come out here just to turn back around again. It doesn't make a bit of difference that our people are all gone. I knew all along that was likely. I still want to go on to the south, Rab. In fact, I'm even more convinced now that it's the right thing to do."

"For God's sake, *why*?"

"Because of what we found here. What we've seen. Aren't you even curious? Don't you want to know?"

"Know what?" Rab tried his best to sound calm, although he certainly didn't feel it.

"What happened here. What those flying things really are. Where they come from."

"I'd like to know," Cloud muttered. "Well, I would," she snapped when Rab turned to glare at her angrily.

He hadn't been so deluded to expect her support, but he had hoped she'd at least keep her opinions to herself.

"So we're decided then," Fin said, rising.

"I wouldn't go that far," Rab replied, coming to his feet as well.

"That's enough!" Cloud dropped her boot and scrambled up from the ground.

"You," she poked Rab in the chest, "sit down," then pointed at Fin, "and you. Go for a walk. I'm on your side. So you just let *me* talk to Rab. You know he listens to me."

Shocked, Rab gazed at Cloud.

Since when did he listen to her?

"Go," she snarled when Fin hesitated.

It was enough to get the young man moving. He stepped around the fire, passed Rab without so much as a glance and headed out the doorway.

Slowly, Cloud's attention swung to Rab and she smiled. "Oh, don't look so wounded. I only said that to get him out of here so we could talk."

"You couldn't think of another way?" Rab asked.

"No," she replied, motioning for him to re-join her on the floor, "actually I couldn't. Now do you think we can discuss this calmly?"

"That's what I was trying to do, Cloud, but neither of you will listen to reason." He folded himself down beside her.

"Fin thinks you're the one not listening to reason." She drew up her foot and began to put on her boot. "And I'm inclined to agree with him," she said, glancing up. "We know what's back at the tunnels and it's all just more of the same. We don't know what's south. Oh," she said, raising a hand to ward off his protest, "I know what you're going to say. But Rab, unless you've been lying to us, you don't *know*. And as I see it, those bird things only prove it. You never looked south for Gift. Why is that?"

"I told you why and you know it as well as I do. Top-siders don't go south."

"Yes, I admit I've never heard of Top-siders going south. Mine never did. But that doesn't mean others didn't. I'm with Fin. Sometimes I think you've intentionally avoided going in that direction. You could have tried. Even if you found you had to turn back, you could have tried. But you never did. Not even once. At least that's what you've told us." For an uncomfortably long time, she held him with her gaze. "I think you know a lot more than I do, Rab, and I think whatever it is, it's something you don't even what to admit to yourself. No, that's not right. I don't just think it. I'm *sure* of it. What is there in the south you don't want to face, Rab? You say you don't know about those bird things." She shook her head. "Well, maybe you do and maybe you don't, but I'm absolutely sure you've been lying about *something*. And I think I deserve to know what," Cloud said, then turned her attention back to her boot.

Of course he'd been lying. Well, evading the truth anyway. Sooner or later he was going to be trapped into breaking his promise to Sunny. She had played the game better than he ever could. She'd made a poor choice in him, but then she had been denied the opportunity to choose anyone else. He could tell Cloud the truth right there and then and it wouldn't make a shred of difference to Sunny. It wouldn't matter much to Rab anymore, either. He'd learned to accept the truth; had had no choice about it in the long run. But Cloud and Fin, they were different. They still had something to believe in. Sunny wasn't right about much, but she was right about that. *'Let the believers go on believing.'* On this planet, it was all they really had. But if he told Cloud everything he knew then he'd be forced to explain why he'd never gone south.

The day after he'd found Gift missing, he'd made a vow never to stop searching for her until he found her. But to have trekked south in a vain search for more refugees would have been an admission that his quest to find Gift was hopeless and just might have seen him stumble upon the wreckage of other ships. Perhaps he hadn't accepted the truth so well after all. Sunny and that wrecked ship out there in the desert—they were the stuff of a past he could imagine never happened. As long as he never found another ship, and as long as he kept telling himself and everyone else that the south was uninhabitable and never found proof otherwise, then he could put what he had done to Sunny away from him, along with the truth she had passed on.

"Cloud, I have nothing to tell," Rab answered at last.

"Then that's it, isn't it?" she snapped, looking up, her boot fully laced. "You can't honestly expect me to go back simply because you ask me to," she replied, fixing him with a challenging stare. "Just how many times in the past have I asked you not to leave the tunnels again? And how many times did you do what *I* asked? None! Now it's my turn. And if you want my opinion, though I'm sure you don't, *my* turn is long overdue."

Rab glanced from Cloud to the doorway, anxious for the distraction of Fin's return. But the doorway remained empty. He could feel Cloud's eyes still on him, patiently waiting on his response.

A piece of wood crackled and popped in the fire in front of him.

"After snow time, I promise I'll go with you," he said, turning back to Cloud. "But not now. We should return to the tunnels and wait. If you and Fin will do that then. . ."

When Cloud began shaking her head, Rab didn't bother to finish.

"Now or never," she said. "If we return, you'll find some way to back out. I'm not going to give you that chance. You can return to the tunnels by yourself if you want, but Fin and I are going on. We've broken with that place and you can't make us do that twice. Snow time hasn't come yet. It's still warm enough to travel on and, well, if it looks like snow time is coming and we haven't found shelter or food in the south, then we'll come back here and wait it out. I'll make that much of a deal with you. What do you say? It's your choice alone now because Fin and I have made ours."

And so it came again. . .that 'better choice' Fin had talked about the day after Stitch had died. . .Cloud's 'better choice' in allying herself with Fin.

Rab sighed and, reaching out, took a small stick out of the fire. Although it was warm to the touch, the end he held hadn't yet been touched by flame; the other end glowed brightly. He tapped it and a little cascade of white ash fell from its tip.

"We'll have no fire," he reminded her.

"That's possible."

"There'll likely be no more water."

"That's possible, too."

"No more food."

"Things that should suit you well. We'll have to come back here then." She edged closer to Rab. "Fin and I aren't trying to get ourselves killed, Rab. We're not stupid. We'll do the smart thing when we need to."

Rab tossed the stick back into the fire and turned again to Cloud.

"I haven't seen much evidence of that. The smart thing was never to have come here in the first place. What good did it do anyone?"

"It showed us there's something else out here, Rab. Those bird things are out here and even you must be curious about what else could be out here."

"Like?" Rab pressed her, glancing up.

"Food we could eat maybe. Wood we could use." She paused a moment before adding "Maybe even other survivors."

"And if there are other survivors, what guarantee do we have that they'll be friendly?"

"None, I guess," Cloud agreed. "But I'm willing to take that chance and so is Fin."

"If I go with you, Cloud, it's on the understanding that I make the decision about when we turn back."

"But that's not fair, Rab. At the sign of the first snow flake, you'll want to turn around."

"That or nothing. The call is mine."

"Fin won't like it."

No sooner had she spoken his name than Fin came walking back through the ragged doorway. He glanced at Rab but his words were directed towards Cloud.

"I've just come back from the well. There's water. Good water as far as I can tell. We should start harvesting the 'shrooms as soon as possible. There'll be plenty left," he continued, casting Rab a brief look. "Enough to get him back to the tunnels."

"He isn't going back to the tunnels, Fin," Cloud announced, rising to her feet. "He's coming with us."

News to Rab. He hadn't agreed to anything just yet. But Cloud was right. He owed her. And not just for every time he'd left her, but for every time he'd pushed her away from him. And now it seemed that she'd given up on him. Well, why not? It was a fine time to at last do something she had asked. His timing had been predictably bad and it wasn't clear if Cloud had actually agreed to his terms, but after ten long years of avoiding it every and any way possible, it seemed his path would finally turn south. Whether it had ever occurred to her or not, Cloud was asking him to choose between her and Gift. Had been all along. When all was said and done, what real choice did he have? Gift was gone. And there was nothing for him back in those tunnels.

Rab tried to judge Fin's reaction to Cloud's announcement, but Fin's face remained expressionless. He simply turned, walked to the spot where his packs were lying and upended the contents of each onto the ground. He should be pleased; it was the outcome he'd wanted from the start. Likely Fin did suspect he was hiding something but he was sadly mistaken in thinking it was knowledge of what lay ahead of them in the south.

"We'll need some way to gather the mushrooms, bring them back here to dry," Cloud said. Stamping her feet on the ground, she looked down at Rab and smiled. "Hey, these feel pretty good."

"Glad some of my ideas are appreciated," he replied. "I'll help you bring in the harvest, Cloud. Leave Fin to see about water," he added, glancing towards the young man who was seated on the ground, back turned, slowly picking through his meagre possessions.

"Fine," Fin agreed without turning around. "And I'll search the village again, too. There's got to be something we can use."

"Well," Cloud said, addressing Fin, "the harvest isn't the only thing we have to attend to. Someone has to fix your pack. Guess that's my job." She held out her hands and Fin flung the empty ripped pack towards her across the fire. "We've got some good enough scraps of cloth to patch it with now but," she shook her head as she settled herself down on the floor with the torn pack in her lap, "without a needle, I'll just have to weave the patch in as best I can, tying off the loose ends. It'll be bunched up a little. Is that all right?" she asked, glancing across the flames at Fin.

"Just so long as it holds," Fin replied uninterestedly.

Rab watched as, selecting a small nail from the jumble she had brought into his space, Cloud began to gently tease out the frayed ends of cloth on either side of the tear. It would hold. Rab had no doubts about that. But the likelihood of Fin finding anything else of use in the village was another matter. Apart from the 'shrooms he and Cloud would bring in to dry, and the well water, which Fin had deemed drinkable, the only other substantial thing the village had to offer them was shelter, hardly something Fin could stuff into that mended pack and carry.

***

"Any suggestions how we're going to dry these 'shrooms fast enough for Fin?"

Before they had set out for the 'shroom field, Rab and Cloud had scoured the village in search of something in which to haul the harvest back from the field. In one of the spaces that had been less thoroughly stripped, Cloud had found a good-sized length of cloth. The cloth was too worn and threadbare to be serviceable as a garment any longer but, if they handled it with care, it would suffice as a sort of sling in which to carry the 'shrooms. They'd laid the cloth out upon a stretch of clear and flat ground as close to the field as possible and, together, had begun to fill it with the 'shrooms they gathered. Cloud worked the fastest and most efficiently and it was hardly any time at all before his back began to remind Rab of just how long it had been since he'd laboured in the 'shroom fields.

"What do you mean?" Cloud asked, looking up. She had a smudge of dirt across one cheek.

Normally the cold air or, when they could spare the tinder, the large drying hearths did the job of drying the 'shrooms but there'd be no time for that now. Besides, the drying hearths were located inside the warehouse and it would be madness to cart a healthy harvest of mushrooms into such a diseased environment. Fin would want to start out immediately and, now the decision had been made for Rab to move on with them, he didn't want to risk waiting around any longer than necessary. Snow time was still on the horizon and before it came he either wanted to find shelter in the south or confirm there was no shelter to be had, and so make it back to the village before the first hard snow ensured they never would.

"We can't dry them the usual way, Cloud," Rab replied, placing a gloved hand to the small of his back to help himself straighten. "Or hadn't you thought of that?"

"Way ahead of you," Cloud said with a smile. "We'll dry them over the fire inside our shelter."

"On what? There's no pots and pans stall here."

She waved his concern aside and bent to the task again. "There's more of that tin you used on my boots somewhere. I saw it. That'll work," she said, lifting a shoulder and further dirtying her face. "You just have to make me some sort of rack to sit it on so we don't have to continually hold a piece of hot tin over the fire."

"*I* have to make you a rack?"

Cloud glanced towards Rab over the top of the expanse of 'shroom caps. "You did such a great job on my boots. Metalwork seems to be something you're good at," she said, looking away. "Which is more than I can say about harvesting mushrooms."

Rab threaded his way carefully between the unharvested stands of 'shrooms and, reaching Cloud, bent to tap her shoulder. "Well, at least I've got sense enough not to try and overload us." He pointed to the cloth with its load of gathered 'shrooms. "That'll tear if we try to carry too much more."

Cloud straightened and looked towards the heavily laden cloth. "Maybe you're right," she said at last. "We don't have to gather it all at once."

With the tip of a gloved finger, Rab attempted to remove the smudge of dirt from Cloud's face, but only made the smudge worse.

"What happens if we leave part of the harvest over snow time?" she asked, glancing around, taking in the remaining untouched field. "Will it ruin?"

Rab shrugged. "I don't know. We always harvested the entire field and stored it in the warehouse. You're the 'shroom expert. You tell me. Why are you worrying about that anyway? We aren't coming back here, are we?" Rab would have moved away then but Cloud grabbed the tail of his heavy coat.

"But what if we have to? We'll need every mushroom here to survive."

Rab threw up his hands. "Why don't you ask Fin what he wants to do."

He loosened Cloud's hand from his coat and began to walk away.

"We're all in this together, Rab," she called after him. "I was just ask-ing for your opinion."

"And I gave it to you," Rab sang back over his shoulder. "You know more about 'shrooms than I ever did and Fin *is* in charge."

"So you're just going to walk off and leave me here with this load of mushrooms to carry in by myself?"

"No, Cloud, I'm not. I'm going to make my way through this field without stepping on every 'shroom in my path and walk to that cloth over there and grab one end of it." Rab stopped and turned around. "I was kind of hoping you might come over here and grab the other end."

***

Rab estimated that it would take at least two full days of harvesting, carrying, slicing and drying over a constant fire to accumulate a barely adequate supply of 'shrooms. And although he had managed to fashion a suitable rack, freeing them of the obligation to constantly hold the piece of tin he'd beaten thin and flat over the fire, his ingenuity didn't free them of the need for constant vigilance. He and Cloud took it in turns to watch the precious fire and the layers of 'shrooms they set to dry, over and over again, on the thin plate. Fin, as self-appointed scavenger, saw to maintain-ing the supply of tinder. There was little left in the village to burn but Fin still managed to keep the fire hot and alive. Cloud and Rab rarely left the shelter but Fin was infrequent company; when he wasn't sifting through the ruined village, he occupied himself by wandering around its perimeter. Rab suspected that the young man spent most his spare time in the cemetery. But it was only a suspicion, one he didn't share with Cloud or feel inclined to confirm with Fin who was growing noticeably more impatient and irritable by the second.

Ultimately Fin's forays about the village netted them some scavenged pieces of additional clothing and a rusted though still serviceable knife. During one of his frequent absences, Fin had come upon a curiously mounded patch of earth in the far corner of a neighbouring space. He hadn't disturbed it but returned immediately to Rab and Cloud with the report of his find. Unanimously they agreed not to investigate what may, or may not, lie beneath the ground. It wasn't common practice to inter inside the home, so either the burial had been undertaken in haste or someone, other than a villager, had performed the interment. If the latter, then likely there were other such burials scattered about the village and perhaps it was better not to know if the space they were obliged to inhabit for some small time yet was shared with someone's remains. In his heart, Rab hoped that if it was a grave that Fin had found, then the interment had been an aberration. He wanted desperately to believe the story Cloud had conceived for his old friends and neighbours; he wanted to believe that, against all odds and likelihood, every last person in his village had simply moved on.

And a possible answer to the fate of the villagers wasn't all that Fin's restless searching brought them. Twice again they heard that strange whooshing sound coming from the direction of the sky and, on the first occasion, Fin had been laying a fresh batch of tinder on the fire. On hearing the noise, he'd dropped the tinder and run outside. Too late. Whatever had been passing overhead was gone. But on the second occasion, Fin was inside one of the ruined spaces at the far end of the village. When he returned to their shared space, he recounted an incredible tale about the thing that had whizzed directly over the top of the roof above his head. He'd seen it clearly this time, he maintained, through the large, jagged holes in the rusted-out sheets of roofing iron. It was kind of a mottled black, he explained in a stop-start fashion that was entirely reasonable considering his excitement, with a sharp projection of some sort at the spot where its nose should be, a long thin neck, two equally long and skinny legs, and, splaying out from either side of its body, broad wings that angled sharply backwards at the midpoint. He insisted it was roughly the size of a grown man. . .a very *big* grown man. When Rab asked about its skin, Fin shook his head.

"No skin," he explained, "this," and then held out his hand. "It came floating through the hole in the roof. Landed right at my feet. Almost like that thing meant it to."

In the palm of his hand rested what Rab, with his limited knowledge gained only from pictures and drawings he had seen in some of the books in the library, decided was a feather, a very large feather that, from base to tip, would have measured at least three times the length of Fin's hand.

"What is it?" Cloud asked, briefly abandoning her vigil at the fire.

Fin moved to show her and, as she touched the strange object lying within his palm, her gaze shifted to Rab.

"It's soft," she said, stroking a finger along the shaft before she turned her attention back to Fin and gently lifted the thing from his hand. "And light. Why it hardly weighs anything at all."

"It's a feather of some kind," Rab told her, taking up her abandoned position by the fire. "And as far as I'm aware, only birds have feathers. Fin must have been right all along."

Bringing the feather up to her lips, Cloud set the vane fluttering with a gentle breath.

"Next time it comes back," Fin said, "I'm going to kill it. Then we'll see what it is. Maybe eat it, too."

"Eat it?" Cloud said, lowering the feather.

"Why not? It *might* be good to eat." Using a small flattened strip of tin, Rab systematically began to flip over one slice of 'shroom after another. "But I'm curious how you're intending to kill it, Fin."

"A rock maybe," Fin replied. "Or I could make a spear."

Rab kept his eyes trained on the precious 'shrooms while he shook his head. "You'd need awfully good aim to bring it down. But it's worth a try I suppose."

"What a shame to kill it," Cloud said, garnering Rab's attention. "There's so little left on Earth, it doesn't seem right just to go around killing living things."

"It would have killed you," he reminded her. "And as for eating it?" He shrugged. "You ate grubs when you could get them, didn't you?"

"Yes, but this is. . ."

". . . different?" Rab prompted.

She didn't answer, but turned to Fin and made to hand back the shed feather.

"You keep it," he said. "I'll have a lot more soon."

With that, he turned, leaving Cloud alone with Rab once again.

"Now where's he off to?" Cloud asked.

The question was more to herself, Rab suspected, but he answered just the same.

"To make a spear would be my guess."

Cloud wandered back towards the fire and, placing the feather to one side, nudged Rab out of the way.

"Do you think he can do it? Kill one, I mean?" she asked.

Rab coughed. Smoke from the constant fire was beginning to seep into every nook and cranny of their cramped shelter. Even a breath of cold air would have been welcome but Rab felt obliged to remain inside with Cloud.

"Maybe," he replied. "If he can get close enough. It's fast."

"Aren't birds supposed to be fast?"

Rab found a spot on the ground where he could be free of the draught from the fire for a while. "I guess."

Cloud swung around, flattened piece of tin raised in one hand, and levelled one of those ice-melting looks of hers at Rab. "You don't mean to tell me those books you keep reading don't say?"

"There's a lot those book don't say."

Cloud shrugged. "You'd never know it," she said before turning back to her task at the fire, "the way your head's buried in them every time you come back to the tunnels."

The last part was delivered in a mumble, but though he'd heard her, Rab didn't bother to respond. Instead he got to his feet, grudgingly, and moved to relieve her at the fire.

"These are ready," she said the moment he approached. "You can set them aside to cool. I'll start the next batch."

After winding a strip of cloth tightly about his hand, Rab took the hot piece of tin from the rack, tipped the dried 'shrooms onto the level rock they'd specifically brought into the shelter for the single purpose of cooling.

"There's something we haven't thought of," Cloud said as, with her hand similarly protected, she took the tin from Rab and set about reloading it with freshly sliced 'shrooms. "If we do have to come back here," she began, glancing slyly towards Rab, "I mean if we do find nothing in the south, then what are we going to do about fire?" She slid the loaded piece of tin onto the rack Rab had fashioned and stood to face him. "By the time this is finished, we'll have used up all the tinder."

"I thought of that," Rab told her, picking up the small piece of tin they used to turn the 'shroom slices from the spot where Cloud had laid it. "As I see it, we'd have two options. To head back to the tunnels or to barricade ourselves in here."

Cloud's face collapsed into a frown. "Barricade? What do you mean?"

"We'd have to pull down some of the walls from the other spaces, build new walls in here, lay them around in circles," Rab explained, gesturing with the piece of tin, "right up to the roof with air spaces between. Two extra walls might be enough. Three would be better."

Cloud glanced around. "But that would leave us hardly any room at all," she observed.

"That's the idea."

"But it's not possible. We couldn't stay confined like that. It may snow for a long time, Rab."

"It may," he agreed, looking up from his task. "Otherwise we'd have to try to make it back to the tunnels."

"Through the snow?" Cloud pressed him.

"Happy for you to come up with a better idea."

Cloud worked in silence for a time.

"No," she said at last. "We won't have to do either. There'll be shelter in the south. I'm sure of it. That bird thing proves it. Fin was right about the bird and he's right about the south."

"I hope so, Cloud," Rab replied, as he set about turning the 'shrooms. "I really hope so."

Chapter 8

CONSIDERING the time and resources he had, the spear Fin made wasn't too bad at all. The major drawback, though, was that he had no expertise in throwing it. Each night, while Cloud set about rationing out their meal and Rab scouted the perimeter of their camp, Fin diligently practised his skills. On the second night out from the village, he managed to blunt the spear's thin metal tip by smashing it into a rock. It had taken him the better part of the next day, working the point during every break they had taken, to sharpen it once again. If he ever got the chance to launch the weapon, Rab remained unconvinced it would result in a kill. When Fin's obsession with the weapon had finally got the better of him, his appeal for the young man to cease his endless practicing had predictably gone ignored.

Since they had left the village, there had been no sight of the 'bird'. To Rab's way of thinking that was both a good and a bad thing. Even if its swoops were only intended as some sort of warning, the creature was big enough to inflict serious injury, perhaps even capable of delivering a killing blow. But its absence suggested that they were heading in the wrong direction. If the same thought had crossed Fin's mind, he didn't mention it. Though Rab was beginning to suspect Cloud might be growing concerned. She'd turned unusually quiet.

The weather was still holding and Rab hadn't felt obliged to rein in Fin's enthusiasm for pushing them as far into the night as possible. The terrain they had been trudging through, day after day, had been unpromising: low and barren-looking hills way off to the east, as Rab judged the direction, hills that never seemed to appear any closer or any farther away; beneath their feet, sharp and angular rocks that cut through the bottom of Fin's and Rab's boots and sent Cloud slipping and sliding on her metal soles. Overhead, a low-slung swath of dirty-coloured cloud neither shed its moisture nor lifted, but simply dimmed as each night encroached upon them, then lightened again to that same familiar sombre grey as dawn edged closer. The sooner they reached the point where Fin either proved himself right or conceded that he'd been wrong, the sooner they could turn back.

Rab had promised to show Cloud the river once they reached his village; he'd reneged on that promise. Though no one knew for certain, Rab had always suspected that the river, which swung around his village, veered slightly west in its southerly progress. As a child, he'd actually attempted to track it and with only Jep for company, had braved the foul air and a trek as close as they had dared to the cloying mud of the bank for one full day and night only to return home with little achieved but a vow never to repeat the folly. Now the river had become one of Rab's arbitrary turning points. If they reached it even before half their supplies were consumed, then he'd still insist they turn back. Even Fin wasn't foolish enough to argue in favour of crossing a body of water that seemed too deep. And in all likelihood it would be deep enough to deter an attempted crossing. If they didn't reach it, then the turning point came the moment their packs reached that half empty mark unless, and it was an unlikely 'unless' in Rab's mind, something about the terrain to the south showed unequivocally the promise of food and shelter.

And so they journeyed farther and farther south; Rab religiously assessing their remaining supplies each night; Fin, spear in hand, striking out ahead of them each morning; and Cloud looking ever skyward. It was on the evening of the fifth day out from the village that they uncovered the reason for the disappearance of the 'bird'. Fin was the first to come upon the remains. . .what there was of them. Mostly just feathers and bones and a broad patch of discoloured stones around the site. More disturbing was the nauseating smell, reminiscent of the rotting 'shrooms in the village warehouse, and Cloud's discovery of an abandoned fire nearby. Though the coals were cold, there was still an abundance of ash left undisturbed by the wind, suggesting that whoever had killed the 'bird', stripped it of flesh and likely cooked it, were not all that far away.

"Same people as before?" Cloud asked as, bent to her haunches, she began to pick among the discarded bones.

"Probably," Rab agreed, sloughing off his packs to kneel down beside her. "Whoever they were, they had the same idea as Fin." He glanced up and caught Fin standing over the bones. The arm with which the young man held the spear was extended and the end of the spear was punched into the ground. For an instant, Rab was reminded of Sunny and the way she always stood, holding that wretched gun of hers.

Though he'd seen plenty of broken bones in his time, Fin had probably never seen a real skeleton before. Cloud maybe. . .during her days wandering on the surface with the Top-siders.

During his last search top-side, Rab, himself, had come upon the remains of a long-lost Top-sider, although the discovery hardly fazed him. How could it after the things he had seen and done inside that ruined ship all those years ago?

"Like you said, Rab. If there's one, there's more," Fin said. "We'll have meat yet."

Rab rose from the ground. "I'm more concerned about who made that fire right now, Fin."

The young man shrugged. "Got to be either bounty hunters or Top-siders. They might have even been killing these things for years. Not likely either one of them is going to tell us."

Cloud, who was still hunched over the bones, shook her head. "It can't be Top-siders. We never saw anything like this."

"Then by your reasoning it can't be bounty hunters, either," Rab observed.

"Then who?" she asked, glancing up.

"I haven't a clue," Rab admitted and, reaching down, offered his hand to assist her up from the ground. In her free hand, Rab noticed two thin slivers of bone.

"Needles," she said, pre-empting his question. "I can make needles out of these. Pity I didn't have them back in the village."

Rab gestured towards the abandoned fire. "Any suggestions where the tinder came from for that? There's nothing out here to burn."

"That's obvious," Fin replied, lifting the spear to point back the way they had come. "Our village."

"No, that can't be, Fin," Cloud protested. "We couldn't carry anything, so how could they?"

"I think Fin might be right, Cloud. All they'd need would be a cart of some sort."

"But. . .," Cloud began, then hesitated. "I guess that explains those tracks in your village then, doesn't it?" she said at last.

"I guess it does. And that means it *is* Top-siders. Bounty hunters travel light."

"Do you think it was a Top-sider fire we came across in the forest as well? We wouldn't have seen any tracks there because it had rained."

"And we wouldn't see any tracks here, either," Fin said before Rab had the chance to answer. He kicked at the stones in front of him, "not on this," then bent to examine the bones more closely, placing the spear on the ground beside him. "I wonder how they killed it."

Cloud pointed to the ruined, featureless head. "Its head's smashed."

"Yeah, but that was probably done after they brought it down," Fin said, glancing back at Cloud. "To finish it off."

Cloud grimaced. "I don't like it," she said. "Killing things like that."

"Are you saying *you* wouldn't do it?" Rab asked.

"No." She shook her head and turned away to make her way back to the cold fire. "I'm just saying I don't like it."

Rab followed, leaving Fin to pick through feathers and scattered pieces of bone.

Cloud was on the ground again, this time sifting through the remains of the fire.

"We're not going to leave these coals here. They're good medicine. And we can still get a small fire out of some of them."

"Strange they didn't take them," Rab said as he lowered himself down beside Cloud to help.

"Maybe they don't know."

"Doubtful," Rab said with a smile.

"Maybe they don't care."

"Again doubtful."

"So?" Cloud stopped her scavenging to look at Rab. "Why do you think they didn't take them?"

Rab passed her a coal. "They didn't need them."

Cloud dropped back on her haunches. "No, that can't be it. Even if they'd brought a good supply of tinder from the village, no one passes up medicine."

"Unless they have more than enough already."

Cloud offered up a wry little laugh. "Who *ever* has more than enough?"

"Don't know. But if we keep going south, I guess we're going to find out." He handed her the last of the usable coals and rose to his feet. "I'll bring you something to hold those."

Abandoning her collection of coals, Cloud hurried after him.

"Then you think they've been ahead of us all the way?"

"Makes sense," Rab said as, together, they walked back to the spot where Rab had dropped his packs. "It explains the fire in the forest, the tracks in the village like you said. The fact that nearly everything in the village had been gone through and rearranged."

"And the absence of your people?" Cloud prompted.

"Not that," Rab said. "I doubt we're following them, Cloud, if that's what you're thinking. I suspect Fin did find at least one of their graves. The rest are buried there somewhere. If the graves were recent, I think we'd have noticed more of them. Whoever did the burying, did it some time ago. But it's my guess it's the same people."

"But that *doesn't* make sense. Top-siders who took the time to bury someone else's long dead and then come back again? Why?"

"If I knew that," Rab answered, "I'd know who we're following."

"Whoever they are," Fin said, catching the end of the conversation, "they've only just learned how to kill." He passed Rab a thin piece of metal. "Too thin," he explained, pointing to the broken point of the spear head lying in the palm of Rab's hand. "Mine is thicker."

"By intent?" Rab asked, glancing up.

"By accident," Fin conceded with a shrug.

Rab handed the broken point back to Fin. "Keep practising," he said, then bent to collect one of his packs.

***

Fin was excited when they came across the bridge, while Cloud took the discovery more in her stride. None of them had ever seen a bridge and coming upon it had certainly surprised Rab although, in hindsight, perhaps it shouldn't have.

Just as he had always suspected, south of their village, the river did sweep westward although they encountered it much farther to the south than he had anticipated. Save for the water the tunnel-dwellers sieved and filtered, the river water looked the freshest he had ever seen. There was no fouling of the air in the immediate vicinity, either. . .an added and unexpected bonus. But the bridge itself had been the biggest surprise. Though they hadn't encountered it immediately, Fin had spotted it, or rather something that looked unusual, a little way downstream. A short walk along the unspoiled bank of the river had brought them to the bridge. This wasn't Earth; Rab knew that. But there had been other life on this planet once; still was, evidently, if only a few straggler 'birds'. It should have come as no surprise to him that whoever had built those roosts up north so very long ago would have left other evidence of themselves behind. In fact, it was perhaps more surprising that, in all his travelling, Rab had never come across any of it before. And a bridge was just a bridge after all. They, too, had to have devised some way to get across a river and Rab had seen perhaps a dozen pictures of bridges in the books in the tunnel city library. Still, stumbling upon a structure that was so strongly reminiscent of the bridges his own kind had built on Earth had rattled him. Fin didn't seem to notice his distraction. Cloud, predictably, did, though she said nothing about it immediately.

The one and only time he had come across evidence of this planet's lost inhabitants, those roosts, the structures had been largely in ruins. Superficially the bridge looked to be intact and seemed to Rab to be constructed of the same material as the roosts he, Sunny and Gift had come upon out on the plain, a modified rock or brick of some kind. Rab remembered all too well how time and the elements had compromised the walls of the roosts, but the bridge appeared to have fared much better. Although the five arches that supported the deck of the bridge bore the inevitable scars meted out by time, water, and ice, they seemed remarkably well preserved. Down at water level, the supporting pillars that held the arches aloft had been gnawed and eaten into on the upstream side. Downstream, although dirtied, the pillars looked smooth and wholly undamaged and, from where he was standing, Rab couldn't spot a single broken piece of rock or brick on the underside of the bridge. The deck itself had suffered the most damage and what Rab assumed had once been an even and easily passable surface was now roughly pockmarked, irregularly lifted and, in some places, cracked to perhaps the width of man's body and, more worryingly, an unknown depth.

When Fin made to cross the bridge, Rab called him back.

"It may not be safe," he explained when Fin turned around, one foot shy of stepping forwards.

"Well, someone needs to find out," Cloud said and, once she shrugged off her backs, pointed towards the sloping bank. "I'm going down there to look from underneath."

"Know a lot about bridges, do you?" Rab asked, taking hold of her arm above the elbow to prevent her from rushing headlong down the shallow slope.

"As much as you do, I'm guessing."

Fin came up just as Cloud was shaking herself free.

"I'm not going to stand around here while you two argue about who goes first," he said and flung both his packs to the ground.

Once Fin began to shinny down the bank, Cloud turned to Rab.

"This was it, wasn't it?" she said, arms akimbo. "The place you were going to make us turn back?"

"The bridge?" Rab asked in surprise. "I didn't even know it was here."

"Not the bridge, Rab. The river. You were counting on it blocking our path."

"It crossed my mind," Rab confessed.

"Then it's a pity for you that the bridge crosses it," she said and, kneeling, peered down the slope in search of Fin who had gone out of sight completely.

"Well?" she prompted, glancing back towards Rab. "Assuming he finds the bridge safe, are we going to turn back or go on?"

"You'd turn back if I asked you to?"

"I promised, didn't I?" Cloud replied, coming to her feet. "But if I'm given a choice, you know it will be for going on with Fin."

Oh yes. He knew that all right.

Rab looked past Cloud towards the opposite bank.

If only they hadn't come upon the bridge. . .

They hadn't reached that crucial halfway point in their supplies and it seemed that the river wasn't going to be the certain deterrent Rab had hoped. Not only was the bridge offering them a way forward, it was offering them a way back as well. They could go on a little way farther. Let Fin find what he was always destined to find. Nothing different to what they had already found these last few days. Maybe other straggler 'birds' and, if they were unlucky, a few lost nomads. Nothing more. If there were any more ruined ships to be found, they wouldn't be found this far north. Rab felt fairly certain of that. And when they found that nothingness, would Fin be satisfied and turn back towards his home in the tunnels?

It was a question Rab doubted that the young man, himself, could even answer. . .not yet. . .not until the nothingness out there, on the other side of the bridge, convinced him that there was no alternative. And yes, Rab admitted, to himself at least, that perhaps, just perhaps coming upon the bridge had sparked his curiosity, rekindled just a little bit of the flame he'd thought extinguished long ago. But unlike Fin, when they found that nothingness, he would finally be satisfied. He'd return to the tunnels, find a home there among a people he could never hope to fully understand. He was done with traipsing this top-side, done with searching for Gift. She was lost. Had been already these ten long years.

"*If* the bridge is safe, we'll go on," he said to Cloud, "until half the food and water is gone. I know I can't make you turn back then, but I'll be asking you to. Begging you to."

"I'm not stupid, Rab. Really I'm not, although I know you think coming with Fin on this journey proves otherwise. But I had to know if the only choices that are left are those tunnels or a life spent aimlessly wandering the surface." She reached out to touch his cold face. "Understand?"

Better than she knew.

It occurred to him then that Fin had been gone a long time. The same thought must have crossed Cloud's mind, too, because suddenly she turned from him and looked back down the slope in search of Fin.

"Fin?" Rab called at the same instant Cloud shouted the young man's name.

It seemed like a long time before Fin's voice sounded somewhere below them.

"You'd better come down here."

Cloud looked briefly at Rab before she began to scurry down the slope ahead of him.

They found Fin directly underneath the bridge. When he saw them, he gestured for them to follow him towards a spot just upstream of the bridge.

"Take a look," he said, nodding towards the ground.

It was even colder in the gloom beneath the underside of the bridge and Rab hurried past Cloud, reaching Fin ahead of her. But it was Cloud who bent to her knees first and Cloud who thoughtlessly stripped off her gloves to touch the strange greenish growth Fin had found nestled in the crevices between the smooth rocks of the river bank.

"I've never seen a colour like this before," Cloud said, leaning closer.

Rab dropped to his haunches beside her.

"I found more of it up that way."

Rab turned and caught Fin pointing upstream.

"But what is it?" Cloud asked faintly.

Before Rab even realised what she was about to do, she had two of her bare fingers wedged inside the crevice.

"Don't!" he cautioned her too late.

Effortlessly she peeled out a long and narrow flap of the oddly coloured growth. She had ripped it the way an expert tailor could rip a thin strip from a larger piece of cloth.

"It's sort of spongy, "she said, "and it smells funny," she added, bringing the flap up to her nose. "Like mushrooms but stronger. Not very nice at all."

"Then put it down," Rab suggested.

In an instant, she had a tiny piece of the stuff broken off and popped into her mouth.

"Cloud!" Rab shouted at her.

Her face quickly contorted and she spat.

"Tastes worse than it smells," she said, still spitting.

"What do you think it is?" Fin asked, dropping to one knee beside Rab.

All Rab could think of was that the stuff was some kind of plant. But here? Now? When they'd never seen any kind of living plant before?

"Whatever it is, I'm taking some of it," Cloud said.

"What for?" Rab objected.

"Could be good medicine," she explained as she set about peeling out more of the plant-like growth from the crevices between the rocks.

"Who's going to test it?" Rab asked, getting to his feet.

"You let me worry about that and concentrate on finding me something to put it in," Cloud told him, intent on her task.

Fin stood, looked at Rab, then shrugged.

"I've got nothing," he said. "The bridge seems safe enough to me, I'll wait for you on the other side."

With that, he strode past Rab, made for the gentlest part of the river bank and began the easy scramble up the slope.

"Well?" Cloud said, getting up from her knees. "What have you found me?" She had three short strips of the greenish plant cupped in her bare palm.

"I don't have. . ." Rab began, then stopped abruptly.

Reaching inside the deep pocket of his heavy outer coat he withdrew the draw-string pouch that contained Gift's little blue stone. He stripped off his gloves, loosened the string and tipped the stone into the palm of his hand. Without wasting a second to think about it, he pitched the stone as far as he possibly could. It landed in the river about midstream, soundlessly, with only a transient little ripple in the water to mark the place where it had gone down.

"You. . ." Cloud started to say but, instead of finishing, reached out and took the now empty pouch from Rab's hand. "Thanks," she muttered not meeting Rab's eyes, as she stashed the tiny fragments of spongy green plant inside.

"You keep it," he said as she made to pass the pouch back to him, and headed towards the place where Fin had made his way up the bank.

By the time Rab, with Cloud a step behind him, started over the bridge, Fin was already halfway across it. Rab watched the young man as he jumped each gap he came to, relieved to see that Fin was taking some pains to ensure that he landed softly. Behind him, the tap-tap-tap of the metal soles of Cloud's boots on the rough blocks of the bridge was starting to irritate him; another reason to be glad when they reached the opposite shore. But Cloud insisted on stopping when they came to the middle of the bridge.

"Hey," she protested when Rab tried to hurry her on. "I've never seen a river before," she said and leaned over the crumbling edge. "And you promised me."

"You'll be *in* it if you keep leaning over the edge like that."

Rab made a grab for her sleeve, collecting a wad of material.

"Move," he snapped, dragging her away.

Fin was waiting for them at the end of the bridge.

"There's a road here," he said.

"Wasn't on the other side," Cloud observed, glancing down to inspect what Fin had found. "Not much of one on this side, either, if you ask me."

"Look back the way we came, Abby," Fin said.

Rab looked back, too. And there, on the opposite bank, he saw what Fin must have already seen: the ghost of a road.

"We could have been walking on it and never even noticed," Fin said, then looked southward towards a terrain that, to the best of Rab's knowledge, no Top-sider, villager or tunnel-dweller had ever set foot upon before. "I wonder if they came this way, too."

So did Rab. It seemed a little ironic to him that, perhaps within the span of only days, two separate groups of wanderers might have traipsed the same unknown ground, moving towards the same unknown destination. Cloud, Fin and he were aware that someone might be travelling ahead of them. But were the people ahead of them aware that someone might be travelling towards them from behind?

Chapter 9

"WHAT do you think it means?" Cloud asked, bent at the knee, examining the stain that looked suspiciously like dried blood to Rab.

"Could be from another one of those birds," Fin suggested. "Doesn't have to be human."

"Doesn't have to be," Rab agreed. "But even if it isn't, explain that," he said and pointed to the piece of wood in Fin's hand.

The going had become tougher on this side of the river, the terrain less predictable—rockier with intervening hills and depressions. Though more than once they suspected they might have lost it, they managed to stay on the road through its many twists, dips and rises. It was just shy of nightfall when Fin had come across the length of wood and, at almost the same moment, Cloud had stumbled upon the blood-stained rocks.

Fin hefted the wood in both hands. "Looks like a piece of an axle to me," he said. "Broken," he added, carefully fingering the sharply splintered ends. "Which does explain that."

Lowering his hand, he pointed to a wide gouge in the ground by his feet. The ruined road was littered with sharp-edged stones and if a cart had been dragged along, a sort of berm would form on either side, leaving the middle ground disturbed. And that's just what Fin was pointing at.

"Didn't happen too long ago," Rab said, taking the wood from Fin. "We're still following them."

Fin shrugged. "Kind of expected we would be what with the road and all." He walked towards Cloud and dropped down beside her to examine the blood-stained rocks again.

"Been better if we *had* lost the road," Rab said, more to himself than to Fin, and tossed the broken length of wood aside.

"Hey," Cloud shouted, getting to her feet. "I could use that."

She hurried over to the spot where the wood had landed and picked it up.

"One of them must be hurt," she said, rising. "Maybe badly. Looks like a lot of blood to me."

"How old is it? Any idea?" Rab asked.

Cloud just shook her head. "I don't know. It's dry. But then I don't suppose that means much."

"No," Rab agreed. "And they'll be moving slower now."

Cloud glanced back at him.

"Broken axle," he explained. "They're dragging the cart now. Four wheels are best; two wheels will do. Three won't work at all. That piece of wood you've got there must have fallen off the back of the cart without them realising it."

Cloud swung the length of wood in her hand. "Then whatever is in that cart must be pretty important to them."

"Like everything they took from our village?" Fin suggested. "But I say we keep going the same way," he added, getting to his feet. "Down the old road. Sure they took everything from our village, but it wasn't like they stole it. We'd have done the same."

"I agree with Fin," Cloud said, walking back towards Rab. "Anyway, they're out here and maybe they know something about what lies to the south."

"Why?" Rab asked her. "We're out here and we don't know a damn thing. Could be they just stumbled on the road same as we did."

"Maybe. But you, me and Fin, we know why we started going south in the first place. Why did they?"

Rab shrugged. "They're as mad as we are?"

"Speak for yourself," she replied and tapped him lightly with the length of wood. "Only a mad person would toss aside a nice piece of wood like this. I can make a small fire with this and those coals I collected before. Knew they'd come in handy sooner or later. . ."

She was mumbling to herself, wandering back to the place where she'd discarded her packs.

"And yet again," Rab said, looking at Fin, "they weren't careful enough to make sure they hadn't left something useful behind."

"So?" Fin said with a smile as he passed Rab, following Cloud. "You tossed it aside."

Yes, he had. He hadn't been thinking when he'd done that, being more concerned with those blood-stained rocks and what they could possibly mean for them in the future.

Cloud set about making a fire and there, beside it, they ate their one substantial meal of the day in silence. The warmth lasted for only a short time, long enough though for Rab to slip into sleep. He woke when it was still dark, cognisant that, once again, one of his small party had gone missing. He found Cloud a short distance away, startling her when he approached and barely avoiding a crack to his head from the sizeable rock she hefted.

"You shouldn't have come up on me like that," she said by way of apology.

Rab couldn't see her face; he could hear the tremor in her voice though. Something had frightened her.

"I heard something," she said, confirming his suspicions. "Over here."

"That bird of yours again?" Rab asked, hoping she'd reply in the affirmative.

"Wasn't from the sky," she said. "Whatever it was, it was on the ground. I'm sure of it. What I heard was sort of a crunching sound like someone was walking there."

"In the morning, we'll look," Rab told her, suddenly feeling more chilled than he had just a moment ago. "If there was something there, maybe we'll find evidence of it when it's lighter."

"On these rocks?" Cloud said out of the darkness. "We can't even see where we've walked."

Rab didn't need to be reminded.

When dawn came, all three of them scoured the site but, just as Cloud had predicted, they found no evidence that something or someone had visited them during the night. But Cloud didn't usually jump at shadows; Rab had no doubt that she had heard something close to them in the darkness. There was nothing for it but to press on, follow that deeply gouged track that had been left by whoever had passed this same way before them, possibly the same someone who had backtracked this way during the night although Rab couldn't imagine why they'd do such a thing.

"If they're using a cart," Cloud said, tromping along beside Rab, "then they have to be Top-siders."

"I thought we already decided that," Rab replied, glancing towards her boots.

He was beginning to regret having covered both soles entirely with tin. Whoever was travelling in front of them would hear the tell-tale ting-ting-ting of Cloud's footsteps long before they arrived.

"Bounty hunters don't use carts," Cloud continued as though Rab had never spoken. "But now it looks like the cart is broken and someone in their group is badly injured. And still they don't turn back. There is something out here, Rab. Something they are trying to reach," she said, tilting her head to look up at him. "There must be other Top-siders in the south and they're going to them for help."

"Or they're running," Rab suggested.

Cloud just smiled. "From what?"

"Could be they *escaped* from the Top-siders."

"What?" Cloud said with a little laugh. "You think we're following a group of little girls who somehow broke free of the Top-siders who took them? That's ridiculous. How could a few little girls steal a cart without someone discovering them? No," she said, with finality. "I'm right. You're wrong. And when we come across them, you'll see for yourself." Suddenly she stopped and reached out to grasp Rab's arm, pulling him up beside her. "And that might be sooner than I thought. Smell that?"

Rab sniffed the air. Fire!

"Stay here," Rab cautioned her and made to race off after Fin.

"Why?" Cloud asked, gripping his arm.

"I told you before Fin can't smell anything until he's right on top of it. I'll bring him back. Don't worry."

She let go of his arm, though Rab suspected it was unhappily.

He quickly caught up with Fin, who hadn't noticed the smell that Rab had finally identified as the pungent aroma of camp fire.

"It's almost night," Rab said once he had returned with Fin to Cloud. "I suggest we get as close as possible, without them seeing us, and wait."

"You want us to sit here all night and spy on them?" Cloud asked. "Why? Seems to me we have to approach them sooner or later. Why not now?"

"That would be stupid, Cloud," Rab replied.

"Really?" she snapped. "They have a fire. We don't. Who's being stupid?"

"She has a point," Fin said.

Rab shook his head. "They're armed."

"So are we," Fin reminded him, brandishing his spear. "And mine isn't broken."

Cloud stepped forwards and placed a gloved hand on Fin's spear arm. "Maybe Rab has the right idea after all, Fin. Maybe we should wait. They're armed; we're armed and, if they do have someone injured with them, the first thing they're sure to think is that we're going to take advantage of that."

When neither Fin nor Rab answered her, Cloud spoke again. "Well? Am I right or not?"

"You're right. You're right," Rab hurried to say. "But I wouldn't have expected you to think of that before either of us did."

"Don't know why," Cloud replied. "I have years of experience living with these nomadic Top-siders to fall back on. *You* don't," she said, pointing a finger at Rab. "Best to stay here for the night. Find out how many of them there are. Maybe even how badly one of them is injured."

"All right," Fin agreed, sloughing off his packs. "But it's a shame to miss out on that fire of theirs. . .made with *our* wood," he said, casting a reproachful glance at Cloud.

"I thought you didn't blame them for taking what they could from our village," Rab said, dropping his own packs to the ground.

"I don't," Fin agreed. "Wouldn't stop me from taking it back though."

***

They had to leave Cloud behind. The sound of those boots of hers would have been audible long before they came anywhere near the Top-sider camp. The moment it turned dark enough, Fin and Rab had left her. They didn't have far to walk before spotting fire glow. The Top-siders had chosen a good place to make camp, a nice expanse of level ground that was protected on three sides by low hills. Just off the side of the road, Rab found a depression where they'd be out of earshot but within seeing distance, thanks to the generous size of the Top-siders' fire. To combat the cold, Fin sat with his knees drawn up tightly and clutched to his chest. It wasn't long before Rab did the same.

"Has it occurred to you," Fin said in a whisper, "that we might be doing to them what they did to us last night."

"It occurred to me," Rab replied, shifting position to relieve the growing numbness in his feet. "But if it was them Cloud heard, then they must have decided we weren't any threat to them."

"Or too few in number to worry about."

"Maybe that," Rab conceded.

"They're well equipped. Better than we are and that cart of theirs must be full of wood. Otherwise they wouldn't be burning such a big fire."

He wished Fin hadn't mentioned the fire. Bad enough just looking at it. Knowing that there was warmth to be had such a short distance away could become maddening by the end of the long night.

"How many do you count?" Fin asked.

"Eight," Rab replied. "No children."

"Same here. That's kind of small to be the entire band, isn't it? Where's the rest? And where are the children?"

"In front of them," Rab suggested.

"Or behind *us*, Rab."

"Well," Rab said, shifting position once again, "either way, we're going to have to approach them. Find out what they're doing here."

After a long moment of silence, Fin spoke again.

"I'm guessing that's exactly want they'll want to know about us."

"And that," Rab replied, turning to Fin in the darkness, "is for you to answer because I'm still not entirely sure myself."

***

Cloud was jumping up and down on the spot when they joined her back at their camp, lee-side of the wind at the base of a gentle rise.

"Cold here all by myself," she said by way of explanation.

"Cold there with him," Rab replied with a touch to Cloud's shoulder as he made his way to his abandoned packs.

"So?" she called, chasing after Rab. "Isn't someone going to tell me?"

"Not a lot to tell," Rab answered and, unstrapping the largest of his packs, delved inside seeking food. "We counted eight of them—"

"Only eight," Cloud interrupted. "Isn't that too small?"

"That's what we thought," Rab said, dropping to the ground.

"What did they do all night?" Cloud asked, slipping down beside him. When Rab offered some of his food, she shook her head.

"Already eaten. Did any of them leave camp? Do anything unusual at all?"

Either his hearing had gone in the night or Cloud was speaking very softly.

"No," Rab said, halting with a piece of 'shroom loaf halfway to his mouth. "Why?"

Cloud glanced at Fin, who seemed more interested in the contents of his packs than anything Rab had to recount to Cloud.

"I heard that sound again last night," Cloud whispered.

"The bird?"

"No, the other," she told him. "That sound like someone walking around. At first I thought it was you or Fin coming back, but it wasn't."

"It wasn't anyone from the camp, either. No-one left it."

"You didn't maybe fall asleep?" she asked, inching closer. "Miss someone leaving?"

Rab shook his head. "Impossible."

"Then there's more of them," Cloud announced, confirming what he and Fin had already begun to suspect.

"When we saw how few of them there were," Rab said at last, "we more or less expected there might be. Better tell Fin." He started to get to his feet.

"Don't," Cloud asked.

"Why not? He already suspects it."

"I know. But Fin's grown too fond of that spear of his for my comfort. He's just as likely to act first then think later and start something someone else is better equipped to finish."

"He's the leader, Cloud, not me. You went with him."

"And I still think he's right. About coming south, I mean. It's just that when it comes to situations like this. . .well," she snapped, jumping to her feet. "It's why I wanted you to come along in the first place."

***

"Not like that," Fin grumbled, "like this."

He wrenched the spear from Cloud's hand and repositioned it, tip up.

Cloud cast Rab a 'see what I mean' glance that Fin clearly missed.

"You look like you're about to stir a cooking pot with it."

"Maybe I'd prefer to," Cloud shot back, plunging the end of the shaft into the ground by her feet. "I don't see why I have to take this anyway. They'll clearly see I don't know what I'm doing whether I hold the spear tip up or down."

"They don't know what they're doing, either, Abby," Fin reminded her. "Not really. They're new to using spears, too."

"Look at it this way, Cloud," Rab interrupted. "If you hold the tip up, you're not likely to stick it into your foot."

"And that," Cloud said, swinging the tip of the spear around to point it at Rab, "is the only good advice I've got from either of you so far."

"I agree." Stepping forwards, Rab took a careful hold of the tip of the spear to raise it back to its upright position. "I'm going with you."

"No," Cloud barked. "We've been through this. I go alone. They won't be so alarmed if they see a woman, but they could easily take the two of you for bounty hunters."

"You, too," Rab pointed out.

"Really?" Cloud stabbed the end of the spear into the ground once more. "Just how many female bounty hunters have you come across?"

"At least one," Rab replied, glancing at Fin.

"Well, Sunny was an exception," Cloud snapped. "You've said so yourself enough times."

Untrue. Rab rarely spoke of Sunny at all. If Cloud had learned anything about Sunny, it had been from Fin's limited experience.

"Let her go," Fin said. "We'll be right behind her. If anything happens—"

"We could easily be too late," Rab cautioned him.

"She'll have time. And so will they. With those boots of hers, they'll hear her coming long before she gets there. And we'll be watching. If it looks like something could go wrong, we'll call her back."

"And what exactly do you mean by 'wrong', Fin?"

"Shut up," Cloud shouted. "I know more about Top-siders than the both of you put together. This is the best way. Like Fin said, they'll hear me first, so they'll be sure to see me coming. I'll tell them who we are. What we're doing here. And I'll tell them about the two of you. That we have no intention of harming anyone."

"All well and good, Cloud. But what about *their* intentions?" Rab asked.

She patted the pack on her back, the only one she had elected to carry into the Top-sider camp. Rab was to shoulder the other for her. "They have a badly injured member of their party. I have the medicines they need. Purple mushrooms are considered poisonous top-side, Rab. You know that. Even if they've learned how to use it, they can't possibly have enough. Here." She thrust the spear towards Rab. "If there's anything that's going to make them suspicious of me, this is it."

Rab pushed the spear back towards her.

"And if Fin walks in with it later, they'll be convinced. You have to take it." He glanced towards Fin. "Or you have to leave it behind."

Predictably Fin just shook his head. For once, Rab welcomed Fin's obstinacy. Now that Fin had more or less mastered the weapon, Rab didn't really want to let it go.

"Fine," Cloud snarled, tightening her grip on the shaft of the spear. "I'll take it. Now can we get started? They'll get too far ahead of us if we don't get moving."

Fin led the way. Rab had been counting on the band of Top-siders to be advancing slowly, encumbered as they were with the cart, but it surprised him how soon Cloud drew up, claiming she could smell smoke. He smelled it then, too, and hurried to catch up with Fin, who hadn't even made it as far as the shallow depression they'd hidden in last night.

"They haven't broken camp," Rab explained to a startled Fin. "Their fire is still burning."

"Then something is wrong," Fin said, glancing ahead although the Top-sider camp had not yet come into sight. "Maybe that injured Top-sider has died."

"Or this is a far as they ever meant to go," Cloud suggested, walking up to join them.

Fin shot her a dry look. "Out here? In the middle of just more noth-ingness? I don't think so."

Rab turned to Cloud. "Fin's right but they're wasting fuel. If one of their party died, then they'd just bury him and move on. They wouldn't bother to keep a fire going."

"No they wouldn't," Cloud agreed and threw back the hood of her heavy coat. "So, I guess this is it then." She glanced at Rab. "They'll see I'm a woman this way," she explained pre-empting the question Rab was about to ask, then hefted Fin's spear. "Even if I do have to go in armed with this ludicrous thing."

Without further word, Cloud started off, leaving Rab divided in a battle between anxiety and guilt. He should never have let her go.

Fin took to pacing beside him. "We've got to get closer," he said at last. "If Abby gets in trouble—"

"Go," Rab said, "as quietly as you can," and started after Fin.

"I can see their camp now," Fin whispered shortly. "Abby's almost on it."

Rab saw it, too. . .a cluster of figures huddled on the flat ground about the fire, the cart with its low end tipped towards the fire, a mound of something beside it, and Cloud. . .drawing closer. Why hadn't the Top-siders heard her? Even from where he and Fin had stopped, Rab could hear every step she took and each tell-tale ping of her boots sent a new shiver of dread down his spine.

Suddenly one of the Top-siders rose up from the ground. They'd heard her all right but were only choosing the time to reveal it. When Rab saw what the Top-sider who'd stood held in his hand, he almost abandoned their plan and rushed forwards. Would have, probably, if Fin hadn't reached out to stop him.

"It's all right," Fin whispered. "He's just holding the spear. Same way Abby is. Got to expect that."

He should never have let her go! And both he and Fin should have thought more carefully about what they might be sending her into. He'd just assumed that the blood they'd found was from one of these Top-siders and that it had been spilled through some sort of injury. What if it was something else?

Sunny would never have acted so rashly. The first time she encountered Rab and learned he had a sick boy with him, what had she done? Backed away, of course, until Rab had told her that Stitch's fever was the result of a fall. But Rab and Fin, they had just sent Cloud into the unknown. And it was too late now to call her back. She'd moved so far away, he couldn't even hear her footsteps anymore. Still she walked on and that Top-sider had started walking towards her. Got to expect that, too, Rab reasoned. Best to keep her some distance from camp.

Cloud was the first of the two to stop, then she bent and placed something on the ground. The spear! Had she done it voluntarily or been ordered to do it? Rab would give a week's worth of 'shrooms to know.

"What's she doing?" Fin whispered anxiously.

"Showing good faith," Rab replied. At least he hoped that was why she'd abandoned her only defence.

Rab risked a brief glance away from Cloud towards the Top-sider camp. No one else had moved but it seemed to him that all eyes were on their leader. They, like he and Fin, seemed willing to wait it out for the moment, so he turned his attention back to Cloud. She and the Top-sider elder appeared to be talking. It bothered him that the Top-sider hadn't relinquished his spear the way Cloud had but, so far, he just kept holding it almost casually, much in the same manner Fin usually did. Suddenly Cloud raised her arm and pointed and there was no mistake she was pointing directly towards Fin and him. In an instant, Rab decided. He raised his arm in reply.

Immediately Fin turned on him. "What'd you do that for? Now they know exactly where we are."

"Don't see it matters much, Fin. All they've got to do is look."

"Yeah. . .but. . ." Fin began but didn't finish.

"She's coming back," Rab said. "Alone. I suggest we stay where we are 'til she gets here."

The moment she approached close enough for Rab to see her face clearly, he could tell that she was smiling. The ping-ping-ping of those boots preceded her and Rab never thought he'd feel grateful to hear that irritating sound.

"They've agreed to let us come in," Cloud called to them, "if we give them some of our medicines."

Top-side, even an enemy can become a friend under the right circumstances.

"But you two can't count," Cloud said on reaching them. "There are nine of them, not eight. There's an injured man in that cart of theirs." She handed the spear back to Fin and looked relieved to do it. "Ten really if you count the baby."

Rab exchanged a surprised glance with Fin. "They're travelling with an infant?"

"Seems so," Cloud replied, retrieving the second of her packs from Rab. "They didn't tell me as much but I heard it crying."

"Did you at least ask what they're doing here?"

"Look," Cloud said, sounding exasperated, "I didn't have time to get their entire story. I thought the faster I got you two to the fire, the better you'd like it. There are nine of them and, as far as I can tell, one baby. Three women and six men. As to what they're doing here, I'd suggest you ask them yourself."

"Then they're about three, maybe four family groups travelling together," Fin suggested.

"I'd say so," Cloud agreed. "I couldn't really see the rest of them all that well. But I didn't see any other children."

"Then it's just like we thought. That's probably not the whole band," Fin said, turning to Rab, who glanced briefly at Cloud.

No it probably wasn't, which posed a couple of worrying questions. Where were they now? And why hadn't they come forward to help the others with the injured man?

"I don't suppose you had time to find out how that Top-sider got injured?" Rab asked.

"No," Cloud answered with a shake of her head. "Why?"

"Just hoping it was an accident of some kind," Rab said, starting out ahead of them. "That's all."

He could hear Cloud's puzzled voice behind him.

"What's he mean by that?" she asked of Fin.

"Don't know for sure," Fin replied, "but I've got my suspicions."

Rab turned at the sound of Fin's footsteps.

"You're thinking whoever's lying in that cart might have some sort of disease, aren't you?"

"I don't know what to think, Fin, but it's too late now. We let Cloud walk into it and now she's walked back to us."

"I wish you'd thought about that before."

"So do I," Cloud informed Rab coldly as she passed.

When Fin made to stride out ahead of her, Rab called to him. "Fin, if you're going to walk out in front like that then you've got to give that spear of yours back to Cloud."

"Give it here," Cloud snapped and wrenched the spear from Fin's hand. "I hate this thing. All it's good for is killing."

Fin fell back and walked silently beside Rab who was agonising on what might happen when they reached the Top-sider camp. Sure he'd encountered any number of Top-sider bands during a decade of wandering the surface, but none quite like this one, and never in a place so remote. Before now every encounter had happened out on the wide plains and the Top-sider bands had been larger and, as a consequence, less inclined to be fearful. He lacked the look, skill and demeanour of a bounty hunter, something no Top-sider leader had failed to recognise within a few moments of their first meeting. He wasn't big enough; he wasn't bold enough; and he never travelled armed. . .not since the first year when he'd carried Sunny's rusted, defunct gun and found it more of a hindrance to shoulder than a reliable deterrent against any Top-sider with a mind to kill him. Then there was also his obvious lack of interest in all but one particular child, Gift, and the fact that, travelling as light and as far as he did, he was possessed of something useful to trade: information, which, for the sake of his skin, he freely offered. He could tell them where the wild mushrooms were flourishing best, whether a water supply had dried up, where they were most likely to encounter competition in the form of other Top-sider bands and where they weren't. But now, with this small band of Top-siders, Rab didn't know what to expect. All he, Fin and Cloud had to offer was a little of their medicine and all Rab could do was hope that such an offer would be enough.

The leader hadn't moved from the spot where Cloud had left him and it wasn't until he drew closer that Rab began to suspect the man was no ordinary leader. Rab had expected someone far older, but the Top-sider who stepped forwards to intercept them appeared hardly ten or so years older than Rab. Age was a difficult thing to determine in a Top-sider; constant exposure to the elements aged them swiftly, so, if anything, this

Top-sider could be even younger than he appeared. The hood of his coat was thrown back, revealing dark hair largely untouched by time, an angular face, which though lined, was not yet marred by the deeply incised grooves about the eyes and cheeks so common among a people whose constant companions were the wind, the cold, and the dust. The man's mouth was concealed behind an unkempt beard but his dark grey eyes betrayed no hint of suspicion or subterfuge. Rab's first impression was that he could trust this man and that alone put him on alert. Where Top-siders were concerned, it was better never to rely on first impressions.

"My name is Glint," the man said in a voice that bore the typical rasping of the nomadic Top-sider. "You're welcome to share our fire. But this woman, here," he glanced briefly towards Cloud, "says you have medicines that you're willing to offer in return."

Rab nudged Cloud's shoulder, a prompt for her to produce the stone-encrusted vial of purple mushroom extract Lilly had given her. For a moment, Rab thought Cloud hadn't understood until suddenly, thrusting the spear towards Fin, she bent to one knee, dropped her packs and began to rummage around inside one of them.

"We have medicines," Rab agreed, "and we'll do what we can to help you." He pointed towards Fin. "I'm Rab. This is Fin and the woman's name is Cloud."

The Top-sider's grey eyes narrowed and his hand tightened around the shaft of his spear. "She said her name was Abby."

"It's both," Cloud explained, glancing up. "I lived top-side for many years. He's the only one calls me Cloud. Here it is," she said, rising, and made to pass the vial of extract to the Top-sider. "You can test it if you like but be very sparing, too much of it will kill you."

The Top-sider, Glint, declined to take the vial. "You have medicines that powerful with you?" he asked, sounding surprised.

Cloud glanced briefly towards Rab before responding. "It's purple mushroom extract. I thought that most Top-. . .I mean people who lived on the surface had heard about it even if they didn't have the means to make the extract."

The man's eyes crinkled slightly about the corners. "Yes, we've heard of it. And we've heard the term Top-siders before, too."

"I'm sorry," Cloud hurried to explain. "I didn't mean to be rude. It's just that. . .well, I was born a tunnel person and it's a while since I've lived on the surface, so I speak like a tunnel person."

The Top-sider nodded. "Heard of them, too. Never seen one."

"Actually Fin and I aren't strictly tunnel people," Rab interrupted. "We were both village born. I think you know the place." He nodded towards the fire. "It's where I suspect all that fire wood of yours might have come from."

The Top-sider stiffened. "Then you've really come to claim what you consider to be rightfully yours."

Rab shook his head. "No. That village and everything in it hasn't been ours for a very long time. You found it. It's yours. But I would like to know what you're doing so far south."

"I could ask you the same question, young man," the elder replied.

Rab glanced at Fin who wisely remained mute.

"Yes, you could," Rab said, looking back at the elder. "Seems we're agreed then. We have the same initial questions, but very different immediate problems. It's been many days since we've been able to have a fire. We need it and you need the medicines we have. If you take us to your injured comrade—"

"Only the woman, Abby," Glint interrupted. "His wife will only allow her to see to Staunch."

Rab looked over at Cloud, curious if she was already aware of the arrangement. Judging by the furrow that had suddenly appeared across her brow, it didn't seem so.

"That's fine," she said before Rab had the chance to say anything. "I'll go now," she suggested, "if that's all right with you?"

Glint pointed towards the cart on the other side of the fire. "He's there. His wife's name is Dee. The woman with her is Poppy, Staunch's mother. They're expecting you."

Cloud hurried off, vial of purple mushroom extract in one hand, her packs in the other.

"Dee doesn't entirely trust you," Glint explained.

Top-sider candour. It was something Rab was accustomed to. Fin wasn't. Rab placed a hand to Fin's spear arm just in case the young man took it in his head to respond.

"Understandable," Rab agreed. "Nor do we trust you entirely as you'd expect."

"Of course," Glint agreed and ushered them towards the fire. "Please. Warm yourselves. We have food to share."

Rab shook his head. "That isn't necessary. We have enough for now."

"You harvested the 'shrooms?" Glint asked, walking abreast of Rab and leaving Fin to follow behind.

"Did you intend to harvest them yourselves on the way back?" Rab asked, conceding it probably wasn't the most subtle attempt he'd ever made to wring information out of someone, but it seemed to work.

"No," Glint replied freely. "Until this happened," he nodded towards the cart and its injured cargo, "we had no intention of going back. Now though? Who can say?"

Rab cast a glance behind, checking on Fin. "What happened to your friend?" he asked, turning back to the Top-sider.

After a long pause the Top-sider replied. "I suppose there's little point trying to hide anything. You must have seen them, too. Those things that appear at dawn?"

"The birds," Fin said at their backs.

Glint stopped walking and turned to the young man. "You know what they are? You've seen them before?"

"No," Rab answered, garnering Glint's attention, "to both questions. Might be birds, but whatever they are, one of them nearly took Cloud's head off."

Glint nodded. "I'm afraid we underestimated them, too. Staunch killed one of them—"

"With that spear you've got in your hand?" Fin prompted. "The tip's broken. We came across the broken end of a spear among the remains of one of those things."

Glint glanced towards the tip of Fin's spear. "And the tip of your spear is undamaged. I'm guessing you haven't made a kill yet."

"Not yet," Fin agreed. "But your Staunch made the tip of his spear too thin. Mine won't break."

Again the skin around the Top-siders eyes creased. "Those birds as you call them are tougher than you might think. Have you had a chance to look at their feet?"

"Their feet?" Fin shot a glance at Rab. "No. Not really. What about their feet?"

"They have claws, young friend. Very sharp claws. Sharper than that spear tip of yours," he said, nodding again towards the weapon in Fin's hand. "If you come across one again, I'd advise you to be exceptionally careful. Staunch wasn't and got himself gutted for his carelessness. He can't survive."

Instinctively Rab's hand went to the Top-sider's forearm. "If you know that, then why—"

"Did I allow you into our camp? I've already told you. We need your medicines."

"For someone else?"

The Top-sider shook his head. "For Staunch. To ease his pain. We didn't suspect you'd have purple mushroom extract with you though. It's a stroke of good fortune for us but mostly for Staunch, of course."

"You're not suggesting what I think you are?" Rab exclaimed.

"What's he suggesting?" Fin asked, clearly growing suspicious.

"What you do with your medicines is up to you. We simply ask that you do what you can for Staunch."

"No, I'm sorry. Cloud will do her best but I'm afraid you'll have to rely on time alone and, if it's as bad as you say, then you won't have to wait too long."

"Likely not," Glint agreed. "But to watch someone suffer that way—"

"Then use that spear of yours if you have to but you can't ask us to. . .no, I'm sorry. We can't. He's of your people. Not ours."

Rab strode off towards the fire, with Fin hard on his heels.

"Is he seriously asking Abby to—"

"Stop," Rab snarled. "Right there. I *don't* want to hear it."

No! Not twice in a lifetime! Wasn't once more than enough? He wouldn't do it. And he wouldn't let Cloud do it, either.

Rab had his packs off long before he got to the fire. When he reached it, he dumped them to the ground, startling Glint's already wary comrades and sparking a fountain of embers from the fire. He looked over the bright yellow and red flames towards Cloud, the cart and the two women, who sat silently on the ground, backs turned. Neither of the women appeared to have noticed his abrupt arrival and, if Glint were telling the truth, the man in the cart was too far gone to have been disturbed.

Chapter 10

"IT'S bad, Rab. Really bad," Cloud said, lowering herself to the ground beside him. "I can't fix it. I don't think even Ruby could."

"Don't waste your time trying," Rab told her. "They know it already."

"What's that supposed to mean?" she asked as she tightened the straps about one of her packs.

"That's why they wanted our medicines, Cloud. It didn't have anything to do with saving him, but. . ."

Rab stopped talking when the woman, the one who had the baby slung in some sort of pouch arrangement across her back. . .he thought she said her name was Sandy. . .came towards them from the opposite side of camp. She passed a handful of food to Cloud, then turned around and wordlessly walked back towards Glint and the clutch of Top-siders who had gathered around Fin. Rab hoped he was doing more than expounding on the virtues of his spear the way it appeared. He should be gathering information.

"There's two!" Cloud said, sounding surprised as she gazed after the woman.

"Two what?"

"Babies," Cloud replied, looking back at Rab. "There's another one sleeping over by the cart."

"Guess Fin and I aren't the only ones who can't count."

Cloud's attention turned to the food in her hand. "What's this?"

"She brought some for me earlier," Rab said, showing Cloud what was sitting on the top of one of his packs. "I haven't tried it yet."

"Not hungry," she said. "Not after what I just saw. How do you know they think he can't be saved?"

"Glint just about said so."

"Then what do they expect of us, Rab?" she asked, placing her food beside Rab's on his pack. "Why did they allow us in?"

"They want us to use our medicines to finish him."

"Oh." Cloud was silent for a long time before she spoke again. "Then I think that's what we should do."

"No. I won't allow it."

"*You* won't allow it? Rab, you can't tell me what to do."

"Then I'm asking you, Cloud. I'm giving you the best advice I can. If you do it, you'll regret it every moment for the rest of your life."

"I'll regret it more if I don't do *something*, Rab. You can't say how I'm going to feel. You don't have that right. You can't even know how *you'd* feel if. . ." Suddenly Cloud hesitated. "Or maybe you can."

Rab didn't answer.

"I always suspected you were hiding something," Cloud said soberly. "You should have told us."

"Why? It wouldn't have made a bit of difference. Sunny asked me to do it and I did it." He reached out to grab one of Cloud's packs. "Where's that vial? In this one?"

Cloud wrenched the pack out of his hands. "You can't have it. I'm still using it."

"Then promise you'll only give him enough to make him comfortable."

Cloud let out an exasperated-sounding breath. "Rab, all the medicine in the world wouldn't be enough to make him comfortable. He's suffering terribly."

"Promise me."

She didn't get the chance.

"You haven't tried our food," someone said.

Rab looked over his shoulder and found Glint standing there.

"We have our own, Glint. You should save this for yourselves."

"There's more where that came from," Glint replied, pointing with the broken tip of his spear towards Rab's pack. "Try it," he prompted.

Rab took the morsel of food from the top of his pack. The thought occurred to him that these Top-siders might just have it in mind to poison them and simply take the vial of vital medicine. But they'd heard of purple mushroom extract and anyone who'd heard about it would have known that administering it correctly was a delicate balancing act. It took just the right amount to cut the pain; a little too much would kill you; a lot too much just made you violently ill. These Top-siders wouldn't know enough about the stuff to get the balance right. For that matter, he wasn't even sure Cloud did.

Rab took a bite of the food. At first he found it tough and quite bitter, but thought he could soon adjust to the unfamiliar taste.

"Your young friend has developed quite a liking for our meat," Glint said, nodding towards Fin who was still spiritedly talking with the others.

"Meat?" Cloud retrieved her share of the food from Rab's pack. "Is that what this is?" She took a bite, screwed up her face, and passed the remainder to Rab. "It's very strong," she said, working on the piece in her mouth. "Couldn't eat much of it."

"It takes some getting used to," Glint agreed.

"How long will it keep?" Rab asked, examining the half-eaten chunk in his hand.

"Staunch killed it some days ago and it's still good."

"My bird," Cloud said soberly, eyes focused on the meat in Rab's hand.

Rab ignored her. "You said there's more. Are you planning to kill another?"

"With the help of your young friend. He's going to show us how to make a better spear tip. One that won't break so easily."

So Fin hoped. He was hardly an expert. In the back of his mind, Rab wondered if it was such a good thing for Fin to do, but then quickly dismissed any fears. Today! Tomorrow! The Top-siders would soon hone their craft, with or without Fin's assistance.

"You've seen Staunch," Glint said, turning to Cloud. "What do you think?"

Cloud glanced briefly at Rab while she hesitated. "It's not good," she said finally, rising to her feet to answer the elder. "There isn't much I can do."

"You can't save him," Glint said although it was clear to Rab that he wasn't pressing Cloud for an answer.

She shook her head just the same.

"Then you'll understand if I go and sit with his mother and wife for a while."

"Wish he wouldn't carry that spear around with him all the time," Rab said once Glint had walked out of earshot.

"I should go back, too," Cloud said.

When she reached down to retrieve one of her packs, Rab caught a hold of her wrist.

"Promise," he said.

Cloud slipped her hand free and gathered the pack from the ground. "All right. I'll only give him enough to cut the pain some. But I don't agree with you, Rab. I don't think I'll ever agree with you about this."

Rab didn't care whether she agreed with him now or ever; all he wanted was her promise. He knew she'd keep it.

Half-heartedly, Rab finished off the meat. Food was food. Besides, there was little else for him to do but rest and eat. Cloud was employing what skills she had with the injured Top-sider. Fin was busy with what was fast becoming a favoured occupation: weapon making. But rest was the last thing on his mind. Lowering his head into his hands, he propped his elbows on raised knees. The heat from the fire felt good on the top of his head. He heard someone move towards him but didn't look up, not even when he sensed them sit down beside him. This was the Top-siders' fire; if anyone had a right to its warmth. . .

"So Top-sider. . ."

It was a woman's voice; perhaps Sandy had come back.

". . . still chasing after that launch pad?"

Rab's head shot up.

He'd fallen asleep; he hadn't meant to. Wasn't even aware that he'd done it but it was the only explanation.

"You're not seeing things," the woman said, lifting the corners of her mouth ever so slightly as she looked directly into his face. "It's me."

That didn't help him a lot.

"Gift," the woman said quite casually.

No. That wasn't possible. He had to be dreaming. He'd done enough of that over the last ten years—dreamed he'd found Gift—alive and safe and waiting for him—and then woken to find it just wasn't so. But he wasn't dreaming this time. He could see that now. This wasn't the Gift of his dreams. The Gift of his dreams had remained that same little girl, never aged. The woman sitting on the ground beside him was all grown up. She was older. Of course, she was older. Ten years older. But it was her. Gift of the round dark, knowing eyes. Gift of the soft voice and the gentle ways. She threw back the hood of her coat and revealed the long, black hair he so well remembered. It had always seemed to be in such a mess; now it was tidy and tended.

"How have you been, Rab?"

The question just sounded ridiculous.

"I. . ." he began but couldn't seem to finish. The words wouldn't come. The thoughts wouldn't come.

"I didn't know it was you until your friend happened to say your name. She can't help Staunch, but I understand. Is she a healer?"

Rab's thoughts seemed to be all jumbled up. He'd once watched Cloud untangle a dense knot of threads, seen her grow progressively more frustrated as she'd been forced to slowly pull and pluck and cautiously work her way through the snarl. That's just how he felt now—frustrated that he couldn't seem to pull on the right thread to untangle the snarl of thoughts inside his head. At last something gave and he realised who Gift was talking about.

"Cloud? No. She's a reweaver. . .mostly."

"Oh."

Of its own accord, another thread fell loose.

"But you know her," Rab said quickly. "At least you did once. She was one of the captives Sunny paid for that day. Remember?"

"Oh yes," Gift said. "She said her name was Abby. But I see. And Sunny? Whatever happened to Sunny? Did she die like we thought she would?"

"Yes, she died," Rab replied after a little hesitation.

"Before you reached the launch pad?"

"Before then," he agreed.

"So you never found one?"

"No, I. . .Gift, I looked for you everywhere. I've never stopped looking."

She shook her head. "You shouldn't have wasted your life like that, Rab. I stopped looking for you a long time ago. Oh, at first I hoped you'd come for me but. . .well," she fell silent for some time, ". . . after a while, there didn't seem much reason to hope any longer. These people treated me well. They took care of me. I found friends. Other people to care about." Her focus flicked briefly towards the cart across the fire. "Do you remember the day we came across them? These Top-siders?" she asked, looking back at Rab.

Of course he remembered.

"There was a boy. He gave me a blue stone."

"I remember," Rab replied faintly.

"That was Staunch."

"And now you're one of them," he said. "And you've been with them all this time?"

She nodded. "From the very first. They gave me a new name, of course. Defiance. But I haven't been called that for a long time. Now it's just Dee."

Rab felt like he should reach out and hold her, find some words, any words to comfort her. He couldn't do either.

"I'm sorry," he said at last.

"About Staunch?"

"About everything. That I left you behind in the roost that day. That I wasn't good enough on the surface to find you. That Staunch. . ."

"That's just how things are, Rab." The corners of her mouth lifted again. "Let's not talk about it anymore. I want to know about Stitch and Fin. I haven't spoken to Fin yet but Glint says he's going to show us how to make better weapons. But where is Stitch? Did you leave him behind in the tunnels? And what are you doing down here anyway? It's a long way from the city."

He could lie but what was the point? She'd find out soon enough from Fin.

"Stitch is dead, Gift."

To his ears, the news had sounded terribly blunt, but the expression of Gift's face didn't alter. Why should she be surprised? After all, it was just another promise he'd failed to keep.

"There was an accident in the crop fields where he was working. One of the carts they use to haul the 'shroom crops overturned. He was trapped beneath it."

"Then it was quick?" she asked.

"It was quick," Rab agreed.

"That's good. And Fin?"

Rab shrugged. "Fin is Fin. When Stitch died, I wasn't sure what he'd do, how he'd react. But it was his idea to travel south. He wanted to find out what was out here."

At that, the expression on Gift's face did seem to shift. She seemed. . .well, confused.

"Then you didn't come after those flying things? Your friend, Abby, called them birds. But they don't look like birds to me. I remember those pictures in that book the old man showed us. It's why *we're* here. We've been following them."

"No, we never actually saw one until we reached the forest. Was that your camp fire there? Had to be."

"Yes it was ours. And we went to the village, too. In fact we've been going there for years. I'm afraid we stripped it. There's little left now."

"Doesn't matter," Rab said with a shake of his head. "We won't be going back." At least if Fin gets his way, Rab added silently. "So it was your people who buried the dead in the village?"

"Those that weren't already buried. But that was a long time ago, Rab."

"I don't understand. You must have known where you were. Why did you never try to escape and make it back to the tunnels?"

"They didn't take *me* on their scavenging trips, Rab. Not until much later. And then there didn't seem to be a reason to run away. Besides, I kept remembering those girls, the ones those bounty hunters brought back. Your friend Abby, there. How scared and frightened they looked. And I did try to escape at first. But we kept moving around and I never really knew where I was. The first time I escaped, the elders came and found me. The second time, I found my way back to them by myself. After that, I never tried to run again. And after a while, I didn't want to. I had Staunch, Glint, Poppy, and the rest. Why would I run away from them?"

For him!

But why should she?

"I'm glad you found a home, Gift. Even if it's not the one we planned together."

"It was such a silly thing to do," she said with another smile. "To go looking for something that never actually existed." She shrugged. "But we weren't to know. Now I guess we both do. There's no launch pad. Never was. Sunny was right all along."

Oh yes, Sunny was right.

"So you and these others," Rab said, gesturing towards the Top-siders who were still talking with Fin across the camp, "you're part of a scavenging party?"

Gift's head tipped to one side. "We're all of it. There's no one else."

"But. . ." Rab began to say then hesitated.

Would she lie? A regular Top-sider might, but not Gift. Still when all was said and done, Gift was a regular Top-sider now. Her loyalties would be to them, not to Rab, and he knew from experience how fierce her loyalty could be.

"I'm not lying," she said.

Seemed she hadn't lost the ability to read him all too easily.

"The rest of my people are far to the north-west of here, waiting for us to return." She pointed past Rab into the distance. "We were heading east and, if it hadn't been for those flying things, would never have turned south. Staunch thought if he could just bring one down, we could find out if they were good enough to eat. Well, he did. And they are. But he paid the price to find out." She glanced across the camp site. "If Fin can show us how to make a weapon that won't break, perhaps we can still hunt them."

"How many have you seen?" Rab asked, loathe to share his concerns about Fin's proficiency with such a weapon. He hadn't been tested yet.

"Not sure," Gift replied. "Could just be the same one we kept seeing all the time. But we don't think so. Staunch is certain there are more and, since every time we've seen them, they're heading south, then," she added with a shrug, "that's where the rest of them have to be. And you? How many have you seen?"

"Never more than one at a time."

Gift fell silent a moment. "You don't suppose Staunch killed the only one?"

"I hope not," Rab replied.

He didn't have much of a liking for the strange-tasting meat and evidently Cloud had none at all. But no Top-sider, villager, or tunnel-dweller was in the position to turn their backs on food simply on account of its unappealing flavour.

"Your elder, Glint, said the thing's claws alone were responsible for Staunch's injuries. Is that true?"

"For his worst injuries. Yes. There are some marks about his face and neck that look like bites, but they're nothing in comparison to. . ." She didn't finish.

Rab thought twice about saying anything more but then decided that it was highly unlikely the matter hadn't already been raised with Gift.

"Glint thinks something should be done to help Staunch. And he wants us to do it. Is that what you want, too?"

She nodded.

"I'm sorry, Gift, but we can't. It's not our responsibility. Glint's your elder, not Fin, Cloud or me. It's his responsibility. He has that spear. It's still good enough to. . ." Rab left the rest unsaid.

"Yes, I suppose he could do it. But we'd be asking him to kill his son, Rab."

His son? Rab hadn't stopped to consider that Glint might be the young man's father.

"And as elder, it *is* his responsibility. But he doesn't have the heart to do it and if he can't, he can't ask anyone of us to do it for him."

"I'm sorry, Gift," Rab said again. "I truly am. But you have to understand I can't ask Fin or Cloud to do it, either."

She looked into his eyes a long time before answering. "I know," she said simply.

No! She couldn't do this to him. It wasn't fair. Not after all the years he'd spent looking for her. Not after all the promises he'd made. Not after all he'd done. . .and hadn't done. . .to keep his word to both her and to Sunny.

The long moment of silence was broken by the sound of a child's crying.

Gift's attention shifted abruptly towards the cart and the figures standing about it.

"I have to go," she said, rising to her feet. "That's my baby. Mine and Staunch's," she explained. "Poppy's been looking after her." Gift made to hurry off but stopped almost immediately and turned around. "Her name is Sunny," she said, offering Rab a self-conscious smile. "I know it's kind of strange, considering what I thought about her and all. But well," she added with a shrug, "Sunny saved my life and I felt I owed her for that."

Just what the world needed: another Sunny.

Rab didn't know what to say but then Gift didn't give him long to think about it. Quickly she took the few steps back to where he was seated, dropped to the ground in front of him, and wrapped her arms lightly about his neck.

"I'm sorry about Stitch. I truly am," she said against his neck. "But three saved out of four, Rab. It's better than Blaze could ever have hoped for and I should never have forced you to make that promise." Her hold tightened just a little. "I'm *so* happy to see you again and to know that you've found someone."

With that, she released him and bounded back onto her feet. She was halfway back to her baby before Rab managed to absorb all she'd said.

His promise. The one she'd wheedled him into making. The one to save Stitch above the rest of them. Damn it! He had tried. It wasn't his fault Stitch had got himself crushed beneath a 'shroom cart. But Gift was right about Blaze, their elder. When she had made that bargain with Rab to allow him to have food for his journey if he'd agree to take Fin, Gift and Stitch with him, even Blaze hadn't anticipated a good outcome. He'd argued with her, of course, begged her to accept that they couldn't last the journey and were better off in the village, but she'd countered with the more credible reply: *'they won't last here, either'*. And they wouldn't have lasted; if nothing else, by coercing him into returning to their village, at least Fin had proved that to him.

As to having found someone, Rab guessed Gift was mistakenly referring to Cloud.

"These Top-siders want me to show them how to make better spear tips."

Rab's head snapped around; he hadn't heard Fin coming up beside him.

"We figure we can strip the cart down to half its size, save some of the metal from the straps," he said, dropping to the ground by Rab. "The wood they took from our village is running out and once that Top-sider is dead, they won't need it to—"

Rab placed a hand to Fin's shoulder to stop him from saying more. "What?"

"That Top-sider is Gift's husband," he said.

The expression on Fin's face shifted slowly from one of surprise to disbelief.

"No," he said, "you must be wrong. That can't be."

Rab directed Fin's attention to the cart. "The woman I was talking to—the one who's now holding the baby. It's Gift."

Fin made to jump to his feet but Rab immediately pulled him back down to the ground.

"Leave her be, Fin. For now. There'll be time later."

"But. . ." Fin started to say, then slowly began shaking his head. "How?" he asked.

Rab set about telling Fin all that Gift had told him, anticipating that Fin's interest would be most roused when it came to the Top-siders' experience with the 'birds'. He was right. By the end of their talk, Fin was convinced that the things could be safely killed and that he was the person who could do it.

"Probably just what Staunch thought," Rab warned him.

***

Cloud spent most of the day tending to the dying Staunch. Neither Glint nor Gift made another trip across the camp site and Poppy hadn't left her son's side since the three of them had arrived. Matters weren't going well. Over and over again, Rab willed the young man to die, but all the wishing in the world wasn't going to make it happen any faster. Death took its own course and Staunch must have been a very strong man.

Sometime in the mid-afternoon, Fin and three of the Top-sider men left camp. Rab didn't know what they were doing or where they had gone. Looking for more evidence of those flying things, most likely. Or scavenging. Either way, they'd found a better and more productive occupation than he had. Waiting and watching. It wasn't something Rab did well. When Cloud eventually came walking towards him, he hoped that she'd bring good news. He hoped that young Staunch had died.

"Is it over?" he asked the moment Cloud sat down beside him.

She shook her head. Even though the little light they had was fading, Rab could clearly see the lines of fatigue in her face. The skin beneath her eyes looked dark; if he hadn't known better, he'd have sworn it was bruised.

She brushed her dark hair back from her face and leaned her head into Rab's shoulder.

"They're going to use up all their wood this way," she said. "But he's cold, Rab. So very cold. And worst thing of all, he's conscious. He knows he's dying. He knows it's been a long time. And he knows that they've only kept the fire going because of him. He's begged them to put it out, but Glint won't. And now that night is coming, they can't."

"Can't you knock him out?" Rab asked, raising a hand to brush Cloud's tangled hair.

"It's hard to know how much I can give him with his innards ripped up and open that way. What I've been doing doesn't seem to have worked—"

"And I suppose Glint has been after you again," he said, interrupting her.

"No. He hasn't said another word about it. You told him the way it was going to be and he's accepted it. At least, it seems so."

"You're angry with me still, aren't you?" Rab asked after a moment.

"I'm not angry with you, Rab. I just believe you're wrong. And I think I always will."

Rab had a hard time convincing Cloud to eat the dried 'shrooms he'd retrieved from his pack and when Sandy, the silent Top-sider woman, who must have been watching them from her crouched position on the opposite side of the fire, approached, offering some of their meat, Cloud politely refused it. Still Rab was relieved that he managed to get anything down Cloud at all and, when he set up some bedding, this time accepted from the hands of Sandy, Cloud quickly fell into a fitful sleep. Her tossing and turning ensured Rab didn't sleep. . .that and knowing what he had to do.

It was still very dark when he sat up beside Cloud. Perhaps not even midnight yet. He'd passed the time watching that same old tiny star overhead. Except for a feeble kind of cry coming from the direction of the cart, the camp was silent. The fire was blazing; someone had already stoked it, so if he moved fast enough, there was little likelihood he'd be observed. A little way off, Rab could see Fin asleep; he'd come back into camp without Rab's knowledge. As quietly as he could Rab felt around for Cloud's pack. She heard him.

"What are you looking for?" she whispered.

"Just tell me how much," Rab whispered back.

He could feel Cloud's hand brush his in the darkness. The pack was slipped from his grasp and shortly, in its stead, he felt something hard and small placed into the palm of his hand.

"Half what's left," Cloud said faintly.

Her fingers wrapped around his, closing them over the vial.

"I should do it," she said.

When she started to rise, Rab gently pushed her back to the ground.

"What you should do is say nothing. Now or ever," Rab said and eased himself onto his feet.

He crossed the camp without making a sound; he hadn't spent years and years on the surface without learning some useful tricks. He'd intentionally approached the cart on the side where all the goods they had scavenged from his village had been offloaded, opposite the spot where Glint, Poppy and Gift with her baby were sleeping. At least they appeared to be sleeping and that soft mewling sound that Rab assumed must have been the baby had stopped. He tried to take little notice of the face and the condition of the man who was lying inside the cart with his head tilted towards the high end. But the smell of the young man's opened intestines was impossible to ignore and his eyes were open, reflecting the light of the fire. Rab hadn't seen Sunny's eyes when he'd shot her. He desperately wished he hadn't seen this young man's eyes now.

Rab held up the vial, brought it close to Staunch's face and the light that had previously been reflected in Staunch's eyes shone now in the tiny blue eyes of the little creature that adorned the surface of the vial.

The young man nodded, though it clearly pained him immensely to make even that small gesture. After he removed the cap, Rab glanced towards the young man again, relieved to see that something had changed in his tortured eyes. In them, Rab saw peace, acceptance. . .perhaps gratitude. Had he been able to look into Sunny's eyes, was that what he'd have seen there, too?

Rab tipped the entire contents of the vial into his palm, angled his hand towards the fire light to separate out half, then returned the remainder to the vial. He found a canteen of water by Staunch's shoulder and then finished what he'd come across the camp to do.

Staunch swallowed, thankfully not too uneasily, and then closed his eyes.

Rab didn't know how long it would take the extract to work. Not too long, he hoped, and Staunch appeared to have attained some measure of peace already, so Rab decided to slip away. As he turned away from the cart, he caught another flash of light from the irises of someone eyes. He had been watched by someone lying on the ground. Rab just kept walking but halfway back to Cloud he glanced around. Someone was now leaning over the cart, a figure too short to be Glint. Rab's guess was that it was Gift but he didn't want to know.

Chapter 11

RAB woke with a start. Someone was shaking him roughly. He had no recollection of falling asleep, and the fact that it was such a dreamless sleep surprised him. It was not what he would have expected after he'd returned to Cloud, leaving the cart and its pitiful cargo behind.

"You should get up now, Rab."

He stirred and found Cloud hunched over him. At least he'd spared her the anguish of having to release Staunch. If he'd done little else right in his life, at least he'd done that.

"Everyone else left long ago."

Her words hit like a thump in the chest.

"Left?" he shouted, bolting upright.

"To bury Staunch," she explained. "Glint discovered him dead early this morning."

No. He hadn't. Someone, probably Gift, had already known Staunch was dead long before that.

"Then your guess about the dosage was correct, Cloud."

"Yeah," she agreed with a nod. "Good for me. Come on." She gave Rab's arm a tug. "The fire has been put out but there's still a little warmth left in it. You should eat something now. They'll be back soon."

Rab looked around and, just as Cloud had told him, found they were alone. "Where did they take him?"

"I don't know," Cloud replied, dragging Rab onto his feet. "Fin went but we weren't invited."

"What do you mean 'weren't invited'?"

Cloud shrugged and bent to gather one of her packs.

"I tried to help him," she said as, together, they started towards the dead fire. "You did. I guess they consider our part done."

Rab pulled up abruptly, his impulse to think Gift had told them. "Then they know what I did last night?"

"No one has said as much, but Rab, they did ask us to do it," Cloud replied as she dropped to the ground close to the smouldering embers and motioned for Rab. "You've got to expect them to think one of us did."

"This isn't any Top-sider behaviour I've ever encountered before," Rab said, joining her on the ground.

"Me, either." Cloud opened her pack and began to delve inside it. "They're nothing like the people I lived with." She shrugged again, clearly as lost for any better explanation as Rab was. "Maybe they really are different."

"Not different enough to refuse Sunny's offer of Gift in exchange for some measly clothes."

Cloud's face collapsed into a frown as she offered him a handful of dried 'shrooms. "What are you talking about?"

Rab hesitated but finally took the food from her hand. "I thought you knew. I mean, you were with Staunch's family for a long time. I just assumed—"

"Assumed what?" Cloud pressed him, inching closer.

"Staunch's wife. . .Dee. She's Gift."

If he'd told her the sun was shining, clear, bright and visible in the sky above, Cloud couldn't have looked more startled.

"How did you find out?" she finally asked.

"She told me," Rab explained. "Walked over and told me. Just like that. As though all those years between never happened." He looked at the parcel of dried 'shrooms Cloud had given him and indifferently began to eat.

"Oh." Cloud studied her hands in her lap for a long time before she looked at Rab again. "No one told *me*. Now what?"

"Now nothing," Rab said. He was having a hard time of it. . .getting the dry breakfast down. "These are her people now. She said so."

"Then I think they must be yours, too, Rab. Now that you've found her."

"That wouldn't be a happy arrangement, Cloud," Rab replied with a forced smile. "Considering our past history."

"Yeah. I guess not." Cloud started drawing little circles in the dirt with a stick she found lying on the ground. "Fin and I had a long talk before you woke up this morning. He wants to stay with these people. He intended to tell you about it when they got back. Sorry," she said, glancing across at Rab, "if I've ruined the surprise."

Rab had more or less expected it what with Fin's offer to help the Top-siders rejig the cart and hone their spear-making. "Then I suppose you'll stay, too. It's for the best. You're young. You're healthy. They won't—"

"Oh no," Cloud snarled, cutting him off. "You're not going to get away with that. I'm not going to be some sort of breeder for these people, Rab. I don't care how different they are to the ones I grew up with. I won't."

"But what about Fin? Back in the tunnels, he said—"

"What about him? I told you he wants to stay. I don't."

Rab shook his head. "I suppose it doesn't matter what Fin said. I still think you should stay, Cloud. These people haven't been any threat to you."

"These? No. But these are just their scouts. Sooner or later they'll go back, or the others will catch up."

"All right, all right. We'll think of something. They already think you're a healer. That's got to make you important to them in other ways than just being a breeder."

"Until my supplies run out. I don't know what we might find if we go on, Rab. I only know that this isn't what I came south with Fin to find. You've found what you've been looking for all these years. And Fin," she glanced in the direction of the wasteland where Fin and the band of Top-siders had wandered off to bury Staunch, "he's found something, too. But I don't want to live like a Top-sider again and I won't. You were right, Rab. . .about the Top-siders I lived with. As soon as I tasted that meat from that bird thing, I knew it. I've eaten meat before and it didn't come from any flying thing."

"But these Top-siders aren't like that," he said, trying his best to reason with her. "That meat they gave us *is* from an animal."

"And they're going to go on killing them and eating them, aren't they? And what happens when they can't find any more?"

All Rab could do was shake his head again. "I don't know, Cloud. But if you want to leave Fin with them and go on alone together, then that's what we'll do."

"You'd leave Gift?" she asked, sounding doubtful.

"We left each other a long time ago."

Cloud's mood began to lift. "Then you're willing to continue going south the way we planned. Just you and me? Together?"

"If that's what you want," Rab told her soberly. "But remember these Top-siders will continue south, too, at least for a while and it's possible we'll meet up with them again."

"But they'll have that cart of theirs to drag. They'll be moving slowly. Rab, this is what I want. It's what I wanted all along. And who knows? Maybe we might even find that launch pad after all?" she suggested.

No. They'd never do that.

Rab tried his best to smile. "I thought you didn't believe in launch pads."

"I'm not sure I ever believed in flying animals, either, but they're here. And so was that bridge. And maybe further south, there's something else. Other plants like the ones we found by the river. Plants we can eat. Other animals, too, maybe."

Oh, Rab was sure there were other animals; they'd already been visited by at least one of them, hadn't they? Cloud seemed to have forgotten all about what she'd heard the other night—that rustling sound like someone walking nearby. It hadn't been a Top-sider. Rab believed what Gift had told him; the rest of her people were far away. But whatever it was seemed to have been more curious than hostile. Still before they set out again, Rab intended to have Fin show him how to make an effective spear. Cloud wouldn't like it, but, as far as Rab was concerned, that was just too bad. He wasn't taking another step south without one.

"They're coming back," Cloud said, getting to her feet. "They're going to strip down the cart now. At least that's what Fin told me." She glanced at the now empty cart behind her. "He says it'll be easier to pull at half the size and he'll be able to use some of the wood and metal to make more spears. Do you think they'll let us take something?" she asked, turning back to Rab. "I mean a lot of it did come from your village."

Rab struggled onto his feet. "We can ask but I wouldn't count on it. They found it; they took it. It's just how it goes."

"Yes," Cloud replied, bending to gather her pack. "I remember."

✳✳✳

Fin had reacted badly at first when Cloud told him of her decision. If Rab had been forced to put a name to it, he'd have said that Fin looked wounded. Or perhaps it was simply that Cloud's resolve to leave Glint's band had left him briefly unsure about his own resolve to stay. But in the end, he had accepted Cloud's choice and even gifted Rab his spear, claiming he intended to make a better one from the waste material off the rejigged cart. It was left to Cloud to offer a suitable gift in return. . .half their remaining supply of purple mushroom extract. . .a generous half, though she did keep the little vial it was contained in.

"I can't take this," Fin protested. "Your mother gave it to you. She wanted you to have it."

"And now I want you to have it," Cloud countered, pressing the pouch Sandy had found for her firmly into the palm of Fin's hand. "Anyway, it's long past time you knew since it doesn't matter anymore now. Lilly wasn't my mother. I just let her think she was."

Fin smiled. Evidently he hadn't found that a startling piece of news.

"I often wondered about that," he said and turned to look past Cloud to Rab standing behind her. "Do you think you'll find it? That launch pad?" he asked. "I spoke to Gift, you know, after we buried Staunch. She doesn't believe any more."

"I know," Rab said with a nod of his head.

"You'll track back to us if you find it, won't you?" Fin asked. "We won't be that far behind you." He pointed. "These Top-siders are pretty good at pulling that cart."

Rab smiled. "Trust me, Fin. If we find a launch pad out there, I won't be walking, I'll be *running* back to tell you."

Out of the corner of his eye, he could see the expression on Cloud's face change. She wasn't frowning exactly but something about what he'd said had obviously struck her strangely.

It was as good a time as any to say his goodbyes to the rest of the Top-siders. And to Gift. Rab simply couldn't find an excuse to put it off any longer. He passed Cloud the spear, surprised when she took it from him without comment. On the opposite side of camp, he found Glint, Poppy and Gift together, sifting through the scattered pile of the things they had salvaged from his village. Glint got to his feet as Rab approached.

"I've come to say goodbye," Rab said, glancing towards Gift who was still seated on the ground beside Poppy. He couldn't see the baby any-where. "Cloud. . .Abby and I have decided to go on alone."

"But where will you go?" Glint asked, clearly surprised. "We thought. . ." he looked briefly down at Poppy, ". . . that you'd be asking to stay with us. Especially the woman, considering the circumstances."

Exactly what circumstances, Rab wondered. That she was an un-claimed woman of breeding age? He shook his head. "She wants to continue south. We intend to follow this road at least as far south as it goes and after that. . ." Rab shrugged and left the rest unsaid, it being more or less understood they'd take their chances out there in the wasteland.

"I see," Glint replied. "But we, too, will be moving south. We could travel together."

"I think it best we travel alone. You have enough people to take care of here, Glint. But Fin will stay with you, if you agree."

That seemed to puzzle the elder.

"Fin's skills with the spear will be welcome," he said at last.

With the loss of Staunch, they *were* down one hunter.

Rab turned and saw Gift getting to her feet. Her arm was outstretched as she stepped over the mound of salvaged goods. On reaching him, she took hold of his hand.

"For a long time now we seem to have been walking the same circle but in opposite directions," she said, smiling up at him. "I'm glad we've met up again, Rab. If only for such a little time."

Life top-side was brutal; the little girl who had travelled with him from his village had been born to it and never expected anything different. Long ago, she'd been left behind by the one person she'd relied on to keep her safe. Now grown, little had really changed for her. She'd lost her husband and was left behind again, only now with a small child to care for.

Life went on.

When Gift lifted up on her toes and brushed his cheek with a kiss, Rab freed his hand from hers to touch the long cold veil of her hair.

"Our paths will cross again," he told her and made to step away.

"Wait!" Poppy called to him. Plunging her hands into the pile of salvaged goods, she began to scavenge, finally pulling out one worn boot and, after a moment of frantic searching, its mate. She got up from the ground and hurried over to Rab.

"These are for Abby," she said, holding out her find to Rab. "I noticed her boots are ruined and, well," she stammered, "they're kind of yours anyway."

Rab glanced towards Glint and hesitated.

A sweater, a set of gloves and a second-hand pair of boots! That's the bargain they'd offered the last time.

"I'm sorry," Poppy said, bowing her head. "Everything else we took from your village is in tatters. Only good for patching or burning."

Rab looked away from Glint and took the gift.

"It doesn't matter," he said.

"I'd have given her Staunch's boots but they're too big for her."

"Fin can have them," Glint suggested. He turned to Rab. "I'll walk with you," he said, leaving Rab no opportunity to resist when the elder put a hand to his back, urging him away.

As he walked across the camp site towards Cloud, Rab glanced backwards. Poppy was on her knees, rummaging among the mound of scavenged goods again. Gift had her back to him as she bent and retrieved something from the ground. Sunny, Rab guessed. He turned away.

"I made the bargain with the fair-haired tunnel-woman that day," Glint said as he walked beside Rab.

"Figured as much when I found out you were Staunch's father."

"And Fin knows?" Glint asked, pulling Rab to a halt.

"He's probably guessed, but I didn't tell him as much, no."

"And still he wants to stay?" Glint's focus drifted to the far side of the camp site where most of his companions sat huddled in a silent group, Fin among them. "If the situation was reversed, Rab, would you allow him to stay? We're enemies, after all."

"Are we?" Rab asked, then shook his head. "Perhaps so. One thing is sure, you and I can never be friends, Glint. But enemies? I can't answer that. Not anymore. As for Fin, I wouldn't worry about him. You've got what he came out here to find. A way to survive on the surface. He's not going to let some old grudge jeopardise that. You're perfectly safe with him." Rab met Glint's eyes. "As I assume he is with you."

"We have no intention of harming Fin," Glint assured him. "He's useful to us." He nodded towards Cloud, who was sitting on the ground, industriously reorganising their packs. "So is she."

Rab smiled and looked down at the boots dangling from his hands. "Ah! But you haven't got what *she* wants, Glint. And you never will."

***

They'd been travelling for three days without any signs that the band of Top-siders were anywhere close behind them. Either Fin had overestimated the Top-siders' efficiency at hauling that cart or they'd had some sort of setback in rejigging it for travel. Cloud's new boots fit well enough although she hadn't discarded the ones Rab had patched for her. Time might come when she needed them. Around midday they stumbled on more of that spongy green stuff growing on the bank of a narrow little stream where suddenly the road they had been following abruptly stopped. To Rab's eyes at least, the water seemed cleaner and fresher still than the water they had come across at the bridge. It even had a different kind of smell to it, one that had intrigued Cloud so much that they had lingered overly long on the bank, where she collected more of the green weed, and Rab had been prompted to make a potentially rash decision. But it was now or never! He filled their depleted canteens with the clear water from the river and, so far, neither one of them had shown any hint of sickness.

On the first and every night since they'd left the Top-sider camp, that same strange something had come visiting them again. Only now, Rab heard it, too. It wasn't Cloud's 'bird'; the sound didn't come at dawn but during the deepest and loneliest part of darkness and that alone was more than enough to set Rab's nerves on edge. Even during the daylight hours, he kept looking over his shoulder. On the morning of the fifth day, Rab found evidence of their visitor not far from the spot where they had camped. Actually he'd stepped right on it. . .two ragged feathers ground part-way into the dirt as though the animal who had shed them had been pacing. This wasn't some kill site Glint had neglected to tell them about. There was no blood; no sign that anything had been attacked here. Just those two dirty feathers.

"It was one of my birds all along," Cloud said as she bent down beside Rab to inspect the frayed feathers. "Why haven't we seen them in the mornings like before?" she asked, taking one of the feathers from Rab.

"I don't think it's your bird," Rab said, drawing Cloud's attention to the scuffed dirt about their boots. "It's something else," he added, straightening. "Something that's been watching us for a long time."

"The rest of the Top-siders?" Cloud suggested, glancing up. "Glint and the others could have lied to us you know. Just because they said the rest of their band was a long way away doesn't mean it's true."

Rab shook his head. "No. Not Top-siders," he told her. "Not bounty hunters, either. And not your bird."

Slowly Cloud rose to her feet and the tattered feather she'd been holding fluttered to the ground beside her.

"You know what this is, don't you? You've known it all along."

"I don't know what it is exactly, Cloud. I only know what it isn't."

"Well, that doesn't tell me a lot," Cloud snapped as she stomped away, head bent, studying the immediate vicinity. "There's more here," she called to Rab before dropping to one knee. "It's. . ."

She stood and, in her hands, was what appeared to be a jumbled collection of feathers all matted together. Rab used the tip of Fin's spear to lift the mess from the palm of Cloud's outstretched hand, more or less expecting the individual feathers to break apart and float back to the ground. When they didn't, Rab stripped off his gloves with his teeth, spat them into the dirt by his feet, and with a bare hand collected the matted clump of feathers from the tip of his spear.

"What's sticking them together?" Cloud asked. "Blood?"

Rab dropped to the ground and placed the spear down beside him. Laying the mass of feathers in front of him, he slowly and carefully began to untangle the mess.

Cloud slipped down beside him.

"Oh, Rab," she whispered, leaning around his shoulder. "Look. Those feathers have been knotted together with something."

With the flat of his hand, Rab smoothed out what looked to be a strip of knotted feathers about as long as his arm but only one feather wide. There were perhaps twenty or so feathers bound by some string-type material. After a little careful twisting, Rab managed to get all the feathers lined up, tips all pointing down. The vanes at the base of the feathers appeared to have been scraped away, leaving the shaft smooth and around each shaft that odd string-like material had been knotted to hold all the feathers together. There were tattered threads of the same string-like material running in the opposite direction, suggesting that another strip of similarly knotted feathers had been attached above and below.

"Someone made that," Cloud said faintly by Rab's ear and then fell back on her haunches. "Someone who collects feathers and makes clothes out of them."

Rab swivelled around to challenge her. "You can't know that."

"Oh, yes I can," Cloud said, pointing to the strip of feathers stretched out on the ground by Rab's boots. "They've been woven together intentionally with that stringy kind of stuff. Up and down. That's a piece of someone's clothing. And it's old, otherwise that scrap wouldn't have broken off like that. Trust me, Rab, I've rewoven enough clothes and blankets to know what I'm talking about. Someone made that!"

Cloud's expression went suddenly blank as though her thoughts had leapt far away from this place. It almost startled Rab when, without warning, she stripped her pack from her back and, dumping it on the ground in front of him, began to hurriedly rummage around inside it.

"What are you—"

"Look," Cloud insisted, interrupting him when she found what she'd been seeking. "Look," she repeated and thrust something close up to his face.

It was the vial, the one Lilly had given her the day they had left the tunnels.

"Don't you see?" She sounded almost frantic. "That figure on the side? Those stone eyes? You said it looked like a bird. Well, it is. *Those* birds." She pointed skyward, then towards the strip of woven feathers at Rab's feet. "And the same people who made *that*, made *this*," she said, shaking the vial in front of Rab's eyes. "And it wasn't any Top-sider or bounty hunter or villager." She pushed off with her hands to get to her feet. "Whoever they are, they've been doing it for a long time. There are other people out here."

Other people? No. Not *people*!

"We've got to go back," Rab said sharply, springing to his feet, spear in hand.

"Back? Back where?" Cloud called after him as he started off the way they had come, snatching up his discarded gloves as he passed them. "If there are people in the south, that's a good thing, isn't it?" she asked, gathering her pack to hurry after him.

"And what's the first thing Fin will do if he hears those *people* in the night the way we have?"

"Oh no," Cloud gasped, clutching Rab's arm. "He'll launch that spear of his, thinking it's one of my birds."

"And start something that can't possibly finish well. He may have already done it."

"You think there's more of them around," Cloud said, glancing to the right and left of her as though expecting someone or something to suddenly appear.

"There's more, Cloud. I don't know where exactly. I'd just assumed they were all gone. That they'd died out long ago just like Sunny always thought."

"Sunny!" Cloud barked and, tightening her hold on Rab's arm, swung him around to a stop. "What's she got to do with this? Just what did happen between the two of you on that journey ten years ago? You've never told us a thing. Something happened, Rab. It had to. Oh, I know Sunny died and you lost Gift. But it's more than that. You *found* something. I always suspected you did and now I'm sure of it. Time to tell me what it is, Rab. We're in this together, aren't we?"

Yes, they were in this together. Partners. She wasn't some fragile little thing. She wasn't Lilly. She had the right to know and for oh so very long now, he had wanted to tell somebody. He'd always assumed it would be on his death bed, a confession that would pass on the loathsome responsibility Sunny had given him to some other poor unsuspecting soul. He'd always hoped it wouldn't be Cloud. Didn't matter now because soon Glint and his small band of Top-siders would know, too. And then the knowledge Sunny had begged him to conceal would spread like dust on the wind to every corner of this planet. . .a planet that was not now and, should Fin have already made a terribly grave mistake, never could be their home.

"I've got a story to tell you," Rab said at last. "But you have to listen patiently and not interrupt. And you have to let me tell it on the way back to Fin. There may not be a lot of time."

"Then we'll go," Cloud said and spun around. "But not without that strip of feathers," she called back to him as she ran to collect their find. "Fin will have to believe us when he sees that. And I want the truth. *All* of it."

And the truth was exactly what Rab gave her, beginning from the moment he, Gift, Sunny and her grandfather, old John Braham leading Kix, that ancient horse of his, had walked through the gates of the tunnel city to journey north in search of the fabled city and the launch pad old John Braham had believed would be waiting there for them. He even told her about the struggle they'd had coaxing Kix up the steep stairs onto the plateau. It was a detail she didn't really need to know but, once he got started, Rab couldn't seem to stem the flow of words from his mouth and his memory. He explained what had happened when they'd been obliged to cross the river; how he'd lost his hold on Gift as they'd waded across after Sunny; how the little girl had fallen from his back into the rushing stream and how Sunny had dived back into the river to save her from drowning and, although they weren't aware of it at the time, infected the deep scratches she'd received from one of the young captives who'd been recently returned to the city. When it came to the part about the death of Kix, Rab baulked about how much to tell Cloud. In the end, he related everything—about Sunny and how she'd lied to the old man about that old gun she lugged around with her, about the infected wounds on the horses legs and how Sunny, in her inimitably pragmatic fashion, had raised that gun and shot old Kix with one bullet clean and straight through its head. He'd learned a lot about Cloud lately; she, more than most, didn't like to see things die. But it was easier after that to tell her about the fate of old John Braham who, too exhausted and wracked with grief over the loss of his beloved horse, had drifted into death more peacefully than anyone travelling the barren surface had any right to expect. Once she learned about Sunny's infection and the ineffectiveness of her medicines, Cloud would have known what to expect, but Rab told her anyway, confirming that as each day passed Sunny had grown progressively weaker. He recounted his discovery of the skull and the ragged and empty pack at the base of a ridge near the spot where old Braham had died and that he'd initially concealed the find from Sunny, although ultimately he confessed what he'd found and Sunny had revealed it to be the remains of one of the party she'd travelled north with many years before.

That had come as a surprise to Cloud. Although she'd kept her word and not interrupted, Rab could see the changed expression beneath the hood of her coat. Once it had been common knowledge that Louis, old John Braham's son, had started out with a party in search of the fabled city and that, years later, only Sunny had returned, but over time that knowledge, like many things of the past, had been forgotten. He skimmed over the details of their encounter with the band of Top-siders, Glint's band, although he did explain that it had been the whole band they had come across, not some small scouting party and that, at the time, Glint had not yet attained the status of elder and that it was from a little boy in that party that Gift had received the little blue stone. That little boy, of course, had been Staunch.

Rab struggled in his account of the roosts that Sunny had led them to, feeling that he'd done a poor job describing their size and the pierced cone-in-cone nature of their construction. He had less of a struggle accounting for their purpose; that was kind of obvious now in light of Cloud's 'birds'. He'd expected Cloud to react when, again, he was obliged to tell her about the discovery of Louis Braham's body, but instead she took it in her stride much as she had done with every detail of his story so far. She'd asked for the truth, so he even told her about how Sunny, something of a revered personage among the tunnel-dwellers, had deceived him into leaving Gift behind in one of the roosts. He left out many of the details about the last days of travel before they reached their destination. Cloud didn't really need to know how often he'd been tempted to turn that gun of Sunny's on her. He did tell her about Sunny's deteriorating condition and how, by the time their journey together was almost ended, she was all but dead. And then came the most challenging part of his story—how was he to convince Cloud about what he'd seen and learned out there on the dry river bed where Sunny had brought him? After all, he had seen it for himself. If Sunny had never brought him to that spot and simply told him, *he* would never have believed.

He failed miserably to convey the enormous size of the spaceship, but felt he did a little better in explaining how thoroughly the ship had been stripped. The description of those hundreds of bones and the pens in which the animals had been transported came more easily. Cloud had been rummaging around a little in the library with Ruby; she'd seen some of old Braham's books and looked at the pictures inside them.

When the time came, Rab thought he might baulk at revealing the promise Sunny had forced him to make that day. He didn't. The truth just kept rushing out of him. He told her about the same vow Sunny herself had made—and why she had made it. There was no way off this planet and this planet wasn't Earth. But if the people, be they Top-sider, villager or tunnel-dweller, ever discovered that, what would happen? Stripped of their home and of any possibility of finding a new home that could sustain them, they'd have nothing. No hope. No purpose. Better to live a lie and keep the past forgotten. And so Rab, like Sunny, had vowed to safeguard the location of the ship and everything that lay within it.

It was time then for the worst of his story—time to tell Cloud how, at her own insistence, he had killed Sunny, using the last of the old bullets in her gun. He rushed through the last of it—about how he had returned to the roost to find Gift missing and his discovery of the little blue stone she had left behind—Cloud basically knew the rest.

After he had finished, Cloud remained silent for a very long time. She simply hurried on beside him, keeping pace with his anxious steps. He anticipated she'd have many questions but, when she finally did turn to him and speak, the question she asked first was the last he would have expected.

"Who scratched her?" she said. "Sunny, I mean."

Rab shook his head and smiled.

"That's what you want to know first?"

"If you don't mind," she said brusquely.

"It was either Button or the other one. I can't remember her name. The second girl who was returned with you that day."

"Twist," Cloud replied. "Then it was Button or Twist who really killed Sunny."

Rab had never thought of it that way before. Not that it really mattered.

"Yeah, I guess in some way it was one of them," he said. "But that's not what I was expecting you to take from all I've told you, Cloud. I just—"

"Oh, I got it, Rab. I got it. And now you make a lot more sense to me." She glanced around, taking in the wasteland that surrounded them. "And so does everything else."

"Then you believe me?"

It couldn't be so simple, Rab thought, recalling how vehemently he had argued with Sunny, contending, although wrongly, that there had to be another, more palatable explanation for what she had shown him.

"Do I really have a choice?" Cloud countered. "I'd always thought it was losing Gift that had made you the way you are, but it wasn't, was it? Finding her didn't make that much difference to you. Not really. I mean, it resolved something for you but you were still prepared to let her go. But when I told you about how those feathers were woven together, Rab, that was the first time I saw something in you change. Ever since I've known you, you've just kind of wandered from one day to the next. But you're different now. Or maybe it's just me seeing you differently. Or could it be that you've finally found that sense of purpose you've been so busy defending for us but never had for yourself?" She pushed back the hood of her coat and met Rab's eyes. "You think the people who strung those feathers into clothes are the same ones who made those roosts, don't you? You think they're the real inhabitants of this planet."

"People?" Rab said. He laughed then, though he didn't know why. "I think it's very unlikely they're *people*."

Chapter 12

BY THE end of their first day of backtracking, Rab had grown concerned about how far Glint's band seemed to be behind them. They had travelled fast—he and Cloud—made good time and covered a lot of ground, perhaps half again as much as they had covered in their almost leisurely trek away from the Top-sider camp. But they hadn't stopped to rest or eat and now that darkness had fallen on them in earnest again, there was no alternative but to stop.

Cloud would have pushed on if Rab had insisted but it was pointless to go on to the point of complete exhaustion. If they made the same good time, tomorrow evening they should reach the stream. Surely the band of Top-siders, even encumbered as they were with the cart, would have made it that far by then.

They passed a cold and restless night and, in the morning, set out at the first sign of daybreak. Just as Rab hoped, they reached the stream right on night fall. But the Top-siders weren't anywhere near the stream and there were no obvious signs that Glint and his band had been there. There was still a little light left to travel by, but they had pushed themselves hard these last two days and so made camp by the stream that night.

Rab didn't know how late in the night it was when they heard the scream. He'd fallen into a dead sleep and, if the ungodly scream hadn't woken him, suspected he'd have remained that way until morning. He bolted up from the ground and called out frantically for Cloud. She answered him immediately and it was only then Rab realised that the scream couldn't have been Cloud's; it had come from too far away.

Cloud found him in the darkness.

"What was that?" Her voice sounded ragged, fearful.

For a lone traveller on the surface, the only sounds usually heard were the howling of the wind and the occasional rumble of landslips. But now some living thing had cried out in the night. One of Cloud's 'birds'? Whatever it was, it was not human. Rab's ears were still ringing from the shrillness of its call.

"I don't know but it sounded like it's some distance away from us," Rab said.

"Do we go after it?" Cloud asked.

"In the dark?" Rab countered. "How could we find it?"

"We could if it screams again."

That was the last thing Rab wanted. Whatever had made that dreadful sound had done so out of pain.

Rab made his decision. "We wait until morning."

"And if it *does* scream again?"

"We wait until morning," Rab repeated emphatically.

Sleep eluded him for the rest of the night; he kept waiting for that second scream that never came. Cloud hadn't slept either. At least Rab didn't think so although he never said a word to her, hoping that perhaps she may have dozed a little. They started out early, while it was impossible to see more than a few paces ahead of them, but once they crossed the stream they were back on the road and intended to follow it until they met up with Glint and his band. Or came across whatever had screamed.

When Cloud caught the scent of burning wood, they knew they wouldn't have to travel too much farther. And soon, Rab spotted smoke in the distance.

"It has to be the Top-siders' camp," Cloud said. "They've stopped again."

Yes—it could only be their camp. Did that mean someone else was hurt?

Rab started running then and Cloud came racing after him. By the time he reached the Top-sider camp, the skin of his face had gone numb and he could barely catch a breath. When he hurried past the cart alone, Rab didn't stop to give it or the heavily-hooded couple standing beside it even a brief glance. Glint was by the fire, bending to stoke it with a pitifully inadequate length of wood. He looked up, doubtless alerted by the noise Rab was making. One by one, more of the Top-siders began to notice him and, as he neared Glint, were already beginning to gather. Rab was relieved when he caught sight of Gift among them, but there was no sign of Fin.

Rab pulled up just short of colliding with Glint. Bent at the waist, he gulped for air. Beneath the urgent chatter of the Top-siders, he made out Gift anxiously speaking his name and the sound of Cloud's boots as she pounded the rough stones of the ancient road behind him.

"Where's Fin?" Rab gasped, still unable to right himself, as Cloud staggered to the ground beside him.

Rab felt a hand tightly grip his elbow and recognised Glint's voice.

"Fin? You passed him."

With the aid of Glint, Rab managed to straighten. He had a catch in his side and the weight of the packs on his back had suddenly become unbearable. He dumped them to the ground.

"We heard. . ." he began then was forced to gulp again before he could continue, ". . . a scream during the night. A terrible scream as though—"

Glint's hold on Rab's elbow tightened, prompting Rab to stop talking.

"It wasn't Fin," Glint said. "Not any of us, either."

The elder turned to his fellows and ordered them away. When Gift made to go with them, Glint called her back.

"Dee will take you to Fin. He's over by the cart with Poppy. Best you see for yourself what's inside it."

Cloud was getting to her feet, though she required the assistance of Rab's hand to do it. Quickly he helped her out of her packs before hurrying with her after Gift. The first thing he noticed was the mound of salvaged goods piled on the ground beside the cart. They'd emptied the cart again, the same way they had emptied it so Staunch could be made more comfortable. But Glint had said that none of them had screamed and they certainly wouldn't have gone to such lengths for the comfort of some half-dead 'bird'.

Fin had done it: the very thing Rab most feared. Even though he had no idea what the being might actually look like, Rab knew, with sickening certainty, what he was going to find in that cart.

Fin must have finally realised who had bolted past him because he was watching them as they approached.

"We didn't know," he said lamely the moment Rab drew near enough to hear. "How could we? We thought it was one of those birds and covered in feathers like that, it's what it *looked* like. . .from a distance. . .in the dark."

"Glint calls it the feather-man," Gift said and stepped aside to allow first Cloud, then Rab to peer into the little, rejigged cart.

The feather-man was much smaller than Rab had expected, no bigger than Fin had been when they had left their village those many years ago. Its head was broad at the brow and narrowed to a sharp point at the chin. Its large yellowish eyes appeared to lack any pupils and when it suddenly blinked, Rab was startled to see its lids close across rather than down the enormous iris. Of mouth, there was little at all—just a V-shaped slit above the chin and above that a flattened kind of nose. If the feather-man had ears, Rab couldn't see them, unless the two small holes at the side of its head served that purpose. The skin of its face had a bluish tint to it, although perhaps that was a consequence of its injuries, and it was coarse in appearance. The being was devoid of hair, but the top third of its head was sheathed in some hard nail-like rind that was slightly darker in colour.

"It's still alive," Cloud whispered, reaching out to touch the rough skin of its face. "But it's so cold."

"Perhaps it's meant to be," Rab said softly.

"It can still be helped," Cloud said, sounding unexpectedly optimistic, and turned to Fin.

"We tried," Fin told her. "Everything we did just seemed to make it worse."

"Our medicines aren't theirs," Rab said and watched as Cloud gently began to lift the matted feather cloak off the feather-man's body.

Two arms. The feather-man had two arms but what disturbed Rab the most was its five-fingered hands. If it weren't for the additional joint in each of its fingers, Rab could have been looking at a human hand.

The feather-man had been wearing some sort of clothing beneath its cloak but someone had cut it away and it was now so drenched in the feather-man's darkish-coloured blood there was no way for Rab to tell what it had looked like. Its chest was exposed and there the skin, too, was of that same strange bluish colour but much coarser in texture than the skin of its face. It appeared to be kind of plated. The wound that had been inflicted on it was deep and located directly below what in a human would have been its rib-cage. God only knew what internal organ had been pierced and ruptured by Fin's spear.

"Then we need to find *their* medicines," Cloud countered sharply. "There has to be *something*."

Fin reached into his pocket and pressed a small item into the palm of Cloud's hand.

"This is all we found on him—but it's empty," he said.

Cloud opened her hand and, in it, Rab saw a small metal vial. It was cruder in make than the one Lilly had given Cloud. It bore no ornamentation but the cap opened in much the same way. Cloud sniffed at the uncapped, empty container.

"It's that green plant stuff," she said, meeting Rab's eyes. "I've still got that pouch of it in one of my packs."

Rab was hurrying to retrieve her packs before she'd even finished. No sooner had he passed them to her than she had the contents upended all over the ground: her few spare clothes, the patched boots, containers of food, the strip of woven feathers she'd brought to show Fin and the small draw-string pouch Rab had given her.

"If we could just stop his pain," she said, snatching up the pouch, "I'm sure I can stitch up this wound with those needles I made. It won't be pretty," she said with a shake of her head, "but it would be better than letting it continue to bleed like this."

"Using what?" Poppy asked. "For thread, I mean?"

Cloud shrugged. "Anything as long as it's clean. We could strip thread from some of our clothes or those scraps you took from Rab's village."

"Yes. And there's enough wood to keep the fire going so we could boil the thread before we use it."

"Boil it," Cloud said thoughtfully as she lowered the matted cloak back down over the feather-man's body.

"So it's clean and—"

Cloud cut her off. "Poppy, start gathering that thread."

With a nod, Poppy grasped Gift by the arm and hurried her off towards the fire.

"Are you sure you want to do this?" Rab asked, drawing Cloud aside. "You could kill it."

"I don't see it matters much either way, Rab. His people, or whatever they are, are going to find out about this. Isn't it better that they think we tried to help it? Besides," she said, with a glance towards the prone and bleeding thing lying in the bed of the cart, "we have to help it." She turned back to Fin and handed him the draw-string pouch.

"Get Poppy to boil some of this in water," she told him.

"All of it?" Fin asked, loosening the draw-string to look inside.

"How would I know? Guess," Cloud told him, and gave him a shove to get him moving. She turned to Rab. "You go and get me some rags. But make sure they're boiled first."

***

Rab wasn't a great believer in an Almighty, but something must have been guiding Cloud's hands during the night. With Fin, Poppy and him to help, she had managed to get some of that boiled green plant concoction down the throat of the injured feather-man and, within moments, it had begun to settle, although at first when its breathing started to slow, Rab's immediate thought was that Cloud had killed it. Instead, she had knocked it completely unconscious. And as she began to work on the feather-man's ruined chest, Rab didn't dare speak what everyone had to be thinking. Once she was finished, would the feather-man wake up again?

In the morning, when the feather-man remained lying, still and silent, on the bed of the cart, Cloud insisted she wasn't worried, reasoning that they'd probably only used a little too much green plant. But her professed confidence didn't stop her from repeatedly walking back to the cart just to check, even though Rab, Poppy and Fin had taken it in turns to stand vigil. Gift had Sunny to care for and Poppy had sent her away.

As for the Top-siders, they had stationed themselves about the fire and seemed to have been keeping their own watch during the night. Every time Rab had glanced back in that direction, he failed to catch anyone asleep. With Poppy otherwise occupied, it had fallen on Sandy to distribute the morning's food. For some reason, Gift seemed to hold something of a higher status among the band, possibly because her husband had been the son of one of their elders.

Rab had just returned from another of his vigils by the cart as Sandy completed her rounds. Noticing him, she circled back and offered him a handful of food. Rab took it mechanically, little caring what it was. Out of the corner of his eye, he saw Glint get up from the ground. Gift must have seen him, too, because suddenly she materialised out of nowhere and settled herself down beside Rab, cradling a sleeping Sunny in her arms.

"Glint says you know what the feather-man is," she told him. "That you knew it was coming in this direction and were coming back to tell us. Otherwise you'd have been too far away to hear it scream."

"I understand the feather-man is no worse," Glint observed, folding himself down in the dusty ground by Rab. "I heard what Dee just said and she's right. It's what all of us think."

Rab shook his head as, one by one, the remaining Top-siders began to gather in a circle all about him. Understandably they wanted some answers. After all, he and Cloud *had* come racing back, although they couldn't possibly have known what had happened. And almost immediately, Cloud seemed to have known what to do. Rab wasn't sure he would be able to convince them that Cloud had acted purely on instinct and intuition. She had taken a guess, a good guess if they, and the feather-man, were lucky.

"I don't know what it is exactly. But for a while now Cloud had been hearing something in the night. All we could think was it was more of those bird-like things. Two days ago. . ." Or was it three? Rab was struggling to think straight. "We found a strip of that feather cloak it was wearing." His gaze wandered from face to face, but the Top-siders weren't giving anything away. "That's the first clue we had it wasn't just another animal and we realised there'd likely be more of them, probably to the south. We were running back here to stop Fin. If he killed one of them, then—"

Gift's hand came down on Rab's arm, interrupting him.

"It wasn't Fin who speared it," she said flatly. "It was me."

Gift! She'd done this!

Rab was almost in shock. He couldn't reconcile such an action with the young girl he had known all those years ago. Now, finally, he understood—she wasn't just older, she wasn't the same young girl at all. Just like Cloud wasn't Claudia Caine.

"Seems to me," Glint was saying, "that it's irrelevant who did it, it's done. The problem now is what do we do about it."

"Do?" Rab's attention snapped to the elder. "We have to take it back to its own kind. That's what we do about it."

Glint nodded slowly. "That would be the humane thing to do, but is it the right thing? We know nothing about this feather-man. Where it comes from. What it's doing here. We could take it back and get ourselves killed for our trouble."

There was no choice—Rab realised he was going to have to tell his story again, the one he'd always thought wouldn't be told for many, many years yet to come.

"You think I know what it is, but I don't," he said, glancing briefly at Gift before fixing his eyes on Glint. "But I do know where it came from and I can make a pretty good guess what it's doing here."

Rab told them everything he knew from the moment they had left the tunnel city until the day he had returned to the roosts and found Gift gone. Glint and his people knew about the roosts, of course. After all it's the place where they had stolen Gift. And they'd seen the 'birds', too, even killed one. But they knew nothing about the ship. As he spoke, he looked from face to face among the Top-siders. In their eyes, he saw confusion, impatience, even anger, which if it hadn't been for Glint's staying hand, might have manifested itself. But not once did he see anything remotely like belief. Though he had expected some reaction from Gift, there was none. It was a long time before anyone spoke after Rab had finished his tale.

"You're claiming this is their planet then?" Glint asked. "And for generations we've been living and breeding our children on an alien world?"

From the tone of his voice, Rab still couldn't judge if the elder had trusted a word he'd said.

"That's about the size of it," Rab replied. "I know it's difficult—"

Again Rab felt Gift's hand come to rest on his arm.

"And that tunnel-woman, Sunny, was the only one who knew?" Glint asked.

"She didn't *know* exactly," Rab countered. "Like I told you, if she and her father hadn't found the ship and read the captain's logs, they'd never have worked it out. It was the same for me, Glint, but if you'd seen what I saw, then. . .well, you'd have to believe it, too."

"And you and that woman—you keep this knowledge secret for all this time."

The sharp edge in the elder's voice caused Rab to jump. Glint, too, was angry—disbelieving and angry. He had cause.

"We're invaders, Glint, and we're even more fragile than the world we're living in. But this is the only home we're ever going to have and we need all the hope and purpose we can find, wherever we find it, to survive in it. So yes. . .Sunny and me. . .we kept silent."

The elder's focus shifted and Rab realised he was looking towards Poppy, Cloud, and the rejigged cart.

"I didn't see what you claim to have seen," Glint continued, more calmly now, "and it's likely I never will, but I have seen what's lying over there in our cart. It's not human. It's not animal, either. And I agree that there will be more of those creatures and we have to prepare for their worst response to what has happened here. For the moment that's all that matters."

Abruptly Glint got to his feet and, with his entourage of Top-siders, walked away, leaving Rab alone with Gift and Sunny.

That was it? That was all?

Rab turned to Gift in astonishment.

"Surely that can't be the end of the discussion," he said.

"Of course not," Gift replied, tucking the blanket more tightly about her sleeping infant. "They've gone off to plan what to do."

And Rab wasn't going to have any say in that plan.

"Fin and Cloud had no part in what I did. If I leave with the feather-man, will he let them stay?"

"It's not for me to say, Rab. Glint is a fair man although I suppose you might not see it that way. But I suspect Fin will insist on going with you. I can't speak for your friend."

No one spoke for Cloud.

But Gift was right. Very likely Fin would insist on going with him. Cloud, too. And Rab had no right to ask them not to. His gaze drifted briefly towards Glint and the rest of the Top-siders.

"They don't believe me, do they?" he said, turning back to Gift.

"I believe you, and sooner or later they must, but there's still one thing I don't understand."

"Just one thing?" Rab asked, smiling coldly.

"Yes. I remember the old man talking about 'The Pluming'. About how something from inside the Earth had spilled out onto the surface. He said that was what had happened to make the climate change."

"That's what he said."

"But that can't be what's happening on this planet, can it? I mean, how unlucky can we be to have escaped from one planet just to land on another where exactly the same thing is happening? Where the air is bad and the water isn't always fit to drink?" Gift shook her head. "That doesn't make sense to me."

"No, it doesn't make sense to me, either," Rab said. "Never did. Until just recently when I began to notice things."

"Go on," Gift prompted.

"Well, for instance, the star that's in the sky right now. Surely you and your people have seen it."

"Yes, we see it sometimes at a certain time of the year. But it's just one star. We've never seen another. Glint said it doesn't mean anything at all."

"Then I suppose he says the same about those occasional breaks in the clouds, too. You're top-side all the time, you must have noticed that snow time is taking longer to come and that, when it does come, it doesn't last as long."

Gift took a long time to answer.

"Yes," she said at last. "You're right about that. It's only a subtle change, but we've noticed it."

"I think that's just the way it is on this planet, Gift. That it's cold for a very long time and then, for some reason I don't understand, it starts to warm up again. When it's cold, those feather-people and whatever other life there is on this planet move to the south. When it starts to warm, they begin coming north again."

"And if it cools again?" she asked.

Rab shrugged. "Then I guess they go back south. You saw those roosts, Cloud. Something lived in the north once." He gestured towards the cart. "Makes sense it was the feather-people."

"And they're going to keep sweeping north now, aren't they?"

"I think so, Gift."

She looked away, turning her attention to the ground beneath her feet. "All this time, you kept your silence for us. To give us purpose. But what about your purpose?"

"Sunny told me once that the believers should be allowed to go on believing and the rest should be left to make the best of this planet. She stripped me of my beliefs and turned me into the same kind of calculating killer she was. I hated her for that and I don't think she even cared. But to her mind, she was leaving me with the greatest purpose of all. Staying silent and finding you."

"Was she right, Rab?"

"I always hoped that when all of this was over. . .when I found you. . .when I could finally tell someone about what I'd seen and learned out there, I'd know." He shrugged. "But I don't. Not really. But you and me, we're still here. And our people are still here. That must mean something."

After a long and silent moment, Gift lifted her head. "I'm going with you when you take the feather-man back," she said. "I know that's what you'll do, no matter what Glint decides."

"But you can't," Rab protested. "What about your daughter?"

"Sandy will take care of her," Gift said, turning to look directly at Rab. "If this is the feather-people's planet, we'll be outnumbered, won't we? What chance do *our* kind have? If they don't understand that what I did, I did by mistake, well. . .it won't make any difference whether I come back to her or not." She rose to her feet. "I know everything has changed now, Rab, but what Sunny said about doing the best that we can. . .seems to me she's still right."

***

Ultimately Glint had decided that they should go, although Rab suspected that the elder hadn't been so much motivated by conscience as logic. In sending them, he was ridding himself of three inconvenient travelling companions and one of his own who had brought trouble down on his people. After all, Gift had already done what she was intended to do and she was leaving Sunny behind.

And so they started out, Fin and Gift pulling the cart from one side with Cloud and Rab pulling on the other. Every so often, the feather-man drifted back towards consciousness and Cloud would have them stop so she could administer more of the green plant brew. Its life—and theirs—continued to hang in the balance. Whether the feather-man had the capacity for speech or understood what they were attempting to do, Rab couldn't decide. Sometimes it made a peculiar clicking sound that could be construed as words—but perhaps it was only moaning. Sometimes its strange eyes opened and settled on Cloud with a look that hinted at understanding—but perhaps that was just Rab's imagination or his desperate hope.

It was hard going, dragging that cart over the rough terrain and Rab gained a better appreciation of the strength and will of the Top-siders who travelled this way, day after day, with heavier loads than the small, dying feather-man. Glint had permitted them to take a little of the remaining wood, so at least they had the benefit of a small fire at night, something that perhaps also had helped keep the feather-man alive.

Long before they came to the little stream, they heard the noise—felt it, too, through the ground—a low rumble like the earth itself was moving. But it was almost night-time before they reached the bank of the stream and spotted the orange streaks of smoke whirling low down in the sky just above the horizon.

Once night had settled fully, Rab and Fin, leaving Gift and Cloud behind with the cart, crept silently across the stream. At his first clear sight of the feather-people's camp, Rab lost all hope. There were too many feather-people to count, perhaps hundreds of them. The air was charged with the smoke from their scattered fires, with dust, and the discord of random talk.

Gift had grossly underestimated their situation; they weren't simply going to be outnumbered—they were going to be overwhelmed if Rab's fears proved true, and there were hundreds more of them following behind.

As silently as they had come, Rab and Fin made their way back across the stream. Cloud took the news almost calmly. She had less to lose, Rab supposed, whereas there was every likelihood that, should they follow through with their plan, Gift might never see her daughter again.

There was no fire for them that night as they sat huddled wordlessly for some time about the cart.

"I think we should split up," Rab said at last. "Two of us should go on as we planned; two should go back and warn Glint how many of them there are, get him moving back to the rest of his band. All we've got to do is get the cart a little way across the stream now. Two of us could do that easily."

"If we get that far," Fin said faintly out of the darkness. "As soon as they see us, they might kill us."

"Better two of us than four."

"Or we could just leave the feather-man somewhere they're sure to find him and all four of us go back," Cloud suggested.

"No," Gift said, face shrouded in darkness. "You three can return to Glint, but I'm taking the feather-man back to its people. I can pull the cart by myself."

She couldn't. She'd try—but she couldn't.

"Then it's settled," Rab said. "In the morning, Gift and I will continue on to their camp. But you," he found Cloud's hand in the darkness, "and Fin should leave now. It'll give you a head start."

"What?" Cloud wrenched her hand free and jumped to her feet. "No. Absolutely not. Fin can do what he wants but I'm not leaving you behind. We all go on—or we all go back."

"Cloud, it will only take two to pull the cart now. It'll be slower but that's a good thing—it'll just give you and Fin more time."

"No. We leave the feather-man," Cloud declared, "like I said. Just because Gift thinks she has some debt to pay, doesn't mean you do."

But he did. If he'd never left her there in the roost in the first place. . .

Besides, he'd left her once, he wouldn't do it again.

Rab reached up and, finding Cloud's hand again, drew her back down.

"For all we know, they could be peaceful. Remember the feather-man had been watching us for a while—it could have attacked and killed us any number of times. But it didn't."

"He's right."

Rab heard a rustle; Fin getting to his feet.

"It won't be easy backtracking in the dark. But we have the road."

Another rustle; Fin retrieving his packs. "We'll just have to feel our way if we think we're starting to get lost," he said. "If you won't come willingly, Abby, then I'll knock you unconscious and drag you."

Something dropped on the ground in front of Cloud. Fin must have found her packs.

"You'd have to catch me unaware, Fin," she said, swinging on him, "and I'm not that stupid."

"You should listen to Fin, Cloud," Rab said, turning her face towards him again in the dark. "If the feather-people are peaceful, then we have nothing to worry about. If they're not, then the only chance Fin has to stay alive is if he leaves now. And he's not going to leave without you. If you decide to go with us, then you're not only deciding for him but for Glint and his people as well."

"Gift is deciding for *you*, isn't she?" she protested, grasping his hands so tightly it hurt. "Isn't she?" Cloud insisted.

She wasn't. And Cloud knew that as well as he did.

She fell silent and soon pulled her hands away. "Here," she said, thrusting something into Rab's palm: the pouch with the remainder of the spongy green plant. "You give it some of that in the morning. It would be better in boiling water but there'll probably be no time."

When her arms came around his neck, Rab reached out and held her tightly, never wanting to let go.

No time.

"I'll find you," he whispered. "If there's a way, I'll find you."

"I know you will," she whispered back. "You found Gift."

With that, she was out of his arms. She had her packs retrieved and he could sense she was already gone.

It was a long time before Gift spoke.

"I'm sorry," she said softly.

They were the only words that passed between them during the remainder of the night.

In the morning, Rab checked on the condition of the feather-man. He was still alive, although barely, so as Cloud had instructed, he forced a little of the green plant into its mouth. As far as he could tell, it didn't seem to make a lot of difference.

Gift offloaded their small supply of wood, placed their packs in the cleared space, and walked to the front of the cart.

"Are you ready?" she asked, glancing at Rab.

Rab looked back the way they had come, along the old ruined road. There was no sign of Fin or Cloud. He hadn't expected there would be; they were long gone now. He'd done the right thing, sending them away. With Glint's people, they'd be safe. . .for as long as Fin could force Cloud to stay.

"Ready," he told Gift and moved to the opposite side of the cart. He reached out to take hold of the handle and realised his hands were shaking.

Chapter 13

SANDY'S clucking and her boy's high-pitched screeches of delight were really starting to irritate Cloud. If she hadn't been enjoying the warmth of the fire, she'd have moved away. At least Sunny was quiet, lying blissfully asleep on the ground between them. There was something odd about that child; she was a sedate little thing, causing Cloud to suspect that there was a lot more going on inside that tiny head of hers than anyone credited.

"They're coming back," Sandy said suddenly.

Cloud glanced up. On the far side of camp, just on the edge of darkness, she spotted the scouting party approaching and recognised Fin among them. They'd been gone longer than usual this time. Fin's stride looked a little strange and Cloud quickly realised he was limping and using the end of his spear for support. She jumped up from the ground and hurried across camp to intercept him.

"Are you injured?" she asked as the four other scouts passed her on their way to Glint and the other elders where they'd deliver their report on the latest movements of the feather-people.

"Stone in my boot," Fin explained. Sloughing off his packs, he dropped to his rear, laid his spear on the ground beside him and proceeded to remove his left boot.

"You were away a long time," Cloud said, settling down next to him. She'd have preferred it if Fin had moved closer to the fire but, after so many nights without the benefit of warmth, Fin was habituated to the night-time cold. "Did you see them?"

Fin nodded as he upended his boot. "They're still moving slowly north. Hundreds of them."

"And my birds?"

"Saw them, too. . .moving north as well. No signs either are coming this way yet."

Cloud glanced behind her, towards the sixty or so Top-siders in her band. They'd be all right then—for a little while longer.

"Have they reached the city?" she asked, turning back to Fin.

"Passed it," he told her.

"Do you think they found the tunnels?"

Fin stopped working on his boot and looked over at Cloud. "Hard to miss them what with the smoke from their fires venting top-side."

"I guess," Cloud said thoughtfully. "We should have gone back there to warn them."

"They wouldn't have listened."

Fin had his boot back on and was starting to relace it.

He was probably right about that. They had nothing to prove what they'd seen, not even the strip of woven feathers from the feather-man's cloak. Cloud had lost it somewhere.

"Maybe we still should have tried or at least stood our ground and faced the feather-people. After all, they're not savages." Cloud's hand found the old metal vial that she carried around in her pocket. "They had art. They built those roosts Rab told us about. That bridge."

"And our ancestors built spaceships. Can you build one?" Fin nodded towards the milling Top-siders who had gathered in numbers now to hear the latest report from the scouts. "Do you think any of *them* could?"

"Well, moving further and further west isn't the answer. And we don't know that Rab and Gift didn't get through to them, made them understand. It's possible."

She expected Fin's usual reply; they'd been on opposite sides of that argument many times already. But he said nothing.

"What?" she pressed him.

Fin finished relacing his boot before looking up to answer.

"We tracked the feather-people for five days this time, Abby, and on the last, just before we were about to turn back. . .just for a moment. . .I'm sure I saw a man and a woman walking with them." He shrugged. "But they disappeared and I never did see them again. I can't be certain it was Rab and Gift."

"It was them. Had to be. If Rab and Gift are still alive, then that means the feather-people have agreed to share this planet with us. They survived here. Why can't we?"

"There you go again," Fin said, "ignoring the fact that this planet *belongs* to the feather-people and there's a lot more of them than us. Even if conditions are improving, we're competition. If this was your planet, what would you do if some strange-looking race of people came begging to share it with you?"

Finally. . .the argument Cloud had been expecting.

"But we *have* been sharing it, Fin."

"Yeah," Fin replied sullenly, "out of sight of one other." He shook his head slowly. "You're asking an awful lot, Abby, considering tunnel-dwellers, Top-siders and villagers barely got on together."

"Then why are Rab and Gift still alive?" she challenged him.

"Why are they still with the feather-people?" Fin countered. "Why hasn't Rab come to find you like he promised?" He shook his head. "If it was them I saw, then they've stayed with the feather-people to protect us, Abby. They're giving us time. But someday those feather-people will find us and, when they do. . .well, then it'll all be over. For us. Our kind. We'll be finished."

She fell silent a moment before she spoke again. "The next time you go out, I'm going with you."

Fin laughed and jerked his head, indicating the clutch of Top-siders. "They won't let you come with us, Abby."

"Who said anything about taking them?" Cloud answered with a tiny snort. "There's something you've forgotten, Fin," she said, turning grave. "Rab doesn't know where we are."

"Of course he does. He'd expect us to have stayed with Glint."

Cloud shook her head. "No, Fin. That's the last thing he'd expect *me* to do." She got to her feet. "We're going back to the tunnels. We're going to find out what happened to my people and then we're going to find those roosts. That's got to be where Rab is going."

Fin looked up at her from the ground. "You can't know that."

"I think I do, Fin. The feather-people are moving north. The roosts are in the north and that must be why Rab and Gift are still with them."

"And if we find all your people dead when we get to the tunnels? What then, Abby?"

"Then we still go north." She shrugged. "I won't live like this again. I told Rab that and he'll remember. You don't want to live like this either, Fin. Running. Hiding. Scavenging for something, anything to eat just to give you enough strength to get up the next day and do it all over again. *And maybe all for nothing.* Not if there's a better way. You want to know, Fin. Don't try to tell me that you don't. It's why you left the tunnels in the first place. You claimed it was to bury Stitch's heart, but that was only part of it because if it hadn't been for Stitch, you'd never have stayed there at all."

Fin looked away from her, lifted his hand to run it through his wind-blown hair.

"The better choice," he said at last.

"What?"

"Nothing," Fin replied, stretching to collect his spear. "We'll go, Abby," he said and got up from the ground. "And we won't tell any of these Topsiders where we're going. That way, if you're wrong, they'll still have that bit of extra time Rab is giving them."

"I'm right, Fin. I am," Cloud said, arching her head back as far as it would go to look skyward, "and even if I'm not. . .even if we are finished here, you'll never convince me it's completely over. There's a chance some of us could have survived somewhere else out there."

"Maybe on a planet circling that star," Fin suggested.

He was mocking her but Cloud was accustomed to Fin's ways.

"Or that one," she said, nudging his shoulder to draw his attention to the skies. "See it?" she asked and pointed high overhead towards a tiny light twinkling through a slender window in the clouds.

"You've found another one," Fin said, following her gaze.

"And I'll find another one tomorrow. Or the next day," she added with a smile. "You'll see." She reached out and took the spear from his hand. "Come on. Let's get you something warm to eat. It's a long journey back where we came from."

THE END

Thank you for reading FAITHLESS.

We hope you enjoyed it.

If you would like to be kept informed of further
releases in The Safe Harbour Chronicle, or other new books from
Hague Publishing, why not subscribe to our newsletter at:

www.HaguePublishing.com/subscribe.php

And if you loved the book and have a moment to spare we would
really appreciate a short review. Your help in spreading the word is
gratefully received.

About The Author

SHAUNE Lafferty Webb was born in Brisbane, Australia. Her father was an amateur astronomer and her eldest brother, an avid science fiction reader, so perhaps it was inevitable that she developed an early enthusiasm for writing speculative fiction.

After obtaining a degree in geology from the University of Queensland, Shaune subsequently worked in geochemical laboratories, exploration companies, and, while living in the United States, at a multinational scientific institute involved in exploration beneath the ocean floors.

Her short stories have appeared in AntipodeanSF, The Nautilus Engine, Blue Crow Magazine, and The Vandal and her novels, 'Bus Stop on a Strange Loop' and 'Balanced in An Angel's Eye', were released in 2011 and 2012, respectively. 'Cold Faith' and its sequel, 'Faithless', are the first and the second books in The Safe Harbour Chronicle, a series released by Hague Publishing.

Shaune lives in Brisbane with her husband, a research scientist, and a pair of wayward canine companions.

Hague

Publishing

www.HaguePublishing.com

PO Box 451 Bassendean
Western Australia 6934